Shadows Behind

Ross Richdale

It is 1999 and Kosovo refugee Niana Bolsa is abandoned by the Serbs to fend for herself in the mountains. In freezing temperatures, the distraught woman staggers along an empty road through virgin snow. At the point of near collapse she comes across a tractor and trailer by the roadside with two terrified children hiding there. Their grandparents have been shot and mother taken away. Determined to save the children, Niana takes them and heads for Albania. With all records destroyed, nobody queries her right to the children and they emigrate to New Zealand.

Matt Coleman is attracted to the new tenant of his New Zealand shop, Niana Bolsa, when she opens a food bar adjacent to his antique and furniture factory. Niana is reluctant to commit herself beyond friendship and says little about her life. Eventually, friendship between Niana and Matt blossoms into passionate love as they and Niana's foster children become a family.

But the terror so prevalent in Niana's past surfaces again--with a vengeance.

PURRBOOKS

Purrbooks
Palmerston North
New Zealand

ISBN 0-9582559-6-2

Cover design by Ross Richdale

Shadows Behind is also sold as an Ebook under the title of
Sandwiches and Cuckoo Clocks

CHAPTER ONE

"You can go, woman," the guttural Serb language penetrated Niana's mind as she woke, shivering under the thin blanket. Around her, one naked light bulb glowed from the rafters where the women and girls attempted to sleep. Snores, breathing and the occasional moan or scream filled the barren room. Oddly enough, this stinking overcrowded place was called The Haven, for no attacks took place here.

She staggered to her feet with vomit in her mouth and grabbed her jacket. God it was freezing. The cold eyes of the Serb officer glowered at her.

"Go," the man repeated. "We don't need you any more."

"Where?" the woman replied.

"Albania," he snarled. "Your kind aren't wanted in Kosovo."

"But how? And what of my friends who were in my car."

"They stay to service my men. You have thirty minutes to leave. My orders are to shoot all the pregnant sluts. If you're here after that time..." He grinned and ran a finger across his throat.

"Go, Niana," a shaking voice spoke in her own language. "Tell the world about us. It is stupid to stay and be massacred." It was Shemsie, who was another of those in her car when it had been stopped on the way to the border.

Niana nodded, squeezed her friend's hand and walked away. Outside, freezing air assaulted her face but at least the stink was gone. She was driven for forty minutes up a gravel road into the mountains and told to get out.

"See yah in hell," the Serb driver said, laughing as Niana shivered at the roadside and watched as the Russian jeep reversed and headed away.

*

Silence reigned on that winter's day in 1999. Everywhere Niana looked there was nothing but virgin snow, with no footprints or tire marks beyond where the vehicle turned. A watery sun cast its light from a pale blue sky. The rest of the morning was but a numb memory as the hungry, freezing, pregnant woman staggered along the mountain road. Every bend lead to another and every step crunched through icy snow. By noon the temperature was still barely above freezing. Niana was so cold she was certain her cheekbones had frozen. The woollen gloves barely managed to keep her fingers from being completely numb, while walking helped to keep her feet from freezing.

After four hours, the exhausted refugee came to one more bend and another patch of nothingness. Thoughts turned to her family, husband, father, mother, elder brother and almost everyone else she knew. They were all dead. Her only other friends were those at the army camp. If for no other reason, she owed it to them and the unborn child within her to survive and to tell NATO of the atrocities that had befallen her people.

God, she was hungry. Her stomach rumbled while the unborn baby kicked. She staggered as the scene in front became blurred and the trees above began to spin. No, she was not about to give in. Somewhere ahead was her own kind, someone to help.

She took another shaky step, staggered and fell to her knees. "Oh, Zymer," she cried but by now not even the tears came. "I'm so, so sorry. Our baby."

Niana gritted her teeth and rose once more to her feet. Another bend was ahead, more snow, more trees, the weak sunlight and another bend. She stumbled forward and blinked. There was something else. A farm wagon covered in snow was parked on the roadside as if it had pulled over, perhaps to let an oncoming vehicle pass. Linked to the front of it, looking so bright in the white world, stood a tractor; a red tractor.

Hope surged through her. The depression and fatigue of a second before disappeared as she broke into a slithery run.

"Hello," she screamed. "Is anyone there? Hello."

But all was quiet. Not a sound returned.

She reached the wagon and grabbed a canvas cover tied to the wooden side. Shaking with anticipation, she lifted the corner of the flap and gazed into the dim interior.

Four enormous brown eyes ringed in terror gazed up at her and children's sobbing filled the air.

*

"Don't be afraid," Niana whispered in Albanian, her native tongue. "I will not hurt you."

There were two children huddled in the front corner of the wagon, a little girl who looked no more than four and a boy who was probably three

[4]

years older.

"What are your names?" she asked quietly.

It was the girl who spoke. "I'm Adona," she said as she wiped away her tears. "Mummy's gone."

"Hi Adona," Niana said, and then switched her eyes to the boy. He gazed at her briefly and then glanced away without saying a word.

"Halia doesn't talk," the little girl said.

Niana smiled at the boy. "And you won't talk to me, Halia?" she asked.

Round eyes stared at her but the only response was a slight shrug.

"That's okay," Niana replied, glancing around.

For the first time she noticed several corpses lying almost covered by the snow beyond the tractor. *Oh dear God*, she thought, *it must be the children's family.*

"Mummy told us to hide when the soldiers came," the little girl explained while her brother continued to stare out with wide unblinking eyes. "There were big bangs and shouts then it went quiet. We waited for Mummy but she didn't come back."

"How long ago was that?" Niana asked.

"A long, long time. It got dark and snowed all day and it got dark again." For someone so young Adona's explanation was amazing. She knew the corpses were those of her father and grandparents and she also realized her mother wasn't among the dead. They had waited at least two days, possibly three and had eaten rations in the wagon. They used the canvas covering like a tent and it helped keep the freezing cold temperature within bearable levels.

"Okay," Niana said. "Your mummy must have been held up somewhere so what say, I stay and help you."

"She was crying," Adona whispered. "The soldiers made her cry."

"Oh Adona," Niana replied fighting her own tears. "It will be fine. We'll find your mummy and until we do, I'll stay with you. Okay?"

"Yes, please," the girl said while her brother gave a smile of approval but still said nothing.

"Right. So let's see if we can get the tractor going, shall we?"

*

The tractor seemed to be in good condition but, when Niana tried the starter motor, it grumbled but nothing fired.

"Did the soldiers touch the tractor?" she asked Adona.

[5]

"I don't know. We were hiding. When we came out, Daddy, Grandma and Grandpa were lying in the snow. The bad men and Mummy were gone."

Niana realized that if she continued to turn the starter she'd just run the battery down but what could be done? The tractor could be their salvation. Even with food she doubted if they could walk out. "Have you a stove or burner?" she asked.

"I think so," came Adona's vague reply, but it was her brother who nodded and ran to the front corner of the wagon. He returned with a small methylated spirits burner and box of matches.

"Oh Halia," Niana praised. "What a great help you are."

The boy smiled.

Half an hour later, the trio had their first hot meal, canned stew with potatoes and other vegetables added. A hot chocolate drink followed this and warm water to wash dirty faces. Afterwards, Niana boiled up another kettle of water and tipped it over the engine cowling of the tractor. She doubted if this somewhat amateurish effort would help but she had to try something. The starter motor whined and, on the second attempt, there was a chug and a puff of black smoke rose into the air.

"Almost," screamed Adona.

The next attempt worked. The engine fired, roared into life and the two children jumped up to a small wooden bench behind the driver's seat.

"We sat here with Daddy," Adona shouted above the rumble of the engine.

The young mother-to-be smiled warmly and said, "Let's go."

She selected a low gear and the tractor moved forward along the snow-covered road, past the corpses that were once the children's family and, Niana hoped, towards the Albanian border.

*

"...So what are you going to do?" The Serb border guard ran an eye down Niana's rotund figure, across to the two children clinging to her jeans and back to her. "Take your choice. You can take the boy or the girl. The other one remains in Kosovo."

"You mean I have to choose between them?" the exhausted woman replied in a hushed voice. "But why?"

The soldier, a junior officer no older than herself, held her gaze. His expression was devoid of any compassion. The eyes were blank, those of a robot or ruthless killing machine. Niana had seen eyes like those before.

[6]

Back at the internment camp, the Serbs were like that, that look of utter disdain caused, probably, by years of indoctrination and generations of ethnic hatred. She shuddered and stifled a retort by swallowing. The stress of those terrible days, the physical deprivation, freezing conditions in the mountains and lack of food all combined to add to the turmoil passing through her mind. She gripped a wooden pole beside her and attempted to focus on the soldier.

"Why?" her voice came out as a sob.

"Hurry up, woman. You're holding up the line."

"What's wrong, Niana?" The little girl's voice was a terrified whisper. She stared, ashen faced, at the uncompromising guard.

The young woman staggered and glanced down. Halia was shivering in the cold room with his eyes showing the same helpless expression that Niana remembered when they had first met.

She could not abandon the children. She would not take one and leave the other. This was one last sadistic manoeuvre by the enemy to humiliate a defenceless Kosovar. Anger, burning and violent swelled in her throat. She wanted to scream and attack the vile creature behind the wooden counter. Her eyes turned. In front, beyond the opened end of the building, was the no man's land backed by a flagpole. The red with black flag fluttered in the dull light and falling snow. It was fifty meters to Albania and freedom but the distance might as well be fifty kilometres.

Could she run for it? Niana swallowed, gripped both the children's hands, glanced at each of them in turn and nodded.

"Children" she whispered. "Remember what we practiced. Don't let go."

Both children squeezed her hand twice, a prearranged signal to show they knew what to do.

"Now," hissed the desperate woman.

She ran.

With the children's hands gripped, Niana crossed the bare boards of the floor in seconds, dodged behind a guard and jumped to the snow covered ground.

She almost toppled but the momentum carried her forward. Shouts, some harsh and demanding, others high pitched as women refugees screamed encouragement, reached her ears but her only thoughts were to reach the red flag ahead.

The trio had covered half the distance when the first shot rang out and a spasm of agony cut through Niana's shoulder. The terrified woman screamed, staggered but remained on her feet.

"Only a few more meters, Niana," a child's petrified voice pierced her mind.

The two children were now in front. A second shot thundered and another blow hit her with such a velocity, her moving body spun around and she crashed into sludge. Blood gushed out from a fresh wound in her abdomen. More poured down her legs and onto the ground.

But someone was pulling her. The two children had not been hit. With tears streaming from their faces they dragged her forward.

Niana blinked back tears of pain and noticed two camouflaged soldiers holding shiny automatic weapons in their hands aimed across her shoulders.

Another shot rang out; an explosive bang rang in Niana's semi-conscious mind. A whine reached her ears and she saw a flash of orange. The soldier had fired across the frontier to protect her.

"Come on!" screamed Adona. "You can do it."

Now almost to her knees, she staggered forward and shrieked in agony. To people within earshot, her screams were incoherent but Adona and Halia understood. "Go, children. Leave me. Get to the border."

"No." sobbed the little girl. "We can't leave you."

Another rifle fired. The world spun and blackness enveloped the refugee woman as she crawled forward through the freezing slush in her last gallant effort to escape. The two children, though, pulled her relentlessly on.

In the whole desperate episode, neither of them would let Niana's hand go.

*

CHAPTER TWO

A rectangle of late afternoon sunlight shone through clouds of fine dust inside the small factory as a man, in shorts, black t-shirt and work boots, worked with a sanding machine to smooth out an old wooden framed couch. He grinned, ran a tanned hand over the section just completed, released the trigger on the machine so the grinding roar dropped to a faint whirr. That was when he realized somebody was watching and glanced up.

A woman in her twenties stood by the door, attractive and slim with brown hair tied back into a ponytail. She wore a white blouse, denim skirt, white anklet socks and sneakers. A shy expression crossed her lips as if she didn't wish to interrupt the worker.

"Oh, I'm sorry," the man's muffled voice said. "I never realized I had a customer." He turned to show a face covered in safety glasses and a small cone shaped mask.

The woman jerked back almost in alarm before she hesitated, relaxed and broke into a smile. "No, it is I who should apologize," she replied in precise but accented English. "Please continue. I can come back."

"No, it's no trouble. I need to call it a day, anyhow." He removed his glasses and mask, switched the sander off and all became silent.

"I understand you're my landlord," the woman said. "I've just taken over the bakery."

"Of course. I should have guessed. There's been a hive of activity over there but, like you, I didn't want to interrupt."

"So you must be Mr. Coleman, the factory owner. I am Niana Bolsa." A slim hand was held out.

"Call me Matt." He gripped the hand and stretched to his full height, a full head and shoulders higher than his visitor. "Welcome to Dixon Street. I hope old Annie left everything in good shape for you."

*

Matt walked to the door and gazed at the century old building across the driveway. It had once been a general merchandise shop and included an apartment at the rear. He'd bought property three years back for his antique and furniture restoration business but had since moved into the building the pair were standing in.

A short time later Old Annie O'Neill rented the original building and set up a lunch bar to sell breakfast and lunches to workers in the area. Annie had placed the popular little business on the market two months back but, until now, had found no buyer.

He noticed a sign painter had changed the name Aunt Anne's Sandwich Bar to *Niana's Sandwich Bar*, and frilly lace curtains appeared on the old fashioned windows.

"I must say, I like the improvements," he continued. "Will you have everything ready for opening day?"

"Oh yes," Niana replied. "Mrs. O'Neill has been most helpful and showed me everything. It's just..." She gave a nervous laugh. "The apartment at the back is lovely but I want to convert the store room into a third bedroom. Anyhow, when I went to take down the old curtains the rod holding it pulled out. I wonder if you have a screwdriver I can borrow."

"I'll come and take a look," Matt offered. "It shouldn't be hard to fix. I like the new name you've given the lunch bar," he said. "Forgive me, but you certainly don't look like an old aunt to me."

The young woman stared at him with earnest brown eye and flushed. "Thank you, I didn't want to change things too much but thought the original name wasn't really me." She nodded up at the sign above Matt's door. "I like your firm's name, too."

Matt glanced up at the ornate polished sign that read *The Cuckoo's Nest - Antiques and Restored Furniture*. He laughed. "Yes it's part of my hobby," he explained. "As well as furniture, I restore old cuckoo clocks. Cuckoos hoard things so the name just seemed appropriate. I originally started in the old shop but have been in the new building for three years, now." For a moment, the pair lapsed into silence as they walked across the driveway between the two buildings. "And the back flat? Do you think you'll like it? Annie told me you wanted to live there." He shrugged. "It's been empty for a while but is perfectly serviceable. I did it up when I moved in for four months."

"Oh yes. It is one of the reasons I'm attracted to the business. I look after two children and my present apartment is much smaller than this one. I'll move in next week and open the shop a week later."

*

She smiled and thanked Matt as he stood back at the rear door of the building and let her enter first. Though the apartment was old, Matt had repainted and carpeted it throughout. Simple, but good quality furniture went with the place.

"It's just what I need," Niana explained. "I'll put Adona, that's my little girl, in here and her brother in the other room." She smiled. "At the moment they're both squeezed in one bedroom."

Matt pushed a door open and a whiff of musty air hit their noses. "I'll get this painted for you," he said. "It's the only room I didn't upgrade."

"There's no need," she replied with an appreciative glance.

"No, I insist. I've a friend who'll probably be able to get it done before you move in." He glanced at the sagging curtain. "I see what's happened. The old brass fitting pulled away from the clip that holds it. I won't be a moment." He clambered up the stepladder Niana had been using, twisted the offending piece back in place and smiled down. "Now, if you hand me your new curtain I'll clip it on the runners."

Everything was completed in a few moments and, afterwards, the pair went through a connecting door to the shop itself where Matt noticed the improvements. He inspected the layout as the young woman explained what she'd done.

"I'm open from Wednesday to Sunday. Most of my sales are on the weekend," Matt said when he could find no excuse to linger. "All the best for your move in and opening. If you need any more help, just ask. "

Niana smiled and held her hand out again." You're so kind. I'll get the first month's rent money over to you tomorrow."

"There's no hurry," Matt said with a shrug. "I'm just happy to have the place open again. I reckon my business has dropped ten per cent since Old Annie closed down."

He whistled a few bars of a popular tune as he strolled back, examined the couch he'd been working on and started the sander. On first impression, his new tenant seemed a very pleasant person. As he ran the machine up another section of the couch his mind reflected back. A great figure too, not to mention that cute accent. He wondered where she came from.

"Simmer down, boy," he muttered to himself as he grinned and continued his work.

*

It was late morning few a days later when Matt arrived at his shop with the old truck loaded with second-hand furniture he'd picked up for a song from various auction marts and second-hand dealers. There were a couple of old oak bedroom suites from estates that, when brought back to pristine condition, would be very popular.

He backed inside but the thought of unloading the heavy items didn't appeal. He grinned. This life was certainly better than having to fit in with a clock from dawn to dust.

A little Honda parked next door made his thoughts turn to the woman there. Perhaps she was having lunch too. Anyhow, that was a good excuse to go and visit her. He ran a comb through his short hair and strolled across the alley.

"Come in," came the response to his knock. Niana was sitting at one of half a dozen wooden tables between the door and counter.

"I like these," he commented, nodding at the red and white checked tablecloths and comfortable looking chairs that completed the scene.

Niana glanced up from a thick document she'd been reading and sighed. "Hello Mr. ... I mean Matt," she said in a quiet voice. "They have to go out again, I'm afraid."

"Why?" Matt pulled out a chair and noticed she looked quite tired with dark circles under the eyes.

"Regulations," Niana said, holding up the document. "I wanted to use these tables for customers. However, this means I'd be classified as a restaurant rather than a food bar. I can't comply with all the extra regulations."

"I see. I had the same trouble when I decided to open my workshop as a retail store. The bureaucrats had a field day. I even had to put in male and female toilets. One's never used and is full of old junk."

"That's one thing I need." Niana gave a slight grin. "Oh well, I'll just give up the idea."

"Wait a minute," Matt replied. "I'm your landlord. Perhaps I can help. What exactly do you need?"

"I've highlighted everything." Niana slid the document across the table. "I can't possibly comply. There's the extra toilet, an extra stainless steel work area and, would you believe it--off street parking for seven vehicles. I told them I was going to have six tables so that means seven parking spaces." She chuckled. "One family must be going to drive here in two cars."

Matt's eyes met hers and he burst out laughing.

The woman frowned. "What did I say?" she retorted.

"It's not you. I can solve two of your problems right away."

"How?"

[12]

"Unless they've changed the regulations since I had to follow them, it says the men's toilet can be off premises." He flipped to the back of the document and ran his fingers down the index. "Yes, here it is on page eighty six. It seems it's okay for the men to go outside somewhere but not the ladies."

"But how can that help?"

My unused toilet is directly across the alley. That side door you can see is the one. I'll put in a corridor door and leave the outside one open. Stick up a Gents sign and you have your male toilet."

"You'd do that?" Niana glanced up at him but her face remained serious.

"Well I have to keep my tenant happy."

"Thank you but what about the other things?"

Matt grinned again. "I had parking problems, too so I created eight parking spaces down the back that are never used. I think I only needed four. I'll allocate half of them to you and stick up a new sign. Mine fell down last year sometime. You know, *Parking at the Rear*." He laughed again. "Mind you, I'll have to move junk out of the way."

Niana smiled for the first time. "You're a man of many resources, I see. You make it all seem so easy."

Matt was enjoying himself. "How'd you like to go stainless steel sink hunting?" he asked.

"I suppose you have a couple of those lying around, too."

"Afraid not, but there must be one somewhere in the city. If you give me twenty minutes to unload my truck, we'll go and look."

Niana rose out of her chair and faced him. "If you're doing all this for me, the least I can do is help unload your truck. Come on."

"It's heavy stuff."

"So," she replied in a determined voice. "If you were about to do it by yourself, I must be able to help."

And help she did. For a petite woman, she was amazingly strong and never hesitated to take an end of several large dressing tables that were unloaded. Afterwards, she clambered up into the cab, smiled across at her host and watched for approaching traffic as they drove out.

*

An hour later, Matt found what they wanted at the site of a friend whose firm had just demolished a hotel. Niana purchased two large boxes of brand new dinner sets for almost nothing as they were embossed with the

[13]

hotel's name.

"Who cares if they say Grand Hotel," she said as Matt lifted the boxes aboard the truck. "Perhaps I could call the sandwich bar that."

"Well, it's getting grander by the hour." Matt laughed and turned to the man beside them. "I want the sink top delivered tomorrow, Ted," he said.

"Sure, Matt." Ted Wilson grinned after Niana walked away to climb in the truck. "One sexy lady," he said. "Better than the old model, I'd say."

Matt knew it was a joke but frowned in annoyance. "It's nothing like that, Ted," he retorted. "She's renting the old shop, that's all."

"Oh yeah. How's Judith anyway?"

Matt's expression darkened when his wife's name was mentioned. "She decided not to come back after our trial separation, Ted."

Ted sighed. "Sorry Matt. I knew you were having a rough patch but didn't realize..."

"Oh, it's for the best, I guess," Matt said. "We've no family and she didn't appreciate it when I decided to give up my big corporate job and start out on my own." He laughed with a trace of sarcasm. "It is not so good on the golf and social circuit to have a used furniture husband instead of company director."

"Snob," Ted grunted. "And your house?"

"I'm living in it. Judith's moved in with some guy who has a place over in Western Heights."

"Well, you're a free agent, then." Ted nodded at the truck. "Take my advice and go for it, lad."

"Sure," Matt said, huffing a laugh. "A run down old hack like myself. You must be kidding."

Ted only chuckled, slapped his friend's back and walked away.

*

Matt watched him for a second before, deep in thought; he walked back to the truck. A faint fragrance of shampoo hit his nose as he climbed in and saw Niana smiling on him. Today she wore a dark blue sweater that enhanced her cleavage.

"A good friend?" she asked.

"I suppose." Matt flushed at his thoughts. "Ted helped me when I was getting established and we often refer customers to each other "

"It's good to have friends," came the hushed reply.

There was almost sadness in the way she spoke. Matt glanced across

[14]

the cab but Niana had already turned away. She was a beautiful woman but a bit of an enigma, too. He was curious.

*

A few moments later, Niana glanced at her watch. "Oh, my God," she whispered more to herself than to Matt. "I didn't realize it was so late."

Matt frowned and checked the time. It was twenty to three. "Why, have you an appointment?"

"The children. I have to pick them up." There was almost panic in her voice. "You've been so good but can I ask for one more thing? It's just that by the time we return to the shop and I get my car..." her voice trailed off.

"No problem. Where to?"

"Selwyn Avenue School. Know where it is?"

"More or less. You might need to direct me after I turn off the main road."

"Thank you. It's just that they depend on me." Niana glanced at Matt and continued, "They're orphans who came out with me. I'm all they have." Her cloudy eyes linked with Matt's. "You see, Matt, we're refugees from Kosovo. My family has gone. Halia and his little sister Adona were alone and I, what would you say, decided to look after them."

"I see. That sounds like one hell of a decent thing to do."

"I guess, but I need them as much as they need me." She stared ahead as Matt moved the old truck forward. "I'm sorry. You don't want to hear all my complaints. I'm so thankful for the help I've had since my arrival here and now you've been so kind."

"No, I'm interested," Matt said. He saw that his companion was almost in tears. "Niana," he continued, "I can't even guess at what you went through, but I'd like to help."

"Why?" she replied in a sudden hard voice.

Matt flushed a bright red. "Hell, I don't know," he muttered. "Forget what I said."

Niana, smiled. "You're different from most men I've had contact with," she whispered. "Most are only interested in..." She hesitated. "You know."

Matt thought back to Ted's comments and nodded.

"What about yourself, Matt. Have you a family?"

"No. My marriage is over and we had no kids."

"Kids?"

[15]

It was Matt's turn to smile. "Children," he explained. "Judith was a businesswoman and never wanted any."

"I see." The woman's eyes, still serious, bore into him. "Take the next left turn, then turn right at the third intersection. The school is two blocks further on. "

"Right," Matt replied and slowed down.

"No left," Niana corrected, caught his eye and they both laughed. "I took English up to university level but still can't understand it at times."

Vehicles filled every space outside the school so Matt double-parked while Niana searched through the throngs of children pouring out the gate. "There they are," she said. "I'll go and get them."

"Sure," Matt replied, watching as she slipped between two parked cars and made her way to where a boy about eight was clasping the hand of a little girl hardly big enough to be at school.

A minute later the passenger door opened and two hazel eyes gazed at him as the girl scrambled in, followed by a shy looking boy and finally Niana. "This is Matt, children," she said, and then repeated her words in another language. She glanced up at Matt and added more in her own language. Adona gave a chuckle and Halia a slight grin. "I told them you're the nice man who owns the shop and we'll visit McDonald's. Do you mind?"

"Not at all." Matt laughed.

Adona looked up at him. "I got a star at school today," she said in almost accent-less English.

"Did you now? What for?"

"My writing," Adona said in a proud voice.

"The children speak better English than I do," Niana commented. She glanced at the boy. "Don't you, Halia?"

"Yes," the boy replied, casting a quick glance at Matt before he lapsed back into silence.

"He doesn't trust men, I'm afraid," Niana explained.

"Well," Matt said. "We'll just have to show Halia that most men in this country are okay, won't we? "

Halia looked across at Matt. "Niana said you make furniture and wooden trucks."

"That's right. I've made several toy trucks," Matt said, glancing at his companion. They'd never mentioned the row of wooden toys he had on a top shelf in his shop. "If Niana doesn't mind, I'll show you how to make one when you visit."

Halia nodded and glanced away.

[16]

"Niana bought me a teddy bear," Adona interrupted. "I take him to bed every night."

"Did she?" Matt said. He felt a hand give his arm a brief squeeze and saw Niana gazing at him.

"Thank you," she mouthed.

*

At *The Cuckoo's Nest*, the children ran across to the Honda and Niana turned to Matt.

"I must go," she said. "I'll be back after I drop the children off at school tomorrow. It'll be easier once I've moved into the apartment here."

"What about next week?" Matt asked.

"You mean my early hours?"

Matt nodded.

"The mornings won't be too bad. The children will be with me and can walk to school later. I will be closing every day at two so will have time to clean up and meet them after school. That's one reason I thought the sandwich bar would be so good."

"And who financed you for it?" Matt asked. As he was about to apologize again for being forward, Niana flashed a smile before her face turned sad.

"My parents anticipated the trouble at home and had a little money deposited in an Italian bank. I inherited it and a local bank loaned me the rest. Your government has sponsored a program to help us get credit." She glanced across at her car. "But I must be off. Goodbye for now, Matt. Thank you for your help today." Her smile returned.

"My pleasure."

That evening as he drove into the driveway of his home, a modern house in one of the newer suburbs, he watched his cat crawl out from under a bush. He shrugged. Something was missing. He parked the truck in a space by the garage and climbed down before he realized what it was. For the first time in months, he never had that hollow feeling when he arrived back at the empty house.

"Well Misty," he said as he picked up the little grey cat to pet. "I hope you've been looking after everything for me."

Round yellow eyes stared at him as if the cat understood everything he said. Matt laughed, realizing that Misty was only hungry and knew he had cat food in his supermarket bag.

"Come on, Misty." He laughed. "I bought a piece of fresh fish for

[17]

you."

*

Over the course of the next few weeks Matt found out a little about Niana. She was not, as he had first thought, a Muslim. A little research showed that about a quarter of Albanians were Orthodox Christians or Roman Catholics but Matt could find no facts on the ethnic Albanians from Kosovo.

"When I was a child, our communist government discouraged all religions," she commented one of the few times the subject was mentioned. "I guess it worked reasonably well, but my parents told me it was only after Marshall Tito died that the ethnic differences surfaced. The language we speak makes us the enemy in the eyes of Serb nationalists."

She spoke four languages with Italian added to her repertoire of two local languages and English; and originated from the capital of Kosovo, Pristina. There, she had been a postgraduate student. Her experiences during those fateful days in April 1999 were never mentioned but Matt could tell the memories were firmly embedded in her mind. Often small events would trigger a reaction from grim silence to soft tears before she'd swallow and continue whatever she was doing at the time.

Niana's Sandwich Bar opened without much fanfare, but it wasn't a whimper either. The original clients from Annie's establishment returned and the number of sit-down customers, especially for breakfast in the early morning, was so popular Niana moved her opening time back from seven to six-thirty and hired an employee part-time every morning until ten.

She proved to be an astute businesswoman who altered her menus to suit the clients' tastes. Unpopular choices were eliminated and she soon realized the majority of customers wanted ordinary food and tended to bypass the frilly stuff. As well as sandwiches, scones, muffins and small cakes sold well. Home-baked pies were also popular, with small individual ones preferred to the larger family-sized pies. Take-out coffee in paper mugs also sold well.

Matt noticed that the number of customers strolling through *The Cuckoo's Nest* increased and casual sales of smaller items such as the wooden toys and curiosities improved. He'd even sold two of the six cuckoo clocks that had been placed along the wall for months.

*

[18]

CHAPTER THREE

Bits of a cuckoo clock lay sprawled across the workbench like pieces of a jigsaw puzzle after Matt carefully tapped out the dozens of wooden pegs that held the ancient instrument together and used a special solvent to dissolve the old glue. This particular model had been tossed in a back shed or loft somewhere and had sustained water damage. The gears, chains and working parts were a solid mass of rust beyond redemption but the ornate wooden carvings, though blackened with age and neglect, were unbroken. Waiting along the bench was the mechanism of a second cuckoo clock, this one with a smashed exterior. Between the two, and after hours of careful reconstruction, Matt would end up with a fully working cuckoo clock every bit as perfect as when it was first manufactured a century before.

This was his hobby with little financial gain expected for his efforts. It was a fun way to pass a wet Saturday afternoon. Usually a few customers visited so it was worth staying open.

As he grunted over a stubborn peg that wouldn't come out, a movement caught his eyes and he glanced around. Two children stood in the room with their eyes on him, the little boy behind his sister but with both arms firmly around her.

"Hello Halia and Adona," Matt said. "My, you both look smart. Are those new sweatshirts?"

"Niana bought them for us," Adona replied with a cheerful smile. She swung herself around. "I wanted to show you."

Halia glanced up at the row of wooden toys shelved above the bench. "You said we could see your toys," he said in a hesitant voice.

"Of course," Matt replied. "You know, they've been sitting there for ages, now. Would you both like one to take home?"

"Can we?" Adona gasped.

"Why not? As well as toy vehicles, there were several wooden dolls' cots and a small doll's house in the selection. "What would you like?"

"A tractor," Halia replied. "My daddy had a tractor."

"Me, too," Adona added.

"So you want a tractor, too? Not a doll's house?"

"No." The little girl shook her head. "I want a tractor, too, please." She stopped and big hazel eyes looked at him. "Girls can have tractors can't

[19]

they, Matt?"

"Of course." Matt selected four wooden tractors and placed them on the bench. "There you are, pick one each."

Adona's eyes shone as she grabbed one toy while her brother had a more methodical approach. He examined the remaining three in turn before choosing the middle one.

"This has a latch to join a wagon on," he said in a solemn voice.

"So you'd like a wagon? I haven't any but we could make one sometime."

"Yes please," Halia replied. "One with four wheels."

"So what say we make two of them?" Matt said. "One each."

Adona, as usual, was the first to reply. "Yes please." She clasped her toy in little hands." I'm going to show Niana mine."

She ran out of the room. Halia gave a small grin, clutched his own toy to follow but stopped at the door. "Matt?"

"Yes, Halia."

"That pile of sand by the car park. Can we play in it?"

"It will be a bit wet out there now but later you can."

"Thanks Matt," the little boy answered in his serious voice. "Bye."

Matt grinned and wondered if he could ever get the little fellow to smile. After all they'd gone through, it was probably his way of coping. He placed the remaining toys back on the shelf and returned to the cuckoo clock pieces.

A few moments later Niana appeared with a twenty-dollar note in her hand and looked serious, not unlike Halia's expression. "I told the children they shouldn't have taken the toys," she said in a quiet voice. "But they were so thrilled with them I never had the heart to return them. How much do I owe you?"

"They're a gift." Matt grinned. "Wooden toys don't sell well, anyway. Kids now-a-days want plastic ones with flashing lights and electric motors."

"But Matt…" The young women's eyes warmed. "Why are you so kind?"

Matt flushed. "As I said when we met, I just want to help."

"And no ulterior motives?"

Matt chuckled. "Of course there is, a beautiful young woman alone in the world…" He coughed and glanced away. "That was a damn stupid thing to say. I'm sorry."

Niana fixed her eyes on him and reached out to grab his hands. "You hardly know me," she whispered and, without warning, tears began to

[20]

roll down her cheeks. "You might not like the real me."

Matt blinked at her reaction, reached forward and tucked his arms around her, all the time expecting a firm rebuff but it never came. A soft body clutched into him. He could feel tight breasts pressed against his chest and warm arms around his neck, smell that rich clean hair and the aroma of toothpaste as her face moved a mere few centimetres away.

He reached down, placed a finger under a small chin and felt his lips tingle with emotion. Without really thinking about it he found himself kissing lips placed against his.

At first polite, the kiss soon turned into something more frantic as the woman responded. She held him, opened her mouth slightly so her tongue ran along his.

However, a moment later she placed an opened hand on his chest, gave a gentle push and stepped back. "I'm sorry, Matt," she whispered, wiped her hands down the sides of her jeans and stepped towards the door.

Matt interpreted her action as nervousness rather than annoyance so reached out and, in one deft movement, had her back in his arms. She was now shaking but remained there with more tears flowing and tucked her face into his neck as he, without really thinking of the consequences, ran fingers up her sweater and touched the smooth cleavage between her breasts.

"Matt " She sighed but didn't object when he cupped a breast through the material. He kissed her again, long and with passion.

Niana hesitated, kissed him lightly on the cheek and lifted his hand off her breast. "Not now, Matt, please," she panted as if trying to contain her own emotions. "The children."

"Of course," he replied in embarrassment and relaxed his hold as their eyes met.

"I'm not an innocent virgin," she whispered and continued speaking when he smiled and hugged her closer. "No, Matt. Listen to me." The eyes were dry now but her lips quivered.

"Go on," he replied in a gentle voice.

*

"I was eight months pregnant, Matt, when the soldiers came and shot my husband in front of me." She began sobbing again. "I was certain I'd be raped but they fondled me, stared at my rotund body, laughed, said they preferred slim women and told me to head for Albania." Her body shuddered and tears again rolled down her cheeks. "Thirty minutes later

[21]

they returned, tossed a bottle of petrol over the house and torched it. My husband's body was still inside. I had the clothes I stood in. That was all."

"And your baby?" Matt asked, his voice grim.

"Stillborn." Niana shrugged. "After I reached the border an Italian doctor helped to save my life. It was hell, Matt." Her eyes, full of emotion stared into his. "I don't even know his name..."

"Oh you poor dear," he responded after the story with all its horror unfolded.

He reached forward and passion again erupted between the pair, so intense, Matt didn't want to stop but fought his emotions as he held her in his arms. After what seemed to be an eternity, the kisses stopped and Niana sniffed back stubborn tears.

"So that's me," she finally spluttered and stepped back. "I've made a fool of myself, haven't I?"

"No. You have a life ahead, Niana but never be afraid to remember the past."

"Oh Matt, I thought when you heard about me you wouldn't..."

"Perhaps you think too much," Matt interrupted.

"Sure." She blew her nose, grinned, and straightened the rest of her ruffled clothing. "Come on, the children will miss us."

"Okay," Matt said but noticed the twenty-dollar note placed under a block of wood on the bench. "I don't want anything for the toys, okay?" He reached forward and tucked the money in the pocket of her jeans.

"Okay," she replied and smiled. "But you shouldn't spoil them, you know."

"And you don't?"

"I just try to make their lives normal if there is such a thing."

＊

Together, the two walked through to the shop. It was still raining outside and no customers were around. Matt locked up and they headed across the alley. Under the veranda of the smaller building, two mud splattered and wet children were pushing toy tractors along a muddy little road they'd made in the adjacent garden and chatting away in a blend of English and their own language. They hadn't even noticed the adults watching them.

"Oh goodness," Niana gasped. "They're filthy."

Adona glanced up with a grubby smile. "Hi Niana," she shouted above the noise of the rain on the tin roof," My tractor got stuck and Halia had to come and push me out."

"Leave them," Matt suggested. "Let's have a cup of coffee. They can have a bath later."

"You can play for another ten minutes and use the hose in the alley to wash yourselves down before you come inside," Niana told the children as she led Matt inside. "I baked some scones at home. That was why I came to the shop on a Saturday, I thought you might be hungry." She coughed and continued in a hushed but warm voice. "I miss you on the weekends."

"And I thought it was only me," Matt replied.

"Oh, Matt, with all those sophisticated local women in their flashy cars that visit your shop, I thought you wouldn't be interested in a stressed out foreign refugee. As time slipped by and you continued to visit, I thought you were still only trying to be kind."

"Most of my customers are married, over fifty and have a two hundred thousand dollar mortgage over their heads," Matt said. "Not one of them can compare to your sunny smile." He flushed. "I'm not very good at this sort of stuff."

"You were doing okay a few moments ago," Niana chuckled. "I just about had to fight you off."

"Sorry about that..."

"No you aren't." The young woman snapped, stood on tiptoes and placed a firm kiss on his lips. "What happened is what we both wanted," she whispered and kissed him again. "It's what we both need. Next time we'll wait until the children are away and let things happen." She blushed. "That came out all wrong. I can't find the English words I want."

Matt cleared his throat. "You had some scones, I believe?" He changed the topic but his eyes showed his innermost feelings. Even in casual jeans and sweater Niana looked stunning; so feminine and self-assured. He could hardly believe what had happened those few minutes ago. It was like a dream and he'd wake up in his empty bed at home. He realized how lonely he'd been over the last long months but the emotion he felt now was more than a physical attraction of a lonely man towards a voluptuous woman ... much more.

"Of course." Niana's laughing voice interrupted his thoughts.

"With raspberry jam," Matt added. He plunked himself down on a stool beside the stainless steel bench they'd installed when Niana first arrived and watched as she slid a tray of scones into an oven to reheat.

She turned, smiled and took a container of orange juice out of the refrigerator. "Talking about children, I'd better bring my kids in," she whispered with an emphasis on the word kids. "They can use the shower

[23]

here." She giggled. "Perhaps I guessed it was going to be a different sort of afternoon. I brought them an extra set of clothes."

*

Matt had just staggered out of bed on Sunday morning when the telephone rang. It was Niana but her voice sounded remote.

"We need to talk, Matt," she said. "Can I come and see you? I'll need to bring the children with me."

"Of course," Matt replied with a frown. He chatted for a moment without questioning Niana, gave her directions to his home and hung up.

"Oh, shit," he muttered, running his hand along the stubble on his chin, and dashing to give himself a quick shave before Niana arrived.

Half an hour later the Honda pulled up and the two children bounded out, Adona with a cheery smile and Halia a slight grin. Both were well dressed in warm clothes and carrying their tractors and a bag of other odds and ends. Niana walked around her car with a tight expression fixed to her dark eyes.

"Your house," she said in a quiet neutral voice. "It's lovely."

Matt glanced back at the cream bricks and bay window behind him and shrugged. "It was built to my design. Well, I had a pad full of ideas and an architect put them all together," he added. "I started breakfast," he said, ushering the three into a contemporary kitchen where the smell of bacon filled the air.

"Oh Matt," the young woman sighed. "You are making it so difficult for me."

"Why, Niana? I can tell by your body language something is wrong. If I hurt you somehow, forgive me. That's the last thing I want to do." Matt nodded and noticed the two children gazing intently at him. "Go through to the other room, kids," he said. "I've got cartoons turned on. I'll bring you some breakfast when it's cooked. There's bacon, eggs, fried tomatoes and toast. How does that sound?"

Even Halia grinned before he followed his sister to the comfortable lounge.

"Now, what is it, Niana?" Matt asked when the children were out of earshot.

She'd taken off her jacket and wore a blue dress under a beige knit pullover. As usual, she looked quite beautiful. Her face, though, was serious with downcast eyes and teeth biting against her bottom lip.

"It's last night," she said. "Things happened too quickly. To be

[24]

frank, I don't want to have an affair." Her eyes blinked.

Matt reached out for her but she stepped away. "No Matt," she said. "When you held me last night I was drawn to you. I needed your body but I am afraid."

"But why?" Matt's stomach churned as he wiped a hand across his brow.

"I don't want sex just for the lust. It's not enough. At the moment I am so lonely I am trying to cope and I need you, Matt, but as you were, a generous kind friend, not a lover."

"I see," Matt said with disappointment ringing in his voice." I guess I'm no great catch, am I? "

Niana looked at him and burst into tears, the same tears of emotion that wrenched Matt's heart the night before. "You don't understand," she whispered. "It's not that I'm not attracted to you. It's the opposite, in fact."

"You still have your husband on your mind and feel you're being disloyal to his memory; is that it?"

Niana wiped her eyes and stared across at him. "Why are you so bloody understanding," she sniffed. "I had it all worked out. I'd come here, say I wouldn't go to bed with you and even offer to sell my business if being so close became an embarrassment."

"And how did you expect me to react?"

"Oh I don't know. When friends become lovers, the passion passes and they go their own way, usually with one being hurt. I thought you'd be hurt, but very polite, talk for a while about something neutral, I'd go home and you'd avoid me in the future."

Matt walked across to the stove, turned the sizzling bacon over and tossed some tomato chunks in. He glanced out the window, frowned and turned to where the young woman's eyes had followed every movement he'd made.

Without a sound, he stepped forward grabbed her two hands and, before she could react, pulled her into his chest in a powerful embrace and kissed her fully on the lips.

"Matt. Stop it," she retorted, struggling to get out of his arms but he was too strong.

He held on, waiting until she stopped kicking and squirming, and watched while the inevitable tears continued to flow. Holding her face so she couldn't turn away, he kissed her again. Drawing her body against his, he willed himself not to touch the heaving breasts pressed against his chest. After several kisses, she responded with sobs conflicting with the passion.

Finally, Matt relaxed his hold so Niana was at an arm's length.

[25]

"We're more than friends, Niana," he whispered. "Every day I want to hold you like I'm doing now." He let her hands go and stepped back. "But I promise I'll go no further unless it is what you want."

"Oh Matt," the sobbing young woman replied.

"Well?" Matt asked.

She smiled through her tears and held out a hand. "Mr. Coleman," she said, "I accept your conditions." She flushed. "I don't even mind if your hands drift a little."

"Good," Matt said with a wink. "Let's have breakfast. I'm starved."

He turned and broke four eggs into the frying pan. They hissed and splattered while a cloud of hot smoke rose towards the exhaust fan but he never noticed. The arm around his waist and the head tucked into his neck had distracted him.

"I should be very annoyed with you," Niana retorted.

*

Matt kept his bargain and slowly the attraction he had for Niana turned into love that, he was sure, was reciprocated. Every day, when they were alone, he'd give a slight grin, grab her in his arms and kiss her. She'd respond and, if they were in a private spot, his hand would slip across her dress or sweater to softly massage the breasts beneath. He never went under the material until one afternoon, when Niana, almost in exasperation, undid four buttons of her blouse to show she was wearing no brassiere beneath. With a slight grin, she grabbed his hands and placed them firmly on her breasts, kissed him with a passion he was now becoming used to and rubbed a soft hand up his fly.

"Niana," he gasped as he bent to kiss her succulent body. "How can I keep my end of our bargain when you do this to me?"

"Patience, my love," she replied using that word the first time. She moaned as his lips touched a taut exposed nipple "Oh God, Matt," she moaned a moment later as his hand grabbed her other breast and squeezed. She lifted his head and kissed him before adding, "Perhaps I shouldn't have been so provocative."

"It's too late now," Matt said, lifting her up over his shoulder in a fireman's hold.

"Matt!" She screamed, kicked and thumped his back as he carried her over to an old couch in the corner of his workshop and plunked her down. He bent over and kissed her again, stood back and smiled.

"When one plays with fire," he said, chuckling.

[26]

"You just wait," she retorted as she redid her blouse buttons. Suddenly, she jumped up, tickled him under the arms and ran for the workshop door before he could grab her. "I have to go and pick up the kids," she said, laughing back at him. "See you later."

Matt went charging out after her and almost knocked an elderly lady over who, unnoticed, had entered *The Cuckoo's Nest* and had just been avoided in Niana's quick dash through.

"Oops, excuse me, Ma'am," he panted. "We didn't realize how late it was and Niana, there, has to go and pick up her children."

"You don't need to make excuses to me, young man," she answered in an indignant voice. Breaking into a crinkly smile, she added, "I was young once, you know."

*

CHAPTER FOUR

"Those cuckoo clocks. Are they for sale?"

Matt glanced up to see an Asian gentleman, dressed in a crisp black suit, white shirt and dark tie, addressing him.

"Seven of them are," Matt said. "All except the one at the end. That one is my mascot." He noticed the man frown and explained. "That was my first cuckoo clock and is what my business is named after."

"I understand," the man said. Speaking rapidly in what sounded like Japanese, to an older colleague beside him, he turned back to Matt. "And do they all work?"

"Oh yes, they're all in perfect condition but I usually only have a couple going at a time. Would you like to examine one?"

"Please."

Matt carried a small stepladder across the room and lifted the first clock down, gathered up the weight chains so they wouldn't become knotted and laid it carefully on the counter.

The man studied Matt's movements and gave a slight grunt. "You take great pride in your craftsmanship, I notice," he said.

"They're really a hobby," Matt replied with a shrug, "but yes, I am careful. They're delicate instruments."

"How much?" The second man spoke for the first time.

Matt took a yellow card attached to the clock and held it out. The price, in his opinion was quite high but customers usually haggled for a lower one. The younger man read and handed the card to the older Japanese man.

"A very reasonable price." the first man said, "and the others?"

"Except for the larger one in the middle, they're all priced the same. It is a hundred dollars higher."

A conversation between the two customers continued for a moment before another question came. "You manufacture these cuckoo clocks?"

"No, I restore old clocks. Most originate from Switzerland or other parts of Europe." Matt nodded at the end clock. "That one is manufactured in Canada."

"We'll take them," the elder man said.

[28]

"Which one would you like?" Matt asked.

"All seven," the younger man said, withdrawing a chequebook from an inner pocket of his jacket. "You did say they were all for sale?"

"Sure." Matt said. This was equivalent to the clocks he sold in a year. "I'll find some boxes to pack them in."

Ten minutes later, Matt helped carry the clocks out to a black Mercedes parked out the front. In the trunk among a pile of other items were two more old cuckoo clocks.

"Can you restore these for us?" the younger Japanese man asked. "We'll pay you a fair rate."

Matt examined them and nodded. "I can't see any problems but it'll take time."

"All craftsmanship takes time, Mr. Coleman. Just call us when you've finished."

Matt was handed a business card written in Japanese and English. He wasn't surprised to read that the older man was a Senior Vice President from a well-known Japanese firm.

Conditions were discussed, the two older clocks carried inside, hands shaken and the customers left.

*

Matt stared at the check again. My God. What a sale. He felt so excited he had to tell someone, so he wandered across to the sandwich bar.

"Hi, Roseanne." He grinned at the middle-aged woman working there. "Is Niana around?"

"Hello Matt," the chubby woman replied. "I'm glad you came. Poor Niana is a little distressed. I was going to call you but noticed you had some flashy customers."

Matt frowned. "Why, What's wrong?"

"Some guy made a pass at her. He's been hanging around all this week. Every day about nine after most of the breakfast rush is over he orders breakfast and just ogles her. Today he went up and said something and she just tore out the back in tears."

"Where is the guy?" Matt's voice grated as anger rose within.

"He's gone. Niana's out in the staff room."

"Thanks, Roseanne."

He found Niana standing at the end of the room staring out the window with tears flowing down her cheeks. Matt's heart went out to her. He crossed the room in four gigantic strides and wrapped his arms around

[29]

the weeping Niana.

She jerked back in alarm but realized who it was and turned to bury her head in his chest. Quiet tears turned into shuddering sobs as she reached up and clutched her arms around his neck. Matt stroked her hair gently and waited. She was highly distressed, that was obvious.

"It's only some creep," he soothed, kissing her forehead. "Don't worry about him."

Niana glanced up, smiled through the tears and gave him a bruising kiss before she wiped the tears away and explained. "He propositioned me as if I was a harlot," she sobbed.

"He did?" Matt's voice was hard. "Well, don't worry. He's the one with a problem, not you."

"You don't understand," Niana sniffed. "It wasn't just him. He brought back the memories. I wasn't truthful with you, my love."

Matt held her close and waited.

"Back home," she continued, "it was true I was eight months pregnant but the rest wasn't."

"What do you mean?" Matt asked softly.

"That's why I'm so hesitant," brown eyes stared into Matt's. "I was raped. Even though I was eight months pregnant they raped me eleven times over four nights. I counted them. On the fifth day a new group of girls arrived. They raped them and left me alone. There were over thirty girls in that camp. The ones who resisted were beaten before being raped and several died. That's all I was, Matt, a sex object for those Serbs." She burst into shuddering tears again. "You won't want me now."

"Rubbish," Matt snapped. He held her cheeks and kissed the trembling lips. "Why should that make a difference?"

"Oh Matt," Niana sobbed and kissed him back. "I don't deserve you."

"Niana," Matt's face was tight with emotion, anger at her treatment, empathy, and pity perhaps but those emotions were overwhelmed by love for the woman in his arms. "I love you, you silly woman. Nothing will change that. Understand?"

"Yes, Matt," Niana wiped her eyes. "It's as if a shadow is always behind me. That man looked the same as my captors; unshaven face, black moustache and he used foul words. He spoke in English but his intentions were the same. I'm frightened he'll return and attack me."

"I'll deal with the pervert," Matt growled.

*

[30]

Just after nine the next morning Matt sat unobtrusively at the corner-most table of *Niana's Sandwich* Bar sipping coffee and reading the New Zealand Herald. He glanced up as a man walked in the restaurant and made his way to the counter where Niana was placing a batch of scones in the glass selection shelf.

"Hello sweetie." The man's approach was brazen and without hesitation as he slung his overweight body over a stool. "Fifty bucks for thirty minutes. A hundred if you can be a bit kinky." He grinned. "You European girls aren't inhibited like the locals."

In spite of knowing Matt was close, Niana paled and almost dropped the scones. "Go away," she hissed.

"Oh darling, don't think you can put me off that easily. I know your sort, low cut dress so your tits are on display, pretending you don't want a poke." He laughed. "You turn me on, girlie and I--" the sentence was replaced by a grunt of surprise as his arm was seized from behind and forced up his back.

"That is my girl you're talking to there, creep," Matt snarled just above a whisper. "She told you to leave." His face was mere centimetres from the man's. He glared into the frightened eyes and tugged the arm up.

"Shit man, you're hurting me." He tried to squirm out of the hold but screamed in agony as Matt's grip tightened.

"Shut up or I'll break your arm. Get it?" Matt hissed.

"Stop it, man," the man shouted. His eyes bulged and perspiration appeared on the chalk white face. "It was a joke. God, can't a person make a joke? I only--" his voice rose to a scream as Matt stood, spun his victim around and frog-marched him towards the door. The man swore, lashed out with a free arm and kicked solid work boots into the air. A fist connected with Matt's face, which only succeeded in having the vice like grip on his arm tightened until he was buckled over like a staple. A yell of agony pierced the air.

"I'll open the door," Roseanne said. She beamed as the pair approached the front of the restaurant.

Matt nodded and propelled the unwanted customer out to the veranda. "Your welcome is exhausted here, mate. Come back and I'll set my pit bull on you." He didn't own a dog but this creep wouldn't know that. In one violent shove he sent the man sprawling across the wood floor and then tossed a ten-dollar bill at him. "Your breakfast money, I believe. Go elsewhere."

The man lay on the floor, glowering up at the fire in his attacker's eyes and the two clenched fists at the bottom of bulging biceps, and slithered off the edge of the veranda. He stood, rubbed his sore arm and backed across to an ancient Ford.

"It was just a bit of fun, man," he muttered as he leaped into the vehicle and roared away.

*

Niana frowned with worry when he returned inside. "What if the police come and arrest you for assault?"

"Doubt it." Matt smiled grimly. "Anyhow, I'm only protecting a friend."

"Some protection," Roseanne chuckled. "You scared the shit out of him, I'd say."

"Roseanne," Niana gasped in mock horror. "What language."

The older woman flushed. "Yes, well you know?"

"We do." Matt laughed and tucked his arms around both the women. "Thanks for telling me yesterday, Roseanne. Niana would have kept it to herself."

"I wouldn't," Niana protested, breaking into a smile. "Well, for a while perhaps," she added. "Come on, this deserves a free cup of coffee."

She took Matt's hand and led him inside.

*

The old yellow truck rumbled along the harbour front and pulled in off the busy road into a parking area beside a stone wall. In front, the waves surged towards shore, crested higher and tumbled over into white foam that ran up onto the grainy sand. For a minute it continued, reached the base of the wall and retreated just as the next breaker rose to repeat the action.

"Want to walk?" Matt asked Niana.

She glanced across at him and smiled. "I feel guilty," she replied.

"Why? Roseanne said she'd look after the shop, all the baking is finished and Fran will be in at noon to help with the lunchtime rush."

"But your shop?"

Matt shrugged. "My customers at this time of the week can be counted on one hand. Before I met you I'd often closed my doors for an hour or so when there was something I wanted to do."

"Okay," Niana relented. She slipped out of the truck, kicked her shoes off and walked down a short set of steps to the sand. The water

[32]

curled around her toes and splashed up her ankles. "I love the ocean," she whispered when Matt joined her and slipped his arm around her waist. "We had no ocean at home but I spent a couple of holidays at Italian resorts in my varsity days."

They walked on in silence for ten minutes just happy to be together before they broke into small talk. Niana slipped her jacket off and moved into Matt so her hair tickled his neck. He hugged her close and gazed at the panorama of the city across the bay where towering buildings looked squat beneath the skytower. This gigantic cylindrical structure dominated the downtown Auckland skyline, shiny and white with the blue sky beyond.

"There's a small seafood restaurant built out over the water just around the corner," Matt said. "How'd you like to be just a customer for a change?"

Niana glanced up and smiled. "I'd like that," she whispered.

The food was superb, and the table secluded and sunny. Niana only ate a little and sipped her coffee as Matt finished his substantial meal.

"I want to tell you about some of the things that happened to me," she said in a hushed voice. "That's if you want to hear. It's not a pleasant story." Her eyes turned serious. "If you prefer I didn't, I understand."

Matt placed his knife and fork down, reached across and took his companion's hands. "I want to share everything," he said.

Niana broke into a small smile. "But only if you tell me about your life, your wife and why she left that beautiful home of yours and the wonderful man before me now."

"It's no great story but I agree."

*

Matt listened with intense interest as the young refugee's story unfolded. She'd lived in a small apartment in Pristina when the troubles began. One day Serb soldiers surrounded the building and went through, kicking in all the apartment doors. The men, including her husband, were separated from the women and children and never heard of again.

"We found out later from other refugees they were taken to a football stadium and shot," Niana continued in a monotone. "I was driving my car towards the border with five other women friends when we came to a road block. Serbs surrounded us and we were ordered into an army truck. That was the beginning of our ordeal." She sighed and sipped her coffee. "I told you about that."

"Yes." At the thought of what his Niana had gone through at the

[33]

hands of the Serbs, Matt clenched his jaw tight and closed his eyes briefly.

"I thought I'd die there but I guess my condition helped me." Niana looked up into Matt's concerned eyes. It was warm and peaceful in the restaurant. Outside the waves lapped on the shore, the sand on the beach was now covered by high tide and, in the distance, the sky tower still shone in the sunlight.

"I met Adona and Halia on that lonely mountain road," she continued. "Adona said that when the tractor was surrounded by Serbs their parents told them to hide behind the potato bags in the wagon and keep very quiet. Afterwards they heard shots followed by eerie silence. When they plucked up enough courage to come out, they found their father and grandparents lying dead on the roadside. There was no sign of their mother. They waited three days hoping she would return but, instead, I turned up."

"Adona?" Matt queried. "What about Halia?"

"He was traumatized by the brutality and killings. I never got a word out of him for weeks though, from what Adona said, he talked to her when nobody else was around. It was only after our evacuation that he began to speak. Adona, though, told me everything her little mind could comprehend." The young woman grimaced. "For a five year old she was marvellous. She knew her family was dead and it was she who persuaded Halia to stay with the tractor and not to try to walk home. We joined a convoy of refugees and arrived at the border two days later." Niana smiled up at Matt. "It was still difficult but we were free. After my child was stillborn, I was one of the first offered a flight out but refused to go without the children. All our records had been confiscated at the border. The Serbs even took number plates off the tractors. I said the children were from my brother's family and wrote my surname on their papers the Albanian authorities issued, and here we are. They still use the name Bolsa here. I was too scared to include their proper surname in case they separated us."

"Oh, my dear," Matt whispered. "Thank you for confiding in me. But you're all safe now and I doubt if the government will check back into the children's records, even if there were any available."

"I hope not." Niana frowned. "The two children gave me the courage to keep going, they depended on me and still do. Both of them are so devoted to each other and, I hope, to me."

"They are," Matt assured her. "Even when they're in my workshop making the toy wagons for their tractors, every quarter of an hour or so one of them asks where you are."

Niana smiled. "It was a terrible time but now, as well as the children, I have you." She reached across and kissed him. "I thought I loved

[34]

Zymer but this is different, somehow. Don't ask me to explain but, Matt, I love you." She flushed. "I'm behaving like a lovesick sixteen year old, aren't I?"

"Yes." Matt grinned but before Niana's frown could materialize he laughed, seized her cold hands and kissed her. "I love you too, my sweet, so why shouldn't we be happy together?"

"No reason." She laughed and glanced at her watch.

"I know," Matt chuckled and squeezed her hands again. "We have oodles of time before we have to pick up the children from school. How about another stroll along the shore?"

"That would be great." She rose from her chair and waited while he paid the bill. Hand-in-hand, they walked out into the spring sunshine, two people who had once been a world apart, now in love and not afraid to show it.

*

CHAPTER FIVE

As usual, the street outside Selwyn Avenue School was crowded as hundreds of pupils headed home. This time, though, the yellow truck was waiting for Adona and Halia.

Niana hugged the pair and kissed them both before the little girl gazed up expectantly. "Have you got anything for us, Matt?" she asked.

"Adona," her foster mother scolded. "You can't expect Matt to have something for you every time you see him."

"No," Halia said but he also had a slight glow across his usually expressionless eyes.

"Well, actually I have," Matt said. "Look behind the seat."

Both children jumped up and almost banged heads as they scrambled up on the seat. Adona squealed in delight and Halia grinned as he lifted up two toy wagons made to fit their tractors.

"Thanks, Matt," he said, handing one to his sister.

The wagons were unpainted but otherwise perfect with four wheels, little sides that hinged down and even a green rectangle of canvas attached.

"Oh Matt," Niana said, breaking into a broad smile. "They're perfect. How did you know what they looked like?"

"Photos on the Internet." Matt shrugged. "I thought we could paint them together some time."

"Yellow like the truck," Adona suggested while Halia wanted brown, a colour close to the real life one they had in Kosovo.

Matt smiled again and was about to start the car and drive off when they were interrupted. "So, you're a family man now, Matt," a soft female voice said. "That's what you always wanted, wasn't it?"

Matt flushed as everyone turned. A tall, red headed woman dressed in a navy blue suit stood outside. She had a definite air or authority.

"Hello, Judith," Matt muttered. His smile quickly turned into a frown.

"I thought I recognized Stubby here but with the children and young lady I thought you must have sold it." Judith glanced around the cab interior. "Well, aren't you going to introduce everyone?"

" Judith Coleman, my ex-wife," he spluttered.

"Oh Matt," Judith cut in. "Wife. Nothing ex about it. We aren't

[36]

divorced yet, remember?"

Matt's frown grew darker but the woman was already engaged in a conversation with the others. She talked to the children, admired the toy wagons and asked Niana about herself. Finally she returned to Matt.

"You did well, Matt. All the best to you all."

"And Brian?" Matt asked.

"He left." Judith's lips pursed. "Like you, he wanted someone young and sexy." She gulped as if she'd said too much and flashed a smile, squeezed Matt's arm, and she was gone.

*

Matt grunted and drove the truck towards Dixon Street while Niana remained deep in thought.

"Who is Stubby?" she finally asked.

"The truck," Mat replied, relaxing a little. "When I was Halia's age, my father used to wander around whistling an old 1960s tune called *The Yellow Submarine*. The name was shortened to Stubby."

"Can we call it Stubby, too?" Halia added in one of his rare interruptions.

"Sure."

"Your wife was very pleasant and attractive, too," Niana added.

"On the outside."

"But." Niana prompted. "You promised you'd tell me about your life, Matt."

"I know." He suddenly broke into a laugh. "Did I note a touch of jealousy there, my love?"

"Yes," came the frank reply." The few times you mentioned Judith, I visualized a stern skinny person, completely masculine and ruthless; not a beautiful woman."

"She's what you visualized," Matt retorted. "Don't be fooled by the flashy clothes and make up. She's a viper."

"Viper? I don't understand."

"That's a poisonous snake," Matt explained. "Perhaps a spider is a better comparison. She sucks people dry and spits them out."

"Being bitter isn't like you, Matt."

"I know," he said. He slowed the truck at a corner, changed gears and moved it into a stream of traffic on a major road. "You needn't be jealous, though. Judith and I are finished and have been since long before I met you."

[37]

"I'm glad. I just thought that, compared with her, I must look like a simple little farm girl."

"No." Matt broke into a broad grin. "More like a princess."

He chuckled as Adona added her little bit. "Our teacher read us a story about a princess. She was locked in a tower and... her excited voice rattled on.

*

Later that evening after both youngsters were sound asleep, Niana sat beside Matt on the couch in the apartment's sitting room.

She turned and, without a word, kissed him passionately. A frantic kiss continued into a session of petting that stopped when the panting but smiling woman pushed him away.

"It's hard," Matt sighed.

"What is?"

"To stop. My God, Niana. I know I promised but ..."

"Well, don't," she whispered in a husky voice.

Their eyes met and nothing more was spoken. With a touch of nervousness, Matt took the coffee mug from her hand and placed it on the hearth. She turned her head and placed her arms around his neck. He bent down; their lips touched and suddenly all hesitation retreated.

Her tongue lashed Matt's lips as she placed his hand on her breast. He frantically undid the blouse buttons and pulled the garment beneath aside. A tanned body was silhouetted in the shaft of light from the kitchen and he could see the white breasts heaving below a bikini line of glossy brown skin. He reached forward and cupped them while his lips moved down.

"Not here," Niana whispered. "The children "

She led him to her room where Matt watched as she slipped off her skirt and stood before him dressed only in little blue panties. They came together again in a heated embrace with hands exploring, tugging and fondling as they moved towards the bed.

"Oh Matt," Niana moaned. Matt whispered her name over and over as the pair finally came together joining their bodies in a union of ardent, passionate love.

*

"You naughty man," Niana said an eternity later in mock anger,

[38]

pushing the gasping man off of her. She stood up and slipped into a nightgown. "I hope the children didn't hear."

She disappeared and returned a moment later with a smile on her face. "Come and look," she whispered.

A redressed Matt followed her to the adjacent bedrooms. In the old storeroom, now wallpapered and freshly painted, Adona was fast asleep with a teddy bear in her arms. The new wagon lay upside down on the floor where it had fallen off the blanket. Across the corridor, Halia had his tractor and wagon joined together on a small table beside his bed and was snoring peacefully with his arms hanging out.

"They love you, Matt," Niana whispered as she tucked the blankets back around the little boy. "Almost as much as I do."

Matt flushed. "Yes," he said and wrapped his arms around her. "I love you too but had to prove it, didn't I?"

"Oh Matt, I never wanted a male near me. Not until you came along, my darling. You made me feel like a woman, not a harlot."

"That's because you are," Matt replied, and then realized what he'd said. "A woman, I mean, a wonderful woman that I love."

"Thanks Judith,"

"Judith. What has she got to do with it?"

"After I met her this afternoon, I decided if I wanted to keep the man I loved, I'd better..." She giggled. "Let's just say she motivated me into doing what we did tonight."

"Oh Niana, forget about her. She is my past. You're my future."

Niana's eyes looked directly into his soul. "Thank you, Matt," she said and slid into the bed. Stay with me. I'm always up at five thirty, twenty minutes or so before the children wake up."

Matt didn't hesitate. For the first time in years he had a warm female beside him in bed. With thoughts of love on his mind he touched her soft body and drifted into a gentle sleep.

*

"No," Niana screamed flinging her arms around so violently Matt was hit on the face and immediately woke up. It was dark with only a faint rectangle of grey from the row of windows above the closed curtains.

He reached out and grabbed the shaking body before realizing she was still fast asleep. Words in her own language screamed out and her perspiring body shook.

Matt held her arms by her side in a firm but gentle hold, but she still

[39]

grunted, yelled and kicked. Perhaps it was more than a nightmare. Was she having a seizure of some sort?

"Niana, my love. You're okay," he said, stroking her hair. His heart pounded as thoughts flashed through his mind. He bent forward and kissed her hot, wet cheek. "Niana, wake up. You're home in bed."

She jerked awake. "Matt," she sobbed. "Oh Matt. It's you."

"Yes it's me, my darling," he whispered and held her close. "You were having a nightmare."

"I was reliving the attacks on me," she stuttered. "It was so real. The pain and deprivation. Oh Matt, will the nightmares ever go away?"

Matt bent forward and kissed her. "Do they happen often?"

Niana glanced into his eyes. "Not now." She sighed. "At first it was every night but I was put on medication that helped. Over the last few months I've slowly cut down and now have only occasional nightmares, usually after something has happened. Any sort of stress or excitement reactivates them."

"So it was me that caused it, this time. I'm sorry, my love."

"Don't say that," the young woman retorted. "You are the best thing in my life. Without you ..." She smiled and hugged him close. "God, I'm sopping wet. Wait a moment and I'll freshen up." She kissed him, tossed back the covers and disappeared across the hall.

Minutes later she reappeared in a crisp new silver nightgown and crawled in beside Matt.

"I want you, Matt," she whispered.

Their love making in the wee hours of that morning was more subdued than the frantic effort a few hours earlier but just as fulfilling as the pair consummated their love once again.

*

That weekend, Niana and the children stayed at Matt's house for the first time. The children didn't even question the fact that the adults were going to share one bedroom. After all it was a house with three upstairs bedrooms, one for Adona, one for Halia and one for the adults. Matt shared Niana's bed at the shop so why not here?

Halia gazed at the queen-sized bed in the main bedroom and turned to his sister. "We've got a new mummy," he said, not knowing Niana and Matt were on the landing listening. "And now we have a daddy, too."

"Just like our old mummy and daddy," the little girl replied. She gave a little sob. "I can't see their faces any more, Halia."

Her brother frowned. "What do you mean?"

"I can't see Mummy's or Daddy's faces in my dreams any more but I do see Niana's and Matt's. They'll keep us always, won't they?"

"Yes," Halia comforted and tucked his arms around his sister. "Niana and Matt will keep us always. Come on. Let's go and look at our rooms." He took his sister's hand and headed up the carpeted corridor.

*

"Oh Matt." Niana had tears in her eyes. "Did you hear?"

"I did." There was a lump in his throat "So aren't you glad I persuaded you come?"

She nodded. "I have never, ever lived in such a huge and luxurious house before but I still feel guilty."

"Why?"

"It's you always giving me things. You helped me with my business and now not only invite me into this beautiful home but take the children as well. How can I ever repay you?"

"You already have, and with interest." Matt looked up as the children reappeared on the landing. "Do you like your rooms?" he asked.

They both nodded and tore past, back to inspect the bathroom. "I want first bath," Adona yelled as she saw the kidney shaped blue bath, golden taps and a row of plastic fish glued to the cream tiled walls above it.

Niana looked up at Matt and smiled. "Come on," she said. "I'm going to prepare a special meal for our first night in your home together."

She took his hand and headed downstairs.

*

"I can't drive it," Niana exclaimed while the children giggled and Matt sat in Sub by's passenger seat.

"Of course you can," he said. "It's no different than your car."

"But it's so big." Her eyes were glued to the road ahead as she drove the truck into a line of traffic, reached down and changed gears with ease, smiled at the children and accelerated forward. "Oh my God, there's no room in that lane."

"You're going well," Matt encouraged. "Just remember the tray behind when you go around a corner."

"How can I forget? That's all I can see in my rear view mirror." She shifted and swore, as there was a clunk of the gears, but managed the next

[41]

manoeuvre and, fifteen minutes later, arrived at *The Cuckoo's Nest.*

"You can back it inside," she said. "I'll go and open the garage door." There was a satisfied smirk in her eyes as she gathered the children up and headed for the workshop. Matt laughed and reversed into the loading bay. The truck was half filled with furniture and, as usual, Niana refused to just watch.

"If you say one word about it being too heavy for me, I'll scream," she panted after she'd gripped a chest of drawers and staggered forward while Matt walked backwards with his end.

"Mummy's strong." Adona called from across the landing bay.

"Not as strong as Daddy," Halia argued. "He's got muscles."

Niana's eyes caught Matt's and smiled. Without encouragement, both children had begun to call them mummy and daddy. It just sort of slipped out in their conversations.

The straining adults moved a few meters before the chest of drawers was lowered to the floor. Matt grinned, brought a trolley over, slipped it under the dresser and manoeuvred the load to the nearby storage area.

Meanwhile, Niana glanced down at the deep red creases across her hands and attempted to control her puffing. The furniture had been heavy but she wasn't about to admit it. Instead, she stretched her fingers to restore circulation, climbed back inside the box-like interior of the truck and headed for the last item to be moved, an old oak desk.

"Come on, Matt," she yelled. "Stop bumming around."

"Yes dear." Matt laughed and broke into an exaggerated jog. He leaped across to the tray in one gigantic leap and grabbed Niana in his arms so tightly her feet were lifted off the floor.

"Matt. Stop it. The children are watching."

"We don't care, Mummy," Adona called." Matt's allowed to do that. Isn't he, Halia?"

Her brother shrugged but there was a smile on his face. "I guess," he relented." A bit sloppy, though."

Matt kissed Niana again and placed her down. "We've done well." He chuckled. "You know, I might even keep you around for a while."

Moments later after the desk had been unloaded, Niana grinned and walked to the driver's side of the truck.

"I'll drive home," she pronounced in a determined voice and climbed aboard.

*

Niana's Sandwich Bar wasn't a gold mine, it required long hours of work by a dedicated staff but found a niche in the local area and regular customers now outnumbered the casuals.

Matt, too, was doing well. The cuckoo clocks he restored for the Japanese customers had been finished. He was now designing a brand new clock from scratch to see if it was economically feasible and had found an importer who could get him most of the parts required. The mechanism was modern and battery driven, so Matt designed authentic looking weights and pulleys to give the cuckoo clock a traditional look. The mechanism that made the bird shoot out had not been found but he was sure he could design one himself.

"Of course, it's only experimental," he explained to Niana. "If it is too costly to make, I'll just make this one and keep it in the shop."

"I like the name," Niana said as she inspected a small wooden stylized sign. "Macolansa Products has a nice ring to it. But what does it mean?"

" Matt Coleman and Niana Bolsa. I just left a few letters out to make one word."

"Oh Matt, you are a romantic." She placed her arms around his neck and kissed him affectionately. "Can you make one for my shop?"

"I'll put you on the waiting list. Give me a ring just before next Christmas."

It was a time of prosperity and love for Matt, Niana, Adona and Halia, but, like thunder clouds hidden behind a mountain bathed in sunshine, consequences from their past lives were about to catch up and engulf them all, dark, sinister and without warning.

*

CHAPTER SIX

Ida Azemi would have been an attractive woman but the last months had been hard on her. Lines around the mouth, under the eyes and a small scar that puckered her cheek made her look a decade older than twenty-two, her actual age.

She sighed and reached for yet another folder. If nothing else the Albanian authorities were meticulous in documentation. This was probably an aftermath of rigid Stalinist communist days when the small Balkan country could count only China and North Korea as a friend. Now, of course, but only through the fact that it sat south west of Kosovo, Ida's homeland, it was flooded with NATO and American troops and a friend of the west.

She was about to open the third folder when the young border guard placed his hand on the folder.

"Our agreement," he stuttered in Albanian.

"Oh yes," Ida smiled but the expression never reached her eyes. She followed the boy through to a small windowless storeroom and waited while he shut and latched the door. With no money to bribe the Albanians she used the only commodity she had, her body.

It was all over in fifteen minutes and Ida went back to the real reason for her visit. She nodded as the man plunked six old-fashioned photograph albums in front of her. They all had black pages with eight photographs on each page. Some were collared but most were a grainy black and white as if taken by an old camera from another era. All were methodically stuck in with the ancient triangular corner tabs and assigned a reference number. Hundreds of similar photos showed tired looking women and children clutching their few possessions. Ida sighed. Every person photographed was someone real, with a life, feelings and aspirations. It was so easy for the blur of faces to be thrust aside like the crowd scene at a soccer match.

A few moments later, Ida gasped and slid the photograph album around for the guard to see. "Reference 99/4 3417. Those children." The woman in it was unknown but the children looked familiar to those in the coloured photograph she had with her.

The guard brought up a data sheet on his computer and typed in

[44]

the reference number. "The children have the first names of Adona and Halia and were among the first to be selected to be moved on to a third country."

"Where are they now?" Ida's eyes lit up and there was a quiver of enthusiasm in her body language.

"The information is classified," the boy replied and turned to gaze openly at the woman's breasts.

"No way," she snapped. "You've had your fun. If you don't co-operate, I'll tell your superior you raped me. You know what your authorities think of junior officers who molest women at the border."

The youth gulped and swung his eyes back to the computer monitor. "The children were accepted as displaced persons and airlifted to New Zealand, a small English speaking country in the South Pacific," he croaked. "There is no more information."

"I'd bet my right arm those are Emine's children." Ida whispered more to herself than the guard. She shut the album but when her fingers slipped out, the photograph came with them. In one more deft movement it was deposited in a skirt pocket as she leaned forward to attract the boy's eyes in a different direction. She brushed a hand over her long dark hair, once always so well groomed but now in need of a cut, and nodded at the young guard.

"It was fun," she muttered the half-truth and left the building without a backward glance.

*

It was a three-hour drive in the beat up Yugo car running on black market gas down the Albanian mountain road. The gravel surface was still a vast improvement over the road's original condition. Most traffic was now travelling in the opposite direction and Ida had to pull over twice to allow two massive convoys of NATO trucks and half-track vehicles through.

Her destination was a massive tent city catering to thirty thousand refugees. This one was run by Italian authorities and the green white and red tricolour fluttering beside the red and black Albanian flag at the main entrance almost made her feel secure. It was amazing how one's values changed in such a short time.

She drove along the muddy access road, past the inevitable queues waiting to use toilets and showers and on to Lane R where she parked beside two tractors in a small pull-off area, gathered up two bags of supplies and walked along to Tent R73, home.

[45]

"Hi, Drita," she announced as she moved the flap of the khaki military tent and slid inside. "How are Emine and the baby?"

The young woman inside glanced up from the camp bed she was lying on and smiled. "A bit better," she replied. "Aren't you Emine?"

She turned to the third inhabitant in the tent, a slim dark haired woman who was sitting in a canvas chair suckling a small infant to her breast. "Yes, I'm fine," came the vague reply.

"And she began to feed Agron without being told," Drita continued. "Rokmane and I were thrilled."

"Well, I have news," Ida brought out the photograph she'd stolen and handed it to Ditra. "Information, too."

The other woman frowned. "You didn't sell yourself again?" She sounded like a teacher reprimanding a naughty child.

"Well, why not?" retorted Ida.

"Oh, Ida." Ditra sighed. "Why do you do it after all we've been through?"

"It got me this information and a tank of gas," the other woman snapped. "If we don't look after our own butts, nobody else will." She sat down on the bed beside the silent Emine. "I got something for Bubbs," she said and produced a fluffy toy rabbit.

Ditra sighed again. "Not another male?"

"No." Ida smirked and handed the toy to the mother. "I was given it at that American base down by Beslibek."

"Thank you." Emine gave a brief smile and her eyes flickered acknowledgement.

"I also got diapers, baby powder and ointment. When I explained our situation the Americans literally heaped stuff on me." She opened the plastic bag and placed the items on the table.

"My God, Ida. You're the limit." Ditra laughed. "I have trouble getting out the front gate while you roar all around the countryside gathering up things." She grimaced. "I can't say I approve of your methods, though."

There was a cough and the young woman turned as a teenage girl walked in rubbing her wet brunette hair with a towel. Rokmane was the last inhabitant of Tent R73, all strangers until they'd met in the Serb internment camp, but now friends who had no other family.

"Hi Ida," she said, plunking her slightly chubby frame on an empty bed. "Did Ditra tell you Emine began feeding Agron herself?"

"I had to," the vague woman whispered. "My boobs hurt."

"Well," replied Ida. "That's progress isn't it?" She tucked an arm around the baby's mother and held out the photograph. "I think I found

[46]

your other children, Emine," she said. "Have a look at this. I'm sure it's Adona and Halia."

The young mother switched her baby over to a second breast and took the photo in her thin fingers. Eyes focused on the glossy paper. She stared, frowned and swallowed. For perhaps the first time since her child was born, an emotion crossed her face, her eyes warmed and a smile, not just the usual vacant grin, moved across her lips.

"Halia, Adona." She breathed deeply and stared at the photograph. "That's them. My children. It's them." She glanced up and tears appeared in her eyes. "Where are they, Ida?"

*

A British doctor, Rob Rodgers examined Emine and spoke to Ida in terrible Albanian.

"I understand a little English," she replied in that language.

"Jolly good," the doctor said and instantly confused Ida.

However, between the pair, the doctor's message got through.

"Physically, Emine and the baby are fine," he said. "The little chap is putting on weight and so is his mother."

"But her mental condition, Doctor?"

The young man frowned and ran a hand through his ginger hair. "That's the trouble. In my opinion the birth of her child was not the primary cause of her condition. Her mind couldn't handle the trauma of her treatment and has shut down. She should be showing a greater improvement by now." He shook his head. "The next six weeks will be important. In that time, Emine will either improve or regress. If this happens, I'm afraid it may become a permanent condition."

"Shit," Ida gasped. "What can help, Doctor."

"Continue everything you're doing. She needs friends and loved ones at the moment."

"There are no loved ones. Her parents, parents-in-law and husband were all killed by the Serbs," Ida said bitterly. "She was separated from her children and thought they were killed too." She shrugged. "That's when she began to withdraw."

The doctor frowned. "You said... thought they were killed. Are they alive, missing or what?"

"Alive, apparently. I'm not sure why, but another refugee took them with her when she was evacuated."

"Where to?" the doctor almost snapped.

[47]

"Some place I've never heard of. I was told they speak English there and it's in the South Pacific somewhere."

"Australia?"

"No, New something.

"New York?" The doctor shook his head and corrected himself. "No, that's nowhere near the Pacific. How about New Zealand?"

"That's it." Ida's eyes lit up. "That's where the children went."

"Interesting," Rob Rodgers replied. "It fits in. They have a medical team in the Balkans attached to the German Red Cross. That could be why Emine's children were sent there." He shrugged. "It's only a small country with a population not much bigger than Kosovo so they can't take many but..." He stopped as if deep in thought. "This could make the difference."

"What, Doctor?"

"If Emine finds her two older children it could be just the thing to snap her out of her depressed condition." He glanced across at the other woman. "Look, leave it to me and I'll make a few inquiries."

Ida turned to Emine and switched back to her native language. "The doctor said you are both fine, Emine," she said. "He's going to help us look for Adona and Halia."

"That's nice," the mother murmured. "Adona and Halia are gone. Do I feed Agron now?"

"Yes," Ida said with a sigh. "You can feed him now."

"That's fine," the young mother replied. "When he cries, he's hungry."

"You're right," the doctor said, grinning at Ida. "She is improving, you know."

"A little," Ida agreed as she rose and lifted the baby from her friend's arms. "But not enough."

*

It took six weeks, but Doctor Rob Rodgers was true to his word. After a long tiring journey to Italy, Ida, Emine with the baby as well as Ditra and Rokmane were ushered in though a prefabricated building where Australian and New Zealand Immigration officers were issuing the final temporary papers to refugees boarding the awaiting 747 chartered jet airliner.

Ida glanced nervously at her companions, as there was one last problem. On the doctor's advice, they hadn't disclosed Emine's condition. Sure, her friend looked well and had a healthy tan but if a competent doctor

[48]

asked her questions, it would only take one vague answer to warn them all was not right. Countries taking immigrants had thousands of refugees so were hesitant about taking any with medical problems.

The line was long and as they edged closer to the officials, Ida, somewhat out of character, became more nervous. There were three New Zealand officials and an Albanian interpreter behind the computer terminal.

"Names, please," the impersonal voice said in English.

"My friends speak no English," Ida said and repeated all their names.

The computer monitor highlighted their names on a screen and the man tapped the keys without looking up. A printer cackled and pieces of paper spewed out. These were stamped and handed to Ida.

"Your boarding passes," the interpreter said. "More formal details will be outlined on your flight."

They were about to move on when the officer looked directly at Emine. "Will you require special food for the baby?" he said and the interrupter translated.

Ida's heart froze.

"He's fine," Emine said in a vague way.

Rokmane interjected, "We have everything we need for the baby." The teenager spoke in grammatical English and immediately flushed a bright red. She wasn't supposed to be able to speak the language. In fact, since English had replaced Russian as the main foreign language now taught in high schools, the seventeen year old had a better knowledge of it than any of them.

The official looked up, frowned and studied the teenager before his eyes returned to Emine and back to Rokmane. "I thought…" he said, and Ida's heart jumped up to her throat.

The girl's scared eyes looked fearfully back and teeth bit on her bottom lip while her knuckles clutched her new skirt so hard they turned white. Whether the man felt sorry for her, the four friends never knew but he gave a grin and waved them on.

"Don't be ashamed of your English," he added as they stepped away. "You wouldn't want to hear my Albanian."

"I'm sorry, Ida," Rokmane stuttered as they joined the queue boarding the massive airplane. "I almost blew it, didn't I?"

"No." Ditra spoke for the first time. "I have no idea what-so-ever what you were saying but I saw the officer's eyes."

"So?" Rokmane replied.

"They were kind eyes; most unlike any other officials we've come across. The Serbs treated us like shit; the camp officials were good to us but remote. Nobody except that English doctor really took much notice of us. We were just one of thousands of refugees to feed but this man showed empathy." She grimaced. "He knew Emine had problems, too."

"How do you know?"

"I don't speak English but I believe body language is international," Ditra replied. "I could read his eyes."

Ida nodded. Perhaps the new world they were emigrating to could become a home, after all. Perhaps in this new world, she and her friends could just be humans again.

*

The flight to the other side of the world was long but offered the refugees a luxury most of them had never experienced before. But the war was going to be dragged along with them. It was four hours into the flight when Rokmane came back to the row where they were sitting behind a bulkhead that had a pull down bed in which the baby was sound asleep.

"Ditra," she hissed to the only one she found awake. "Come here." Her face looked terrified.

Ditra frowned and followed the teenager forward towards the restrooms. Everywhere, were dimmed lights and the sighs of sleeping passengers.

"There," gasped Rokmane, pointing to a window seat where a man was asleep.

Ditra stared at the man in question and gasped.

"It's ...it's him, isn't it?" Rokmane stuttered and clung to her friend's arm.

Ditra nodded. The man sleeping less than a meter from them wasn't a refugee or even from Kosovo. He was a Serb and one of the most sadistic officers at the internment camp in southwest Kosovo where they had been kept in terror for over a month.

"That's Konstantin Deuratovich, all right," she hissed, attempting to keep the tremor out of her own voice. "But why is he here pretending to be a refugee?"

*

CHAPTER SEVEN

Even before she opened her eyes, Niana suspected something was wrong. For one thing, it was totally dark. Where was the security light that lit up the alley between her apartment and Matt's factory? The reflection from this always lit the top window above where the curtains were drawn. She glanced at the bedside digital clock. It was also too early for the delivery trucks.

Two of them called every morning, entered the alley via an L shaped service lane that came into Matt's back parking area from the next road. There was a small garage door at the side of the shop, really a smaller version of the one in Matt's workshop; the truck drivers had keys so it could be unlocked, they delivered their produce and remove the empty containers. Usually these vehicles arrived with in fifteen minutes of each other just after four a.m. and were used as a wake up alarm to signal Niana that another morning had arrived.

Perhaps it was another bad dream! The young woman frowned and listened. A very faint hissing noise disturbed the silence.

Oh my God! She knew the sound. In one leap she was out of bed and, not even waiting to grab a dressing gown or flick on the light, tore along the corridor into Halia's room and shook him.

"We have to go, Halia," she cried, not realizing she was speaking Albanian. "Quick. I'll get Adona."

None too gently, she hauled the sleepy boy out of bed, almost dragged him with her as she ran across the corridor and lifted the little girl, blankets and all, into her arms. Two blankets slid to the floor but one remained around the child.

"You're hurting my arm, Mummy." Halia cried in alarm.

Niana ignored him and tore along the totally black corridor to the side door. It was hot outside and stones from the driveway cut into her bare feet. She hesitated and swung her head from side to side. Should she head for the road or back down the alley? No, her innermost thoughts told her there was no time. There was only one possible place.

"Quick," she whispered, this time in English. "Over to the men's restroom in Matt's place."

She guided the now weeping boy in front of her while trying to reassure a half awake Adona all was well. The restroom door was unlocked, as usual. She pushed Halia in, squeezed behind and slammed the door.

"Get down," she ordered, and wrapped the one remaining blanket with Adona still inside around them all.

*

Across the road, a dark figure squatted beside a concrete wall and smirked. Everything had been completed in less than fifteen minutes with the security light cut and the gas turned off, the meter to the house inlet disconnected and replaced by a short hose. Spewing gas had been hissing out beneath the shop's high floorboards for twenty minutes now. That should be enough. He didn't even glance at the remote in his hand but just pressed a button and waited.

Five seconds later, an explosion ripped through the shop.

An orange fireball burst into the predawn air with a blast of air that shattered the windows of *The Cuckoo's Nest* and two other buildings in close vicinity. Charred wood burst into flame. After the initial explosion there was a lull of perhaps two seconds, the flames died as oxygen was sucked away before the dormant gas ignited. A blue fireball detonated and shot a hundred meters through the air before fanning out and dropping flaming debris everywhere.

Matt's building shook like an earthquake, windows shattered and paint blistered. It did, however, absorb the blast and remained intact.

Niana's Sandwich Bar was gone. Instead, three flaming sagging walls surrounded a hole in the ground, an inferno of acid black smoke bellowed into the air above five meter flames that replaced the initial fireballs. The rumble of exploding debris all combined in one fiery hell. Another secondary explosion sent sheets of roofing iron onto the road where they bounced like rubber balls to add to the mayhem.

The man grunted in a foreign language and slipped along a pedestrian alley through a back yard of a factory, over a fence and onto the comparative darkness of a parallel road. From there he climbed into a car and drove away.

*

Matt jerked awake from a deep sleep. He reached out to feel for Niana's soft body but realized it was Tuesday and she was back in her apartment. But something had awoken him. He rubbed his eyes and switched on the light. Two forty in the morning. No wonder it was still

[52]

dark.

He heard sounds. The doorbell was chiming and was followed by a persistent knock.

Damn. What could it be? He grabbed his dressing gown and rushed downstairs to the kitchen door.

Two police officers stood in the glare of the veranda light.

"Mr. Matt Coleman?" asked a young woman with intense blue eyes.

Less than two minutes later the distraught man was being driven in a police car across town. The flashing blue and red lights and howling siren made even the most inconsiderate driver pull aside and let them pass. Matt tried to comprehend the facts he was still being told. The little shop had exploded but his own workshop had been largely unaffected. No, there was no news of anybody being rescued. Sheer heat prevented fire crews from entering the building. Yes, the area had been doused in foam, and three engines were in attendance; his own factory was being bathed in water to prevent a secondary fire starting. Yes, it was instant. Some sort of explosive device could have been used or a gas main exploded. It was too early to tell.

"I'm sorry Matt." Constable Connie Swanson had a difficult time trying to keep the emotion out of her voice. "We'll be there in five minutes and you must be prepared. If anyone was inside when the building exploded they would not have survived. There was no time." She reached across and squeezed the man's arm. "If it is any comfort, nobody would have been in pain."

"Thank you Constable," Matt's voice shook and his face appeared chalk white. "There there were two children as well as Niana," he stuttered. "They survived the slaughter in Kosovo and were rebuilding their lives." He blinked and tears rolled down the side of his nose. "It's not fair."

"It is still not known if your friend was in the building at the time," was all Connie could find to say. The sight of this giant man shaking like a leaf and weeping jolted her own emotions. "There will be a doctor at the site. We will get a tranquilizer for you."

Her voice was interrupted by the crackle of the police radio. The driver gave a crisp identification, spoke for a moment and turned to Matt. "Did you hear that, sir?" he said. "A rescue crew in protective clothing are about to examine the building." He glanced away. "Not that there is much of it left, I'm afraid."

The scene on their arrival was worse, far worse than Matt could possibly visualize. Beyond the roadblock, the road was filled with four or more fire engines, hoses ran across the road and half a dozen floodlights bathed the area in harsh white light. Bellowing black smoke created a fog that clung to the road and everywhere, silhouetted people in fluorescent yellow jackets. Matt's eyes, though, were riveted on the building in front. Where the little wooden building had stood since 1895, was a bellowing cylinder of fire. Five arches of water were being played on the flames and a monstrous machine was shooting white foam across his own workshop.

A look of horror on his face, Matt's lips moved but nothing came out.

*

Niana pushed the children down by the interior door, placed the blanket around them and almost crushed them in her attempt to use her body as a shield, when the world erupted. The corridor lit up in ghastly white light, the building shook and a blast of superheated air crashed through the splintering glass above. Pungent air engulfed Niana. Burning debris hit her hand but she refused to release the blanket. She could smell burning, hair burning. Her own hair!

Now the noise arrived, roars that throbbed on her eardrums, a high pitched ringing and then ... silence. Had her eardrums burst? No, everything was shrieking or pinging. A whine like a bullet made her jump in fright. She remembered the noise from the border where a Serb had taken a pop shot at her as she crossed into Albania.

Thoughts filled her conscious brain. The air was like molasses, so thick she couldn't breathe. Her chest was tight and her head began to spin.

More sounds. The children were crying. She could feel their little bodies shaking beneath her but they were both alive and clinging tightly around her neck. She held them to her bosom and kissed them both.

"We're safe, children," she whispered and lapsed into silence.

*

"I'm sorry, sir, you have to stop." The fireman placed a gentle hand out in front of Matt. "Nobody without protective clothing can go any closer."

"Of course," the distraught man muttered and stepped back. People and voices were all around. He knew they were trying to help but it wasn't him who needed assistance. It was Niana. Oh why did she have to go home? He'd wanted her to stay another night but she had insisted.

"No Matt," she had said in her soft voice. "It's a busy day and the children have to get to school. I'll have a nice breakfast for you when you

[54]

arrive, scrambled eggs, bacon and mushrooms. Your favourite."

Scrambled eggs, bacon and mushrooms. Those were the last words she'd said. A brief cuddle, a kiss and she was off in her Honda, now a burnt out hulk, mere meters away.

"Bye, Matt," Adona had called. Her white hand had waved out the window as the Honda reversed down the drive. "See you tomorrow."

Without warning, the man erupted into uncontrollable shuddering sobs. The grief was so intense, he never noticed the policewoman beside him.

"Matt," said Connie. Both her voice and smile were warm. "They're alive, Matt. Come with me."

In a trance, the man followed to where an ambulance waited with opened doors.

"Go inside, Matt."

He bent his head and looked into the bright interior light; right into two wide brown eyes, an oval face; smiling lips

"Matt," Niana whispered and held up a bandaged hand. "We're okay, Matt."

Across the interior were two other little humans with blankets around them; four more eyes glued on him and two smiling faces, Adona and Halia.

"Oh, my God. Niana Adona Halia! You survived. You're all right." Matt erupted into more tears as he crushed the young woman in his arms.

"Matt," cried Niana as she responded to his bruising kisses, "I'm safe. We're all safe. A bit of blistered skin. That's all."

Niana's face was bright red like an overdose of sunburn and her eyelashes and hair scorched. Worse, though were her lacerated hands. The blast had shattered the wooden door of the restroom and splinters of wood and glass gouged them where they'd held the blanket.

"The hissing warned me," Niana explained. "At home during the war, the Serbs always turned the gas stoves on in the buildings, waited ten minutes then tossed a bottle of petrol over everything. One lit match caused an explosion that literally blew the roof off the structure." She gave a long blink. "Without that noise, I wouldn't have awoken and Matt... I don't think it was an accident. I am always so careful with the gas and check the stoves before I go to bed."

Her body shuddered and she attempted to smile but instead, broke into tears. A nurse on board with them smiled and gave her an injection. "Shock is setting in," she said. "This will help you sleep. Afterwards, you'll be fine."

[55]

"Thank you," Niana responded and lay back with her eyes still on Matt.

"How are the children?" he asked the nurse.

She smiled. "They are one lucky pair," she said. "Their mother used her body to shield them. Without that and the blanket, it could have been a different story."

Adona smiled at Matt but Halia just sat and gazed, expressionless at the frosted glass ambulance windows. Niana also noticed, sat up and hugged the little boy. "I couldn't have done it without you," she said.

"Why?"

"You helped me with Adona, didn't you? She would have been too heavy without your help."

Halia's eyes lit up. "We're a family, Mummy," he whispered. "We have to help each other."

"I was scared," Adona added, and leaned her head into her brother's before she faced Matt. "Mummy and Halia saved me."

"Everyone was very brave," Matt replied. "I have never met such brave people and I am so proud of you all." He felt Niana's hand go slack and glanced down. The injection had worked and she had drifted to sleep. "Sleep well, my love," he said as he gently kissed her forehead.

*

It was late afternoon before Niana and the children were released from hospital and returned to Dixon Street. In the meantime, Matt had gone downtown, bought them all clothes and made statements to the police and insurance officials.

Niana stared at the black ruins with a drawn face. "Even my car is gone, Matt." She sighed. "Everything. You even had to buy us clothes to wear."

"But you and the children and yourself are safe. That's all that matters, Niana. Things can be replaced but not people."

"I know," she said. "I should be so grateful but all I feel is a terrible dread inside."

"It's the reaction."

"No, it's more than that. The fire is too much like home to be a coincidence. Somebody did this, Matt. It was no accident," Her face paled. "And whoever did could easily return and do it again."

"I doubt it," Matt replied as he squeezed her arm. "You can't burn down the old shop twice."

[56]

Niana gave a slight smile. "You know what I mean?"

"I do but don't worry. The police will investigate it, I'm sure. "

"I suppose. But my business and home are gone."

"So you stay with me. That's no problem and, as for the business, I have an idea."

*

Even after initial protests, Niana had to agree Matt's idea could work. Three days later, a sign went out in front of the shop section of *The Cuckoo's Nest* that stated *Temporary premises of Niana's Sandwich Bar. Full service beginning Monday.*

The inside had been converted with Matt's furniture and cuckoo clocks moved out into the workshop itself.

"After all," he said. "Half the time the customers walk through to the workshop to find me."

No stoves were available for baking but the local wholesale bakery quoted a reasonable price to supply pies, muffins and other items Niana usually cooked herself. Matt's friend, Ted procured new tables and other equipment from one of his many sources and the insurance company agreed to pay for them. Even the local authorities were most co-operative and authorized Matt's shop as a temporary restaurant.

Officials and insurance inspectors spent all the week sifting through the remains of the shop before it was handed back for disposal. Matt's insurance company, who became the de facto owners of the burnt out hulk, immediately had the site bulldozed and promised a full replacement building would be constructed.

Niana, while outwardly calm had become quiet and only medication prescribed by her doctor halted the return of nightmares.

"I feel like a zombie for an hour after I take these," she remarked to Matt the next evening as she sat in on the bed and counted out three different pills to take. "I hope they all know where to go."

"Doctor Andrew said that might happen but you should persevere with the full course," Matt said. "From what you said, she sounds like a very understanding and conscientious woman."

"Oh, she is," Niana answered.

*

The Monday opening of *Niana's Sandwich Bar* was a resounding

[57]

success. Nearly all the regular patrons returned as well as several new faces. Roseanne and Niana hardly had time to breathe from seven until nine and an extra supply of food had to be ordered from the bakery to replenish their supply.

"You know," Niana said when Matt walked in at quarter to ten, "I quite like the idea of not doing any baking. The contract I have with Imperial Bakers for the supplies is hardly any more than the cost of ingredients for the food. Of course, I don't have the selection but the customers didn't seem to mind."

"You certainly looked busy. How did the new counter work?" Matt had installed a long stainless steel sink unit in the corridor that separated the shop from his workshop.

Niana gazed at the piles of lettuce leaves, cucumber peelings and empty salad dressing jars clustered around. "A little cramped but I reckon I sold more filled rolls than on a usual Monday. I guess our fire attracted curious customers." She stretched up and kissed him on the cheek.

"And the car? I believe it was being delivered this morning."

"It's out the back." Niana's eyes looked happy. "It's the same model and year as my old one but is actually in better condition. The kids like the bright yellow colour."

"Aye, you two love birds," Roseanne hollered and stuck her head through the corridor door with a grin. "If you can drag yourselves away from each other, I've got a couple of mugs of coffee waiting."

The pair smiled and cuddled closely. It had been a hectic couple of weeks.

*

CHAPTER EIGHT

Niana answered the telephone, frowned, talked a moment and hung up. "Matt, that was a Sergeant Dave Meredith. Have you heard of him? "

"He's the guy working on our case," Matt responded. "I gave him a statement the day of the fire. What'd he want?"

"They have someone in for questioning and want us both to go down to the Central Police Station to pick him out in a line-up."

Matt frowned and placed a piece of a cuckoo clock down. "Why should we be able to recognize anyone?"

Niana shrugged. "Beats me but they want us there as soon as possible. A police car is coming to pick us up."

*

"It's one way glass so take your time," Dave Meredith advised. "There'll be a line of seven men. If you recognize anyone, just note their position from the left end. If you want any of them to turn to the side, just ask."

Niana nodded. Police stations, even in this country, scared her. She gripped Matt's hand as the lights in the long skinny room were switched off.

The men, all scruffy looking, filed in and swung around to stare blankly ahead. There was one she recognized immediately. The one, second from the left was the guy Matt had thrown out of the restaurant.

But it was wrong. This guy, no matter how uncouth he was, couldn't be the arsonist. He was a local. She was certain a Serb torched the shop. She gave Matt's hand a tiny but definite squeeze. His eyes looked down at her, eyes linked and she gave a minute shake of her head before turning to study the men.

"I recognize nobody sergeant," she said in a low voice.

"And you, Mr. Coleman?" the police officer asked. "You seemed interested in one of the men."

"I thought I recognized the middle guy," Matt muttered, "but I now doubt if I know him."

"I hope not," replied the officer. "That is one of our Highway Patrol Constables."

[59]

"I'm sorry, sweetheart," Niana said on the way home. "I know that guy was obnoxious but he couldn't have done it. To use gas to blow the shop up was too much of a coincidence. I'm sure a Serb terrorist did it."

"He could have been working for one," Matt said. " He was one rough customer."

"No, Serbs wouldn't do that. They're too proud to use local criminals."

"So why didn't you tell Sergeant Meredith that?"

"Police, even your police, frighten me," she replied in a whisper. "You can if you like."

"No, I respect your wishes but I doubt if the guy will appreciate what you've done for him."

Early the following morning the sandwich bar buzzer sounded to indicate someone had entered the front door.

"I'll get it," Niana called to Roseanne who was cooking tomatoes and sausages on the one stove they now had.

The man standing there was the one in the line up. Her pulse raced but she continued to walk up behind the counter. The morning rush was soon due so, realistically she had little to fear.

"Can I help you?" she said, pretending not to recognize him.

Crinkly eyes turned up to her. "Name's Tom," he said and held out a grubby hand. "Tom Dench."

Niana took the extended hand and frowned. "Would you like breakfast, Mr. Dench?" she asked.

"And have your boyfriend boot me out?" The man broke into a smile and Niana could see crooked tobacco stained teeth. "No, I just came to say I know you recognized me at the pig pen, yet you never ratted on me."

Niana couldn't fully understand his slang but knew the gist of the words. "I know you didn't burn my shop down... err ... Tom," she said. "However, I'm curious about why the police thought you were involved."

Dench coughed. "I was there," he admitted. "You see that little window in the alley is well lit at night. Often, you get up to go to the bathroom or see the kids and forget to pull the curtain, always between one and three. I like to watch you in those shortie pyjamas. It arouses me, you

[60]

see."

Niana stared, horrified, at the man. Vomit rushed to her throat and her face turned ashen. The thought of this gritty little man staring at her through the window made her ill.

"Don't worry, Miss Bolsa," the man continued and almost looked ashamed. "I only look and won't come back."

"Please leave," Niana whispered. She gripped the counter to stop herself from shaking. "I know you aren't an arsonist but do not condone your other behaviour."

"I saw it all," Dench ignored the request and continued. "A guy dressed in a black balaclava set the gas going, waited for five minutes or so before he crossed the road. I followed. He must've had some remote device because he just squatted down and watched while all hell broke loose and your shop blew up."

"Oh my God."

"Yeah, the bugger muttered something. I couldn't hear him because of the explosion but would swear he wasn't talking in English; some foreign lingo, I reckon." Tom wiped a hand over his grey stubble and fixed his eyes on the now attentive woman. " I followed him through to Stratton Drive where he had a car stashed."

"Thank you, Tom," Niana whispered. "But why didn't you tell the police."

"Don't trust them bastards," he retorted and his frown turned into a grin. "I found out more, too."

"What?"

"A name," Dench grunted. "Two actually. The guy who blew your shop goes by the name of Major Konstantin Deuratovich from " he frowned and tried to get his monolingual tongue around the foreign words.

Niana's already pale face drained even more as her knuckles gripped the counter. "Shit," she gasped.

"Know him?"

"No" she whispered. "But I know the other name. In English it means Section Eight, a Serbian secret service unit. Thank you Tom." She glanced up as two customers walked in the door. "Would you like some breakfast? No charge."

Tom Dench smiled. "Okay," he replied. "You persuaded me." He was about to find himself a seat when he stared, unblinking, back into Niana's eyes. "Be careful Miss Bolsa. He's a dangerous man."

"I know," she whispered. Section Eight comprised of sadistic thugs who terrorized whole villages back in Kosovo and now it was here, across

[61]

the world. She shuddered. How could this be?

Two hours later she confided in Matt. She told him everything; things that had again been thrust into the back of her mind, while he held her close and let her talk.

"This is too big for us, my sweet," he said after she finished. "We need to tell the police."

*

Sergeant Dave Meredith frowned when Niana told him about recognizing Tom Dench but made no immediate comment.

"Old Tom is well known for his nocturnal habits," he observed after she finished. "He's harmless enough, though and we didn't really suspect he was involved in arson." He grimaced. "We really wanted to put pressure on him and it worked because he told you everything."

"So what happens now?" Matt asked.

"We'll keep an eye out for this Konstantin Deuratovich and also have a regular patrol pass your shop at night. You don't still live in the vicinity, do you?"

"No," Niana replied. "I've moved in with Matt over at Summerhill Heights."

"A nice part of town." The sergeant seemed impressed," Far better than Dixon Street, especially at night." He stood up. "We'll keep you in touch of any developments. Just be vigilant in the early morning. The area is relatively crime free but characters, far more dangerous than old Tom, frequent the bars and cheap boarding houses about four blocks further over."

When the pair left, the sergeant reported to his immediate superior. "Do you think there's anything in this, sir," he asked,

"A Serb secret service unit operating here," scoffed the other man. "The rumblings of an old alkie. No doubt, the young lady was very frightened. I'm more inclined to think the shop was torched by the Black Hoods motorcycle gang responsible for several other random arson attacks in our area of town. They get their kicks with petrol bombs. I want you to follow that line, sergeant. Forget this Serb character."

*

Back at the shop during the morning lull Matt, too, was sceptical. "Why would the Serbs bother to cross the world to chase one refugee,

[62]

Niana?" he asked. "You're very important to me but you're just one of hundreds of thousands of your nationality spread throughout the world."

"I told you I remembered who was responsible for those rapes in that Serb Army base." she replied. "They were members of Section Eight and I made statements to representatives of the Hague International War Tribunal about them. NATO soldiers found and arrested one of the men running that camp and three others are on their wanted list. It was my evidence that led to this. Most of the girls were Muslim and, to them, rape is a taboo subject that is kept as a family secret. That's why so many of the Serbs will never be brought to justice for the atrocities they committed." She looked pale. "Tom specifically mentioned Section Eight. I can't see how it can be just a coincidence."

"True so that's even more reason while you should stay with me permanently."

"Oh yeah." Niana broke into a grin. "No ulterior motives?"

"Pure lust," Matt replied. "I can't keep my hands off of you."

"I know that," she retorted, tried to remain serious but she broke into a grin. "Oh Matt, thank you for just being you."

"No problem," he replied, reached across to squeeze her leg and changed the subject. "You know, the builders are coming to start the shop next week?"

"Are they?" Niana replied.

"I had an idea but wanted to ask you first."

"Go on."

"Both our shops are going really well. My idea is that we move the alley over to our boundary and build the new shop adjacent to my workshop. We could have a connecting door for customers."

"Like it is now?" Niana smiled.

"Exactly. I'm amazed at the number of people who wander through."

"Interesting." Niana screwed her nose up. "But how will it affect the builder and insurance company?"

"They don't mind. Basically it will be the same building moved over. I'll need to pay for the new driveway, that's all."

"What say we go one more step?" Niana said. "Instead of just a door, have a sliding panel that can be opened to combine the two shops, you know like those new open plan malls. We could still have our separate areas but…"

"… or we could combine businesses with one big shop."

"You mean *Niana's Sandwich Bar* and The Cuckoo's Nest. Sounds a

[63]

bit long winded and what about…" her excited voice rambled on.

*

Two months later the new shop opened with the name of *Sandwiches and Cuckoo Clocks*. In keeping with the tradition of the old building that Matt and Niana both wanted to keep, the new structure still included the old style veranda with room for outdoor seating.

The interior, though, was completely different. To the right as customers walked in, a polished wooden floor led to Matt's section with the furniture all set out in alcoves designed like rooms. There was an old style parlour, a bedroom and kitchen almost like a museum. One area even had an artificial window with curtains and a rural painting lit up behind it.

Niana's restaurant was almost twice the area of the old sandwich bar. This was obtained by cutting the old living quarters into a smaller two-bedroom apartment. They had thought of having no living accommodation at all, but found that if it was removed from the plan, the insurance company would just rebuild a smaller building rather than use the space to enlarge the commercial area.

"It's all something to do with the original insurance," Matt muttered when they discussed the renovations. "The domestic quarters had a separate insurance. If we don't rebuild a living quarters we just miss out on that bit."

"It sounds silly to me," Niana shrugged, "but you can always rent it out."

"Sure." Matt grinned. "Once it's built, of course, there's no reason we can't alter it if we needed a larger shopping area."

Now everything was finished, though, they realized without the original corridors and wasted space; there was a huge amount of room so the new apartment was really a bonus to use when it was needed.

*

No more was heard of any terrorists and the police reported that the building had been destroyed by an unknown arsonist, the owner and tenant of the property had observed all safety procedures and were not responsible for the fire. Indeed, Miss Bolsa was to be commended on her prompt action that almost certainly saved her own life and that of her foster children.

"That's nice," Niana said. "We've ended up better off but I wouldn't want to go through it all again."

[64]

"And your suspicions about who did it?" Matt replied.

"I'm not sure," Niana said, frowning. "The police don't appear to be concerned. I still believe Tom Dench, though."

*

On Saturday afternoon while Matt stayed on, the restaurant closed early. It was a time Niana spent relaxing and shopping in a suburban mall with the children.

"Mummy," Adona tugged at Niana's skirt as they walked through the wide pedestrian way. "There's Judith."

Niana frowned when she saw Matt's former wife walking towards them but how did Adona still remember her?

"We see her at school sometimes," the little girl explained. "She comes in and talks to us."

"Well, we meet again," the woman's voice interrupted. "How do you like the house? I've heard you've moved in with Matt," She had a superficial smile that a businesswoman might give an acquaintance.

"Hello, Judith," Niana replied in a cautious voice. "Yes, after the shop burned down, Matt offered me temporary accommodation."

"Sure," the woman replied with a laugh. "I must admit I never thought Matt would have the gall to invite a young woman in with him; with a family, too." Her eyes turned cold. "Not yours though, are they?"

Niana glared at the woman. "And why not?"

"Oh, my dear girl, your age and a ten year old son? They're either not your birth children or you were a very promiscuous teenager." She ran her eyes up and down the younger woman. "You'd barely be twenty two. Matt was lucky wasn't he?"

Niana's voice became cold. "You're wrong on both counts. Halia is not ten but thank you for the compliment of calling me twenty two."

"Oh, it's no compliment," Judith retorted. "And, by the way, don't get too settled into my house. I'm sure the novelty of a sexy young foreign girl swinging on his arm will bore Matt after a while." She rolled her eyes. "Especially when he realizes how much it's costing him."

Niana's expression turned dark. She bit back an angry retort and turned to the children. "Come on kids," she whispered in an enforced calm voice. "Say goodbye to Judith." She grabbed both their hands and almost dragged them away.

*

"You said Judith talked to you at school?" she asked a few moments later after she had cooled down and had taken the children into McDonald's where they were now munching hamburgers.

"Twice," Halia confessed.

"She was nice, then." Adona whispered with hurt eyes looking up at her foster mother.

"Oh sweetheart," Niana added. "I'm not annoyed with you."

"The second time she wanted to know our names," Halia continued.

"But she knows them."

"She wanted to know our last names before we were called Bolsa."

"I said I'd never had another name," chipped in Adona.

"And what did you say, Halia?" Niana leaned forward with the frown moving to her lips.

"You said it was our secret, Mummy," he muttered. "I told her I was not allowed to say." His bottom lip quivered. "Was that wrong?"

"Oh Halia," Niana replied, smiled and reached across to squeeze his hand. "No, it was not wrong. You did everything right and I'm proud of you. "

The little boy responded to her action with a smile but Niana noted his concern and purposely changed the topic. Soon, the children were heading towards a movie complex, in their eyes the main reason for their trip to town, and the small event was forgotten.

As they sat in the darkened theatre watching a cartoon movie that the children loved, the encounter played through Niana's mind. What if the authorities found out her surname wasn't the children's and why was Judith so interested? It was more than casual curiosity, she was sure.

*

This concern was further compounded a week later when a very official letter from the Immigration Department, written in both Albanian and English, arrived. It stated that under the humanitarian category of the New Zealand immigration act, Niana's and the children's residency permits had been extended indefinitely and, after the residential requirements were fulfilled, she would be eligible to apply for citizenship.

"Isn't that what you wanted?" Matt asked when he noticed Niana's apprehensive look.

"It is but we have to send back this return postcard. In it, I have to

[66]

list our full names and relationship to each other. She grimaced. "If I lie on an official form and they find out..." She glanced up. "What do I do, Matt?"

"Fill the form in with their proper names and continue as before. Lots of children from split families use surnames different from their legal ones when they are enrolled at schools and so forth."

"Shouldn't I write a letter of explanation or go and see someone?"

Matt studied her worried face. "No. The chances are it will all be stuck on a computer somewhere and forgotten. Even if they query the names, any discrepancy can be blamed on the authorities at the other end. They're not about to deport you all because of a surname."

"I suppose." Niana shrugged. "I also have to send back a form completed by a sponsor. Will you do it?"

"Mrs. Bolsa, I am honoured," Matt laughed.

"What?" Niana responded.

"Your meeting with Judith. My God, with her lifestyle she cost me twice as much as you and the children do."

"She said you'd get tired of us," the young woman responded with a pout. "You'd tell me if we're a burden, won't you?"

Matt turned serious. "Niana, I love you. Forget about Judith and her opinions. As soon as she finds another male to move in with she'll forget about me. Even if she doesn't, that's her problem, not ours."

"But this house. She called it hers."

"The mortgage was always in my name and I've instructed my lawyer to buy her out of the fifty percent required in any divorce settlement," Matt responded. "You're stuck with me, I'm afraid, wrinkles and all."

"Oh Matt," Niana responded with a grin.

*

CHAPTER NINE

Matt didn't mind the rain. It didn't really affect his job and to be working away on his furniture or clocks while rain dashed against the windowpanes was quite therapeutic. He also enjoyed the early afternoon. The rush in the sandwich bar was over and there was time to relax before either Niana or he had to pick up the children. They'd arrive, bubbling with news of their day and settle down in the staff room to watch television or do homework. About four-thirty, Niana would head home and he'd follow an hour later. They were really in a rut but a comfortable one shared by hundreds of thousands of citizens in the city.

The piece of oak Matt was cutting on the bandsaw proved to be stubborn with dust flying everywhere and the high-pitched scream filtering through his earmuffs. He felt a tap on the shoulder and smiled when he realized it was Niana.

"There's a teacher here to see you," she shouted above the noise.

"A teacher?" Matt frowned and turned the saw off so they could speak in comfort.

"Yes. The guy's in charge of arranging work experience programs for his pupils. He's waiting in the staff room."

"Sounds interesting," Matt wiped his hands, gave Niana a brief cuddle, and walked to where a middle aged man dressed in casual clothes waited.

"Pleased to met you, Matt," the man said after shaking hands. "My name's Cliff McCormack. Your partner may have told you I'm in charge of work experience programs at the local high school."

"So how can I help, Cliff?" Matt waved an open hand at an armchair and sat on the couch. "Coffee?"

"Please," the visitor replied. "I have a lad at the school who's going through a rough patch at the moment. He's actually a bright student. This is most unusual for me. I usually help special children or those with some sort of physical handicap."

"And this boy?"

"Family upheaval," Cliff continued. "The mother just up and walked out a few months back. Mind you, from what I heard, one can't really blame her. She took two younger siblings with her and left Kent with his father. Stephen Quinn is a high profile business man who won't admit his son needs a bit of help and basic family love."

"Okay but where do we come in?"

"Every Thursday afternoon our senior pupils have what we call CSSC, community service, sports and clubs, when the pupils do an activity different from their academic studies. It replaces the old sports afternoon. Anyhow, Kent's academic grades have dropped. Old Bill Needham, head of our technology department, found he was very keen on cabinet making and built a professional looking coffee table. "

"And you want us to take him here?"

"Basically, that's it," Cliff said. "The six week block of CSSC is finishing this week. Afterwards, the pupils all have to move on to another activity. We were wondering if you'd take the lad every Thursday afternoon over the next six weeks and do a project of some sort. The school would pay for the materials."

"We have dangerous equipment here," Matt added doubtfully. "I haven't the time to chase up some kid who only wants to hang around."

"If you have a moment, I'd like to show you something."

"Okay," Matt replied without enthusiasm.

The teacher smiled and led Matt down the rain swept drive to a van parked in the back lot. He opened the rear door and waved Matt inside.

"Kent's table." Cliff removed a cloth cover from a circular table wedged between two passenger seats and lifted it to the back.

The table was immaculate with inlaid squares of light and dark wood forming a chessboard in the centre of the circular top. It had a professional finish of stained polish.

"We're going to get a circle of glass cut to sit on the top," Cliff added quietly as the furniture expert turned the table around and examined the symmetrical legs.

"It's well done," Matt said. "I'm impressed." He glanced up and grinned. "Okay but we'll need to sign some sort of contract so my insurance covers him."

"I know," the teacher replied. "I have a standardized document. When he's here, Kent is covered by the school rules so, if there's a problem you just phone me and it becomes my responsibility. All the pupils know that if they don't behave, their program is cancelled immediately and they stay at school."

"Sounds fair," Matt said and reached out his hand. "Send the lad along."

The tall slim youth with prominent Adam's apple and drawn features flicked his eyes away from the factory owner as if he was too nervous to hold the older man's gaze.

"Mr. McCormack sent me," he muttered and handed Matt a small card with the school crest on it. "You have to sign this every Thursday and fill in what I've done."

"Right, Kent." Matt smiled and took the boy's limp hand. "Come on through to the workshop. I've just brought in a load of used furniture that I'm about to renovate. I saw your table and thought you did a great job."

"Yeah," the youth said with a shrug, "Dad reckoned it was okay and stuck it in the patio."

Matt frowned. Even in their first encounter, the lad gave him the impression of someone who had retreated inside himself, almost like Niana when they'd first met. He led Kent through the workshop and noticed a spark of interest as the boy gazed beyond the sawdust, wood shavings, lines of timber and half made furniture to the rows of modern machinery.

"We get a bit messy in here at times," Matt yelled so his voice could be heard above the roar of an exhaust fan.

"You have pretty modern stuff," Kent said. "Better than at school."

"I upgraded most of it," Matt explained. "It cost a mint but it's a vast improvement over the equipment here when I started."

He pointed to a far wall where a row of ancient wardrobes was jammed in beside other furniture in various states of disrepair.

"Your project, Kent," he said. "These were lying out in the back of an old warehouse for years. They're water stained and falling to pieces. However, the wood is solid oak with no borer or rot. Do you think you could cannibalize them and make one good wardrobe from the pieces?"

Kent gave his first smile and opened the door of one wardrobe. He coughed as musty air tumbled out, cast an eye on the wood and wriggled a sagging shelf.

"What do you want done?" he asked.

"Sand them down to the bare wood. Really, you'll be building a new wardrobe from the pieces."

"It'll be a big job to do by hand."

"As long as you wear all the safety gear and use it correctly, you can use the machines," Matt said. "We'll make it a contract. The profit from the sale of the wardrobe you rebuild will be shared fifty-fifty. Is that fair?"

Kent's eyes found Matt's this time. "Thank you, Mr. Coleman." He smiled. "I reckon we could get one good wardrobe out of these, perhaps even two."

"Call me, Matt. We aren't at school here, Kent. I'll get you some safety clothes and you can start. I'll be working on my clocks if you need me. Niana is also around. There'll be a cup of coffee in an hour or so. Go to it."

*

Half an hour later, when Niana saw the high school boy, dressed in goggles, earmuffs and hardhat, working the machine, she shouted to Matt so he could hear her over the din. "Aren't you taking a risk letting him use that sanding machine?"

"Why?" Matt asked, breaking into a grin. "Just because you're too scared to use the gear?"

"I could if I needed to," she retorted. "I don't see you using our ovens very often."

"Point taken," Matt shouted back, grabbed her and placed a kiss on her lips.

Kent glanced up, gave an embarrassed grin and continued pushing the wardrobe door through the grinding cylinders.

"Education he doesn't get at school." Matt laughed when Niana smacked his shoulder and pulled away.

"You mean using the sander?" she said with a sparkle in her eye.

"Of course," Matt said, laughing as he tucked an arm around her waist. "What else? Want to shoot through to the staff room for a bit more fun?"

"I do not." Niana said and hit him again. "Men. That's all you think about." She tried to look angry but broke into a smile. "You can wait until after the kids are in bed tonight. Tell Kent afternoon tea will be ready in fifteen minutes."

She walked out with a backward wave of her hand while Matt crossed the room to his new helper.

Kent switched off the machine and lifted up the smoothed wood. "It comes up well," he said. "I'll need to line the grain up on the opposing doors, though. This door came from a wardrobe in the middle but the original one on the right is smashed..." He continued talking with enthusiasm before, without warning, changed the topic. "I assume Mrs. Bolsa is more than just a business partner."

[71]

"We live together."

"Sorry, it's none of my business," Kent muttered and glanced away. "Good looker, isn't she?"

"I think so." Matt broke into a smile. "Yes, Kent, she is a good looker," he said. "Come and have a cuppa. You've done well, today."

*

Three-twenty on a summer's afternoon was an enjoyable time of the day for Adona and Halia. They had informed their foster mother for the third time that week there was no need to pick them up from school as they could walk the four blocks back to the shop.

Of course, they did have an ulterior motive. Half way home, their journey went by a small park that included a playground with coloured climbing frames, swings, slides and other equipment that attracted children of their age. As usual, when they arrived at the park, a sprinkling of young mothers with toddlers were playing on the equipment. Time slipped by and the people drifted off until the two Bolsa children were by themselves.

"Can you give me a push, Halia?" Adona shouted after she failed to get one of the larger swings moving.

"Sure."

Halia started to pull the swing back when a hand gripped his shoulder. An older boy was glaring at him. It was Hilton Bruwer, one of the Year 6 boys that younger pupils avoided on the school grounds.

"So Sulky Bubby has to play with his little sister." Bruwer laughed without one gram of kindness in the sound.

"So what?" Halia snapped back in defiance.

"Bloody foreigner," the boy continued and turned to a second boy Halia had seen around school. "You know, Andy, this little runt is too scared to even play football. Hangs around with the girls all day."

"Pervert," Andy said.

"Yeah. I reckon we need to teach him how to be a man."

Halia paled. This wasn't his first encounter with the bully but on other occasions he had been on the school grounds with teachers on duty to stop any violence. He glanced around and realized there were no adults nearby to help.

"Leave him alone, snooty pants," Adona shouted.

"Yeah, little girl," Hilton retorted. "You've got more guts than your brother, I'll give you that much."

He grabbed Halia and slung him to the ground. The boy skidded on the concrete and landed heavily on his hands and knees. Blood oozed from grazed wounds but he sniffed back tears in a brave attempt to stop crying.

"Booby boy," the older boy taunted and shoved Halia back to where Andy caught him in an arm hold.

Hilton glanced at the new sneakers Halia wore and a gleam came to his eyes. "You don't deserve those, kid. I reckon we've got better use for them. My little sister is about your size."

The fight that followed was brief and violent. Halia fought bravely but received a bloodied nose for his effort. Adona joined in to achieve a couple of well-placed kicks before Andy lifted up the screaming, kicking bundle of energy and thrust her back on the swing.

"Stay there," he hissed.

Meanwhile, Hilton pinned Halia onto the ground and proceeded to undo the sneaker laces. "You bastard," he grunted when the younger boy managed to kick him in the chin. "For that we'll just have to take your backpack, too. Booby boys don't need backpacks."

Halia gritted his teeth while Andy restrained the shouting, kicking Adona who had leapt off the swing and returned to the fray. She was little but spirited.

Just after Hilton removed one sneaker, a massive arm seized him and a giant of a person lifted him up in a grip of iron.

It was Kent who had finished at the workshop and had strolled along to meet the youngsters.

"I would not do that, if I was you, shortie," he whispered, as he flung Hilton to the side and extended a hand to help Halia up.

He saw the little boy's bleeding limbs and turned to the bully.

"So you pick on someone half your size, do you?" he glowered. "Well, two can play at that game, can't they, worm?"

Before Hilton could react he found himself rising from the ground with his arm pinned behind him. Seconds later, he was the one sprawled across the footpath, hauled up again and a fist, the size of a dinner plate, connected to his nose. He dropped again, buckled over and howled in distress as blood poured onto the ground. When one is eleven, a seventeen year old is something akin to a sumo wrestler.

Kent turned to where Andy stood with fear in his eyes. "Get Halia's sneaker for him," he said in a voice that one did not ignore.

"Sure, sure," the boy muttered. "Sorry, Halia," he muttered, picked up the shoe and handed it back.

"And you." Kent gave Hilton, still cowering on the ground, a light boot on the leg. "If you want a fight, just ask me any time but stay away from my friends. If I hear of you as much as saying a nasty word to either of them I'll come looking for you, worm." He grabbed Hilton by the chin and lifted him so the boy had to stagger to his feet. "Understand?"

"Yes," Hilton muttered.

"Now get before I forget what puny little runts you are and decide I might..." He glowered and cracked his knuckles.

The two boys backed up a step. Hilton made a few cheeky retorts but retreated when Kent stepped towards him.

"So who's the sulky bubby, now?" Adona yelled in triumph.

She ran over, grabbed Kent's hand and watched the boys disappear beyond a nearby fence.

"Come on," Kent said to Halia. "We'll get you home and cleaned up. Look at your clothes. Your Mum will be mad."

"No she won't," Adona cut in. "She's hardly ever mad at us. Is she Halia?"

"Only when she's tired," her brother replied.

"Well, you're lucky to have a Mum like that," Kent added in a quiet voice as he led them away. "They aren't all that kind or considerate."

*

Niana, however, was angry, not with the children or Kent but by the situation. Memories of the crowded refugee camp with its inevitable scraps between children flooded back into her mind. During those long hard weeks, she had become very protective of the two children and soon gained a reputation among those prone to violence as one who retaliated if Adona or Halia were attacked. After the petite woman flung one youth into a puddle of mud, the louts avoided the youngsters and life became more bearable.

"All right," she snapped at the sight of Halia's bloodied face. "I'm not going to put up with this."

She thanked Kent for his help and drove her foster son around to the school.

"Look at him, Mrs. Tregrowth," she complained to the principal who didn't look as if he appreciated having a staff meeting interrupted. "If our worker hadn't come along, Halia's sneakers would have been stolen. They cost a hundred dollars."

"Hilton Bruwer can be a problem," the tall skinny woman in her forties replied. "I'll speak to him tomorrow."

"Then what?" Niana said angrily. "From what I've heard this is

[74]

happening far too frequently."

The principal frowned as if she was unused to having her authority questioned.

"Well, it is," Niana continued. "\I've spoken to several parents about this bullying and they all told me it was a waste of time approaching the school because nothing's ever done."

"So what would you do, Mrs. Bolsa?" Mrs. Tregrowth retorted with a trace of sarcasm in her voice.

*

So what are you going to do?" the Serb border guard ran an eye down Niana's rotund figure, across to the two children clinging to her jeans and back to her. "Take your choice. You can take the boy or the girl. The other one remains in Kosovo."

"You mean I have to choose between them?" the exhausted woman replied in a hushed voice. "But why?"

*

" Mrs. Bolsa, are you all right?"

Niana blinked and stared into the concerned eyes of the school principal.

"Yes," she replied and shook her head. "I think so."

"You look terrible." Patricia Tregrowth's voice was filled with concern. "Come into the medical room and lie down for a moment. I'll get you a glass of water."

"No, thank you, I'm fine," Niana said. "The sight of poor Halia's bloody nose made me feel faint. That's all." She smiled. "I'm sorry I lost the thread of our conversation."

"We were discussing what could be done to punish the boy who attacked Halia."

"Take away a privilege that personally affects him. Just talking to his conscience does no good. He probably hasn't got one."

"Like what?"

"You're the professional, Mrs. Tregrowth," Niana replied. Her anger had now dissipated and she regretted her earlier outburst. "I'm sorry," she continued. "Adona and Halia have been through so much, I guess I'm over protective."

The principal studied Niana for a moment before she broke into a reconciliatory smile. "I'll see what I can do," she said. "I'm glad you

[75]

approached me."

*

The school newsletter at the end of the week included a small item that made Niana smile.

In an effort to improve playground behaviour our staff has decided to exclude children who break school rules from inter-school sports activities. This will directly affect our swimming team that will be participating in next week's tournament. Two pupils have been dropped from the flying squadron and replaced by substitutes.

"It's a bit long winded but I think I get her point." Matt laughed after Niana showed him the article. "Does that affect this boy who thumped Halia?"

"Oh yes." Niana grinned. "He's the school's fastest swimmer. Without him, we have little chance of winning the inter-school relay."

"With the sports crazy locals, Mrs. Tregrowth made a brave move. Your suggestion worked." Matt added with a sideways glance at his partner.

"Mine?" Niana gave him an innocent grin.

"Don't you dare deny your involvement." Matt chuckled. "Halia told me everything that happened when you spoke to Patricia Tregrowth including that you went white, began to shake and almost fell over. Those were his words."

"Oh, Matt," Niana said. "Something in Mrs. Tregrowth's tone brought horrible memories back to me. That's all."

"Would you like to tell me about it?"

"It's not pleasant." She sighed and reached out to wrap her arms around him. "I'll pour us a cup of coffee first."

*

When she finished telling him how she crossed the border into Albania, Matt grimaced, kissed her tenderly and tucked an arm around her shoulders.

"What happened next?" he whispered.

"The soldiers who fired were NATO troops. No doubt they saved my life. If it weren't for the children, I wouldn't be here now. They were tremendous." She sighed. "The second bullet killed my baby. The Italian medical team performed an emergency Caesarean section, patched me up and saved my life. It makes one feel humble, doesn't it?"

Matt nodded and kissed her again. "So that's what made those

[76]

scars," he replied.

"Do you mind?" Niana pouted and pulled her tank top up so a small purple scar below her right shoulder was covered.

"No," Matt said, "It makes you unique."

"So that's my story," Niana whispered. "The children became part of me that day, my only family to replace my unborn child and Zymer, my husband." She glanced up. "But I now also have you, Matt. Thank you."

*

CHAPTER TEN

She knew something was different even though her eyes were still closed. There was no pain in her limbs, no throbbing headache and no unborn child kicking her swollen stomach. In addition was the smell, a fragrance of trees, cut grass and cleanliness.

The noise. Where were the harsh cries of guards, the sobbing women, and the screams?

Emine fluttered her eyelids and, almost in fear, opened them. In front was a window with cream curtains fluffing up by an opened window. Purple flowers and green leaves intertwined on the material. Her gaze shifted and she saw blue, a deep blue stretching to the horizon while above was the lighter blue of sky. She had never seen the ocean before but realized what it must be. To confirm her conclusion, a white boat appeared from the left, bounced across in front of the window to make a vee of white wake.

Where was she? How could this be happening?

The woman's heart thumped in her ribs. She shut her eyes again. It was a dream and she'd wake up back in the stinking camp.

But no! When she opened her eyes a second time, the room was still there, a cosy friendly room. She was lying under a warm eiderdown. Beside the bed was a white baby's cot. The side was down and the blankets curled back. Except for a brown teddy bear sitting in the corner, though, it was empty.

Emine stretched her fingers up across her body and gasped aloud. She had no swollen stomach.

"Where am I?" she muttered and sat up.

Adjacent to the bed was a polished dressing table and her reflection in a mirror. Emine stared. She was dressed in a shiny red nightgown, a beautiful one, glossy and warm against her skin.

Her face. She ran her hands up over it. Her hands.

The reflection showed well-manicured fingers passing over a sun-tanned face with chubby cheeks and only a very slight red line beneath the right eye. Where was the ugly scar? The brown eyes that focused on her were clear with long eyelashes, the ones she was so proud of as a teenager. With trembling hands, Emine pushed back the eiderdown and reached her feet to the floor. Soft carpet touched her skin.

It was real. She was not dreaming. She wasn't even pregnant anymore.

The anxious woman walked to the door and beyond. Perhaps this was heaven. But no! Not with rock music playing.

She reached up, gripped the smooth wooden doorframe and stared in to the next room. A smell of hot toast and coffee filtered by, that glorious smell she remembered as a child in their little village house.

Across the room a tall girl dressed in a uniform of some sort, was facing away from her. The girl was chatting in a foreign language to a chubby, chuckling toddler who sat in a high chair with yellow vegetables all over his face.

"Oh, you are a naughty boy, Bubbs," the girl said. "What will your mummy think?"

Funny, it wasn't Albanian but Emine realized she could understand the language.

"Mama." The little boy chuckled, looked directly at her and held up a chubby hand.

The girl turned and, with the movement, there was another shock.

She was taller, had groomed hair tied back in a ponytail, smooth tanned skin and soft eyes but it was Rokmane. Gone were the sunken eyes, skinny body and bruises. This was a very attractive young woman.

"Hi, Emine," the girl said in that new language. "We thought we'd let you sleep in. We ran out of milk and Ditra's gone down to the dairy to buy a few supplies."

"Rok... Rokmane," Emine stuttered. Tears of emotion appeared in her eyes. "You look so wonderful. Is that really you and whose baby is this?"

The seventeen year old gasped. "Emine," she whispered. "Your voice. Oh my God. It's happened." She dropped a spoon, rushed forward and swept the older woman into her arms. "The doctor said the new drugs might work and it could just happen. Shit, it has."

"Where are we, Rokmane?" Emine's eyes caught a calendar on the wall. The date. It was the new millennium, not 1999 any more. "Is that for real?" she asked in Albanian.

Rokmane turned, saw the calendar and nodded. "Yes. What do you remember, Emine." Tears filled her eyes as she held Emine close, two weeping friends, one perplexed and one relieved who tried to come to terms with the latest development.

"This is your little boy," Rokmane finally sobbed. "Do you remember Agron?"

[79]

"Only as an unborn child inside me. I was in the Serb internment camp and…" She stopped and rubbed a hand over her mouth. "I remember the labour pains beginning and the Serbs taunting me then this."

"It's over a year, Emine," the teenager gasped. She glanced up as the door opened. "Ditra," she screamed. "Emine's got her memory back. I mean she's normal again. Oh hell, I don't know what I mean."

The new arrival dressed in shorts and white top with a gap that showed a tanned middle and navel, stopped, stared intently at the tearful woman and gasped. "It can't be."

"You're looking well, Ditra," Emine, now the least surprised of the pair, said. "But look at your brief clothes."

Ditra grinned. "It's summer and we all wear these." She laughed. "Well the more religious women from home still observe the more traditional dress. After all this time. My goodness, I never thought "

Emotions once again filled the room while the trio embraced, talked, laughed and embraced again. Over the next half hour, Emine was brought up to date on the events of their lives. "Oh look at the time," Rokmane suddenly gasped. "I must be off to school."

"School?" Emine asked.

"Oh yes," Ditra explained. "Rokmane is a senior at New Plymouth Girls' High School. Doing extremely well, too."

"New Plymouth?"

"It's a city in our adopted country," Ditra continued." As we told you, when we arrived here we spent four months in a camp learning English, local customs and so forth then we moved here. The idea of a smaller city appealed to us and it's a beautiful place, Emine. Come on, we'll run Rokmane to school and I'll show you around."

The city of New Plymouth was indeed a scenic place that bordered the ocean with a huge volcanic mountain to the south. Snow covered its higher slopes even though Ditra said it was in mid summer.

"Mount Egmont," Rokmane explained.

Everywhere were cars, cyclists and people walking; girls in uniform the same as Rokmane's, youths in shorts, young mothers with pushchairs and older people. It was a vibrant city with modern houses built on hillsides of greenery, bright clean and at peace with the world.

After a farewell to their charge, Ditra drove along a wide one way street and flashed her eyes across at Emine." What else do you remember?" she asked.

"The children, Adona and Halia. I can't remember my baby." She smiled at the toddler in the safety seat at the back of the car. "But he's no baby now, is he?"

"No, a cheeky little rascal." Ditra chuckled. "And your other children are in New Zealand, Emine. Somewhere here. We haven't found them yet but Ida has headed off around the country looking for them."

"Ida. Is she here, too?"

"Oh yes." Ditra laughed. She stopped the car at a red light. "Just the same. Attracts men like bees to honey and is the dynamic one in our household.

"My children?"

"They were brought here by another refugee woman. We have a name but haven't found her yet. They told us New Zealand was the size of Kosovo but they were wrong. It's almost as big as Italy but has only four million people so there's a big area to cover.

"I see," Emine whispered. "But why did this woman take my children?"

"I can only guess," Ditra said. "I'd say she found the children and began looking after them; a little like us."

"I know," the mother whispered with concern on her face. "After all this time, will they recognize me?" She swallowed. "...Or even want to know me."

*

Ida was frustrated. Her stay in Wellington, the capital city, where she'd been working and trying to trace Emine's children had led nowhere. Officials in New Zealand were as remote and unhelpful as any she'd encountered throughout Europe but, worse still, they were incorruptible and using her feminine charms was useless when females manned nearly all the desks.

She was optimistic that her luck would change. There had been a message left at the youth hostel that asked her to return to the Immigration Department.

The government office was modern and set out in a massive open plan with no partitions between the thirty or forty desks, each with a computer terminal sitting on it. She was directed to Desk Sixteen. Thank God. There was a young man sitting there--that was better than those over-made females.

The man gave her an impersonal smile and read the documents she handed across. "We asked you back, Miss Azemi, as more information on your inquiry has come to our attention." A name card stated that his name was Andrew.

Ida frowned impatiently but waited.

"It appears the children you're trying to trace did enter our country under a different name."

"Can I have her name and address?" Ida asked.

"I'm afraid that's confidential," Andrew replied and shifted the screen slightly towards himself so it was impossible for her to read the text on the screen. "Information can only be given to the person concerned or close relative."

Ida frowned and reached for a letter from her purse. "This is a New Zealand court document naming Ditra Morena and myself as Emine and her son's next-of-kin. Except for her children, she has no living relations. Will that do?" She handed the letter across the desk.

The officer read the letter and tapped more data on his keyboard, "Yes, both your names are here," he read the screen for a moment. "However, there is another complication."

Ida sighed and her eyes narrowed, telegraphing her annoyance. "And that is?"

"The caregiver of the children was given official custody by the Albanian authorities as it was thought they were orphans related to her. The New Zealand government recognizes this authority. Having their birth mother in the country complicates matters but I'm afraid I can't release any more information until the woman is informed of the situation." He gave a slight smile.

Ida she studied the young man. Perhaps her charms would work with him; nothing like that debacle at the Albanian border post, but a few tears. Ida was a fine actress and was by now a very attractive young woman with the war scars largely gone.

She leaned forward and fluttered her long eyelashes at Andrew. "I've been looking for Emine's children for three months," she whispered and included a wee sob. She dabbed her long lashes with a handkerchief. Whether that did the trick or it was her long legs crossed so her short skirt slipped up tanned legs to expose a brief triangle of white panties, she didn't know or care. She hid a grin, though; as the man's professional attention became more personal.

"Can't you help, Andrew?" she cooed and leaned forward so the cleavage of her breasts was evident.

The young man flushed. Thank God. New Zealand men had hormones after all.

"I'll check with my superior," he muttered and stood up. "If you don't mind waiting a moment."

His eyes met hers as he, as if by accident, swung the computer monitor forty-five degrees and walked away. Ida grinned. She could now read the screen.

Niana Bolsa, the name blazed out. There was an address, too and more, lots more but Ida dared not take any notes so concentrated on remembering the main facts.

Andrew returned and nodded at her. "I'm sorry," he said with his eyes once again looking directly into hers. "I am not permitted to disclose any more details. Mrs. Feraj will have to visit one of our offices."

"Thank you," Ida smiled as she stood up, flattened her skirt and gave her brightest smile. "I'll pass the message on. I'm sure she'll be in touch."

Ida laughed to herself as she left the building, found a telephone booth and called home. Minutes later, her own news became insignificant when she found herself talking to Emine.

"My God," she gasped after talking to everyone and returning to Emine. "I'm so thrilled. How do you feel? What do you think of Bubbs? Rokmane, too? Hasn't she matured into a great kid?"

"I'm well," her friend replied. "The doctor told me there was no reason I won't have a complete recovery. I still have to keep up with my medication, though."

"You make sure you do," Ida replied. She was about to tell Emine about her meeting but decided it was prudent to discuss things face to face with Ditra first. "Look, I'm hitchhiking home, so I'll see you tonight."

*

Doctor Frances Hoskin sat beside her desk and faced the two women in her office. "Thank you for coming," she said in a quiet voice. "I wanted to speak to you both."

Ida glanced across, at Ditra before speaking. "Is something still wrong, Doctor Hoskin? Emine seems normal."

"She is and we want to keep it that way," the doctor said. "However, there are a few precautions I have to discuss. Emine has been told most of what I'm about to say but I've kept back a few details."

"She won't go back?" Ditra said. "I mean, is this just a trick?" She frowned. "I'm sorry. English is still difficult for me."

"I understand." The doctor smiled. "We took a brain scan and found no abnormalities. That means there's nothing physically wrong but

[83]

we need to look after Emine. Do you know what I mean?"

"Yes," Ida replied. "What can we do to help?"

"She'll need to continue her medication. The dosage will be gradually reduced over a period of a few months and, hopefully, phased out. As the dosage is reduced she'll become more and more her old self again but, on the downside, she may experience relapses in the form of nightmares, bouts of depression, or find it difficult to make decisions.

I explained all this to Emine and told her that if she feels anything is wrong she should tell one of you, right away."

"And how would we know?" Ditra asked.

"Mainly nightmares but it could also come in the form of headaches or dizziness. She has a fast acting booster pill to take if any of these occur." The doctor stopped and glanced at the two visitors. "Most important, though, is that she should not be exposed to any stress or overexcitement."

Ida frowned. "Such as disappointment?" she asked.

"A major one could very well set her back."

"There is one problem," Ida said. "You see, she has two other children that I've managed to trace. Well, almost." She repeated everything she knew.

The doctor listened intently before she replied. "What do you know about the woman?"

"Nothing. Only a name and address," Ida said

Doctor Hoskin nodded. "My advice would be to take everything slowly. A long drawn out custody battle is the last thing Emine needs at the moment." She jotted a few notes down on a card and glanced up. "If I can help in any way, please phone me."

"Thank you, Doctor," Ida said with a smile. " I thought I'd visit Auckland and visit this Niana Bolsa, you know just as another refugee. I won't mention I know Emine."

"Yes, that sounds like a good approach," the doctor said. "If possible, visit the children and check on how they're being treated but be discreet."

*

Niana crept up behind Matt, flung her arms around his neck and plastered a kiss on the back of his neck.

"You're working too hard, sweetheart," she laughed when he jumped in fright. "Leave everything. It's a beautiful sunny day out there, the kids are at school and Roseanne is looking after the shop. Let's go for a

[84]

walk."

Matt laughed and glanced at the fully assembled cuckoo clock on the bench. "It's no good," he said with a sigh.

"What? Are you crazy or something? It's perfect, Matt. Look at those little leaves, the little Swiss chalet. Even the cuckoo works."

"I know." Matt shrugged. "But the clock runs on a battery, not the traditional chains and weights."

"So," Niana said. "Who would know? You've even included the weights and they can be pulled down."

"But drive nothing inside," Matt said. "I'm going to start again. I can't sell this."

"Then give it to me. I'll hang it above my food counter and we'll see what the customers think."

"Sweetheart, it's yours" Matt laughed and stood up, "I've got those reconditioned ones for our Japanese friends to finish, anyhow." He tucked an arm around her petite body. "Did I tell you Kent has quite a talent?" He picked up a mini wooden deer carved in a sitting position. "He made this one from a magazine picture."

Niana picked it up. "It's beautiful. He's got talent, hasn't he?"

"Yes," Matt said. "He's a strange lad, though."

"In what way?"

"Oh, I don't know. He's always alone. I've never seen him with friends. He talks a lot but never mentions school or his family. It's as if he has no life outside of this workshop."

"He'd do anything for the kids," Niana added. "You know, when he meets them on the way home from school he always takes them for an ice cream."

"I didn't know that."

"I think he's lonely," Niana continued. "He told me once his younger brother and sister were only a little older than our kids. Perhaps that is why he likes their company."

"Could be," Matt said. "I know he's a real asset around here. I even told Cliff McCormack. Cliff said his work has picked up at school, too. Meanwhile, yes, I'd love to go walking with the most beautiful woman in this world."

"Matt," the sun tanned woman said as they walked out into the sunshine. "You're exaggerating again."

*

[85]

CHAPTER ELEVEN

"Come on, Bubbs. We'll go for a walk and let all the other lazy adults sleep in," Emine said as she picked Agron up from the carpet and dressed him in a warm coverall.

On most of the fine summer mornings she was up before six when Agron awoke. She dressed, fed him and set about preparing breakfast before one of the others, usually Rokmane, strolled into the kitchen. If she had time she'd place her child in a backpack and go for a walk along the adjacent beach. Today, Agron awoke at dawn and even now it was only five a.m.

She hummed a tune that danced through her mind as they left the house and strolled down the road. The eastern sky was red and the ocean shone like a mirror. The road wound over a hill where it connected to a wider road that led down to the beach.

"Look at the big bird, Bubbs," Emine said as a grey and white gull glided over and landed on the water rolling into the rocky shoreline. Little waves, only a few centimetres in height, tumbled over and the white foam ran up between the stones and rocks. It was high tide so the water had reached the stone wall bordering the car park.

Beyond, the shoreline curved around showing buildings of the city, a swimming pool sitting on the rocks with a towering waterslide reflecting the morning light, a few taller apartments in front of the chimney of a steam power station. Behind again, was the sugar loaf, a massive rock that rose above the harbour. Emine just stood for a few moments to admire the scenery. It was as if the whole world was at peace.

She hitched the backpack up, felt the tiny arms clasping her neck and little feet kicking out in excitement as she left the parking lot and crossed the mouth of a mountain stream on a wooden pedestrian bridge. She followed the stream inland along a deep wooded valley that cut through the city.

For forty-five minutes, the mother and child followed the path until they came out onto a hilly suburban street. Emine turned downhill to head home pass the modern homes, green lawns and well kept gardens of one of the more expensive suburbs of the city. It was here that her mind was jolted back to realize she was in an urban area. Even though it was still before six a.m. a siren wailed down towards the harbour. The straps from Agron's

[86]

backpack chafed her bare shoulders a little so she found a roadside seat, slipped it off and plopped her son on the grass.

For another ten minutes they stayed in the sunshine, watching as the city awoke around them but something was different. More sirens sounded and a pillar of black smoke rose above the crest of the hillside in front. Emine frowned and decided they should head home. She grabbed Agron in her arms, handed him a piece of crisp toast she'd prepared before they set out and placed him back in the backpack.

"Well darling," she said as she stepped out to the footpath. "We'd better get home. Rokmane will want her breakfast so she can get off to school and you're going to visit the nurse today."

Ten minutes later Emine's face turned to concern. The bellowing smoke was from the direction of home. She swallowed and increased her pace, flames as well as smoke could now be seen in the valley below as well as vehicles and pedestrians converging from all directions.

My God. The area was close to home.

Emine turned the corner and stopped. Her face drained and body began to quiver. Two police cars with a line of orange ribbon between them closed their road off. In front, orange flames bellowed into the air and a cracking roar accompanied them, smoke poured over the surrounding area and fire engines filled the road. Figures in orange and yellow protective clothing were everywhere and canvas hoses bloated with water crisscrossed the road.

"Oh no!" Emine howled. It was their home on fire. The building was one massive inferno of flames, as bad as, if not worse than, the torched buildings of her village at home.

She broke into a run but was intercepted by a police officer. "I'm sorry, madam," he said as he clutched her arm. "It is too dangerous to go any closer."

The woman swung around, her eyes filled with terror. "You don't understand, officer," she shouted. "That's my home, there. My family is inside."

Even as she spoke, there was a tremendous crack and debris shot into the morning air, disintegrated into a million sparks and plummeted to the ground mere meters in front of them.

A second officer, a woman dressed in navy blue uniform and checked hat, placed an arm around the trembling woman's shoulders and lead her across to an ambulance with opened doors.

"Just take a seat, ma'am," she said in a calm voice. "We'll take the backpack off you so your baby won't get squashed. Are you Mrs. Emine

[87]

Feraj?"

Emine found her whole body vibrating. Her hands, arms and even her legs shook, her heart thumped wildly inside and vomit rose to a parched throat. The village was being attacked again. The vision before her quivered, the kind policewoman became a soldier in camouflage and black balaclava waving an automatic weapon and tormenting her.

She blinked. Perspiration poured from her face and the oval policewoman's face appeared again watching her with alarm.

"My friends? Ida, Rokmane and Ditra," she gasped.

Gentle hands held her and she was guided to a seat. "We don't know," the soft English language voice pierced her spinning mind. "We thought you and your baby were inside, too, Emine. I am afraid the news may be bad."

"No!" screamed the distraught woman. "No! No! It can't be true." She swung around in a panic. "My baby. Where's my baby?"

"He's safe," the soft voice continued through cloudy haze of purple. "You had him with you. Look, he's in Officer Timm's arms."

Emine turned and saw the police officer holding Agron; the little boy was no different with his red coverall and laughing eyes.

"Oh, Agron," Emine sobbed and took the little boy back in her arms. As she did this, her eyes glanced out at the crowd of spectators always attracted to tragedies. One person, though, caught her eye. For a second he stared at the ambulance, focused on her, turned away and disappeared back though the spectators.

But that brief view was enough. She knew him. It was the Serb guard from the internment camp, Konstantin Deuratovich.

"He did it!" she cried out and grabbed the police officer's sleeve. She attempted to stand but the world began to gyrate. The faces looking at her became elongated like a kaleidoscope of oil pulsing on water. She blinked, attempted to focus her eyes but failed.

With a low moan she collapsed, unconscious, onto the grass.

*

Visions faded in and out, people in white talking to her, the feeling of sunshine on her face, the smell of disinfectant and polish but she didn't want to wake up.

But she did awaken. Emine's eyes opened to see the ocean again. Somehow the ocean made her confident but it wasn't close but across the city, out a window. She felt a surge of panic and remembered the last time this had happened. Had another year gone by? Wouldn't it be better to drift back to sleep?

She glanced further and relief replaced doubt. No, it hadn't. A baby's cot was beside her bed and her son was asleep in it, a bob of black hair poking out from under a blanket and he was no larger. But the visions of the present returned, the inferno that was her home. That was real. The beautiful summer morning that became another disaster in her life.

She broke into sobs.

A nurse was beside her, talking. "Emine, you're fine. You're in Taranaki Base Hospital, your baby is well and Doctor Hoskin will be in to see you soon. Just relax."

"My friends," gasped Emine.

"The doctor will speak to you," the nurse replied but her eyes filled with sympathy. "Agron and you are safe and everything is being done for you."

An agonizing forty minutes went by before the first familiar face appeared. Doctor Frances Hoskin walked in and sat in a chair by her bed. "I'm sorry, Emine, your two friends didn't survive the fire. " Her voice continued while Emine attempted to maintain a hold on her mind.

Somehow, she knew it was essential to remain conscious and not allowed herself to slip away. She jerked, forced her blinking eyes open and concentrated on the words the doctor was speaking.

"It's been eight days since the explosion, Emine. The local Muslim community has stepped in and everything has been done. Your friends have been buried in traditional fashion facing Mecca and a large crowd of mourners attended the service. They are safe now and wouldn't have felt any pain…" Her voice continued but Emine's mind drifted.

"It's not fair." She screamed and sat up, eyes wide and staring at the doctor.

*

When Emine awoke a second time the doctor was beside her, lights were on but it was dark outside. "Last week Ida gave me a name and address," Frances said. "We know where your other two children are, Emine. They're in New Zealand and living in Auckland. Ida was going to visit them but, unfortunately, she never made it. There's no hurry but think about what you'd like us to do for you.

"Can I have their address?"

"I thought you might ask that," the doctor replied. "So I phoned a colleague in Auckland. She made inquiries and assured me Adona and Halia are being well cared for by a Niana Bolsa from Pristina. The information we have is that she found your children in a farm wagon in Kosovo and has been looking after them ever since."

"All this time?" Emine whispered.

"Yes." The doctor nodded. "As far as we know, her own family was killed in the conflict but she now has a New Zealand partner who's living with her and the children."

Emine nodded and gazed expressionless from the bed. "I'm glad they've been looked after," she said. "Thank you, Doctor." Her lip quivered. "If only…"

"I know," Frances reached across and squeezed her patient's hand. "But you have your beautiful little son and now news of your other children. You are not alone in this world, Emine."

"There's something else," Emine added in a quiet voice.

" And what's that?"

"I remember what happened to me; Agron's birth, our journey out of Kosovo, staying in the refugee camp and the airplane journey to New Zealand." She grimaced. "It's patchy but I'm sure I remember most things."

"That's excellent," Doctor Hoskin answered. "This can happen in cases like yours. It's as if one trauma neutralizes the other. Your mind begins to cope and suppressed memories are brought back to the conscious mind." She wrote notes on a clipboard at the end of Emine's bed and smiled back at her. "I'd like to keep you in hospital for a couple of days until we get your medication stabilized but I'm certain you will be fine now with no relapses."

"Sure," replied Emine. She glanced at the doctor with sad eyes.

"Chin up," Frances said. "I am not about to abandon you, Emine. You'll still need lots of support for Agron and yourself so don't feel you're alone. Understand?"

"Thank you," the woman replied and lapsed into silence. Her manner was brave but inside everything was still in turmoil. She didn't realize it was only the massive dosage of medication in her system that helped her cope with the latest tragedy to hit her life.

*

The young nurse stood with hands held in front and her eyes downcast as Charge Nurse Stapleton glowered up from her desk.

"Patients do not just disappear from this ward, Nurse Bradley," she said in a voice that was barely more than a whisper but cut the air like a

[90]

knife. "You find Mrs. Feraj."

"I've tried, charge nurse," Susan Bradley replied. "When I came on duty, I checked her room and she was feeding her baby in his high chair. Five minutes later she was gone. I believe she had it planned as there was no time for her to get dressed and disappear before I returned to her room."

"I see, and the child?"

"Gone too. I did everything Mrs. Stapleton, phoned security, put out a hospital wide alert ..."

"Yes Susan," June Stapleton's voice warmed. "Thank you. I'll take over the search now." She gave a thin smile. "Did Mrs. Feraj have her morning medication?"

"No, Mrs. Stapleton. That's what I was about to do when I returned and found she'd gone."

"Damn." the older woman said. "Without her medication she could very well have a relapse." She reached for the telephone. "I'll need to telephone Doctor Hoskin. She won't be pleased."

*

Emine shuddered as if a cold block of ice had slithered down her spine. A door banging made her look up. She was in a little room, a women's restroom by the look of it. In front of her sat a grinning Agron with newly changed diapers around his chubby bottom. In fact, the dirty one was still in her hand. She gulped, stared around and found a receptacle to drop it in.

God, her head ached. But where was she?

"Are you all right, dearie?" a voice asked.

Emine swung around and found an elderly lady gazing at her.

"Why yes," she replied and shook her head. She remembered the baby and a throbbing thought on the periphery of her mind told her Ida, Rokmane and Ditra were dead and she had to find someone. But who? "I'm lost, that's all."

"It can easily happen," the lady said. "There are so many buses and routes. Perhaps I can help."

Emine nodded and bit on her lip Her hand reached in her pocket and brought out a small yellow card. Taranaki Base Hospital was printed across the card while beneath, in neat handwriting, was a name and address. Of course, she remembered now. There was a terrible fire and she was in hospital. Perhaps she was still in it.

"Oh you have an address," the lady persisted. "Let's have a look, dearie." She took the card and read it. "Albany, that's way over the bridge. You'd need to go to the other platform. Do you have any money?"

"Yes, of course," Emine replied, felt in her pocket and pulled out a small blue card.

"Oh, you have the ticket," the woman continued. "Good. We'll get you to the bus. Are those things yours?"

Emine noticed a shopping bag and a baby's backpack sitting beside Agron. Nobody else was around so she guessed they belonged to her. She nodded, placed the toddler in the backpack, picked up the bag and followed the lady out into a massive concrete platform with buses, dozens of them, lined up. It was a terminal of some sort and people were everywhere. Emine just stopped and stared. New Plymouth never had a bus terminal this size, she remembered that much.

The little lady waited as the confused mother caught up and, chatting nonstop, led her to a line of blue buses.

"There you are, dear," she said. She made a comment about the baby and disappeared in the sea of faces, an anonymous stranger who helped and moved on.

*

The driver glanced at the ticket and nodded. Emine made her way past the dozen or so passengers and found an empty seat. Five minutes later the bus, now full, moved out of the terminal into a jungle of massive buildings.

"Hell," Emine muttered and gathered Agron in close to her. "Where am I?"

After crossing several crowded intersections, the bus turned onto a motorway. Thousands of vehicles were everywhere, eight lanes bumper to bumper headed along a harbour. She sat and watched as the bus crawled forward and out over the harbour bridge. It continued on the motorway and sped up as the traffic thinned until it, too, drove off and onto a suburban street. Now, every block or so and passengers began to get off.

What now?

Emine examined the card. *Niana Bolsa, Sandwiches and Cuckoo Clocks, 165 Dixon Street, Albany, North Shore, Auckland*, it read.

"Excuse me," she asked the driver after she'd made her way to the front of the bus. "I'm trying to find Dixon Street. Can you help?" She handed the man her card.

"Just about there, madam," the massive Polynesian driver replied.

[92]

"It's two stops away. The shop is near the other end of Dixon Street." He nodded the direction. "You'll have about half a kilometre to walk."

*

"I told you so." Niana laughed as yet another customer made a comment about the new cuckoo clock hanging on the wall behind the counter. "That's four today."

"Okay," Matt replied, grinning. "But why are you still here?"

"Paperwork. I picked the kids up from school and came back," Niana said. "If I go home I never feel like doing it."

"And where are they?"

"In the staff room watching cartoons," she replied. "It's a beautiful hot day and they still want to sit on their butts watching TV."

She glanced up as the doorbell sounded and a woman walked in with a toddler gazing over her shoulders from a backpack. She looked tired and gazed around as if she was uncertain about what to do.

"Good afternoon," Niana said. "Can I help you?"

"Excuse me," the woman replied in a shy voice, "Are you Niana Bolsa?"

"Yes, I am." There was silence as the women looked at each other.

The visitor looked vaguely familiar, something about her eyes and face, but Niana was sure it was a stranger.

"I need help." The woman held a shaky hand out with a card in it. "Your name was given to me but..." Wide frightened eyes stared into Niana's. "I don't know why."

Niana read the card handed to her. It certainly had her name on it. "Taranaki Base Hospital," she said. "So you came up from New Plymouth?"

"I think so."

"And you're from Kosovo?"

"Yes," the woman whispered. "My name is Emine Feraj."

"Well, we'll see what we can do to help," Matt interjected. "You look exhausted. Come on in to the staff room and we'll get you a cup of coffee. The restaurant is closed but I'm sure we can find that much for you."

He glanced at Niana, gave a shrug and guided the woman to the rear of the shop. As they entered the room Adona and Halia gave a backwards glance. The little girl swung back to watch the cartoon but Halia stopped, stared at the visitor and his face drained of colour. He gasped.

"Mummy," he whispered. "You're my mummy aren't you?"

[93]

CHAPTER TWELVE

Niana, who was standing behind her partner when Halia asked his question, stopped, stared opened mouthed at the visitor and felt a flood of emotions surge through her. The first was one of utter disbelief. This was impossible. They were on the other side of the world. Halia must have made a mistake. She looked at the little boy's eyes and her emotion changed to anger. How dare this woman walk in out of nowhere to claim her children back.

But the poor woman looked totally miserable, not cynical or nasty in the way Judith spoke to them. Anger changed to sympathy. The poor woman was so vague and obviously ill. What had she gone through in the last few years?

The name Feraj. Of course, that was the surname Halia had given her. She swallowed and attempted to hide her emotions but couldn't. Tears surged to Niana's eyes; she gulped, muttered a brief excuse and ran from the room. Adona glanced up, saw her distressed foster mother, burst into tears and followed.

Matt had similar but less intense emotions. He studied Halia, noticed the boy's staring eyes, flushed face and shaking hands. He switched his focus to the visitor. She looked as surprised as everyone else in the room, her face also drained of colour and eyes became wide with apprehension.

"Halia!" she cried as tears sprung to her eyes. "Is it really you?"

*

Matt stepped to the door but Niana and Adona were already out of sight. "Damn," he muttered and returned to where the visitor was crying and hugging Halia in her arms.

"I'm sorry," she gasped when she noticed Matt. "I had no idea I would cause such distress."

Matt nodded. "Perhaps you should tell me everything," he said in a kind voice. "Look, take your backpack off, let the baby crawl around, and take a seat."

"But your partner?"

[94]

"I know," Matt said. "Please, relax. I'll go and get her."

He smiled, helped lift the toddler to the ground, patted Halia's head, muttered something to the lad and headed out to find the others.

Niana was sitting in the sunshine by the mezzanine floor windows that overlooked the street outside. Adona, who was in her arms, had stopped crying and the two were watching the traffic flow by.

"Oh Matt, the poor woman. I'm sorry but I've had the children so long..." She cried and blew her nose. "Then to have her arrive from out of nowhere..."

"I know," Matt said. "Let's go back, Niana. We don't know why she's here--and we need to find out."

Niana nodded, glanced at the business card still in her hand and raised her eyes to gaze at him. "You go ahead," she said. "I have an idea."

Matt glanced at the card, his partner, and nodded. "Okay, I'd better get back to her," he said. "Come down when you're ready." He turned to Adona. "Do you want to stay with Mummy, sweetie?"

The little girl nodded and cuddled into Niana.

"All right, see you soon."

*

After Matt retreated down the spiral staircase, Niana sat Adona on the window seat, took a mobile phone from her pocket and punched in the number from the card.

"Taranaki Base Hospital," a voice answered.

"Good afternoon," Niana spoke in a hushed tone. "I wish to make an inquiry about a Emine Feraj."

"One moment, please."

Nondescript music filled her ear before, with a click, a new voice spoke and Niana had to repeat her question.

"And your name, madam?"

"Niana Bolsa. I'm calling from--"

"Mrs. Bolsa," the other party interrupted, "we were hoping you might call. Doctor Frances Hoskin has been trying to contact you. Please wait while I put you through."

Niana frowned. Why would a doctor in New Plymouth be trying to contact her? She waited once more until a third voice came on line.

It took only a few moments for the doctor to fill her in on the situation. "We traced Emine's movements," Frances continued. "After an early flight to Auckland she rode a shuttle bus into the city. That was when

[95]

we lost all trace of her. Tell me, does she appear somewhat vague?"

"Yes, that is exactly how I'd describe it."

"But knows her identity and why she is with you?"

"Not really. From what I could see, she was as surprised as I was when she met the children. It was Halia, that's our little boy, who recognized her, not the other way around."

"It seems she's had another lapse in her memory," the doctor explained. "She's on medication and needs a booster dose. I realize that as the children's foster mother, you're in a stressful situation but would it be possible for you to do one thing to help?"

"Of course," Niana replied.

"Where exactly in Auckland are you?" Niana gave details and the doctor continued. "I'll contact the North Shore Hospital, that's the closest one to you. I'll see if they'll admit her and get back to you."

Five minutes later the mobile phone rang and the doctor told Niana that Emine could be admitted and given an immediate dose of medication to help her recovery. "She had an extremely traumatic experience and is now completely alone in the world," Doctor Hoskin continued.

"I know. It happened to me," Niana said, "being caught in a fire, I mean."

"Did it?" the doctor sounded surprised and she listened without interruption as Niana told of her own lucky escape from death. "This is too similar to be a coincidence," the doctor said. "I think it should be reported."

"The police investigated our fire, had suspects but didn't find the arsonist."

"This often happens," Frances answered. "I guess they have a tremendous workload. Would you agree if I tell the local authorities about you and the fire?"

"That's okay, go ahead. In the meantime we'll get Emine to hospital. That's the least we can do." Niana hung up and gave Adona a hug. "Come on, sweetheart," she said with a sigh. "Let's go and find Daddy."

*

Before walking back into the staff room, Niana stopped and studied the people inside. The visitor could have been herself as she sat on the small couch leaning forward while Matt spoke. Halia was rolling a small rubber ball around to entertain the toddler on the carpet. It could be a domestic scene anywhere.

Emine looked up and smiled in an apologetic way. "I'm sorry," she said. "To have me suddenly appear must be a great shock."

Matt glanced up. "Emine was about to tell me what happened," he said in a cautious voice. "I poured you a mug of coffee."

"Thanks, sweetheart," Niana said and turned to the visitor. "I was talking to your doctor and learned about everything, Emine. The fire, the loss of your friends ... all of it. I'm just glad you found us and I apologize for running out on you a few moments ago." She smiled warmly. "I think we all suffer after affects of the war in one way or another."

She repeated the news for Matt and, in return, Emine brought her up to date on how she came to be in Auckland. The only blank in her memory was what happened that day. She remembered being in the hospital, the elderly lady who helped her in the bus terminal and the bus trip over the harbour bridge but nothing of the middle part.

"Anyhow," she said in conclusion, "I guess I'd better head up to the hospital. If you let me use your telephone, I'll phone for a taxi."

Niana glanced at Matt, saw his slight raising of an eyebrow and replied. "No, we'll go together in my car, I'll get your prescription and you can stay with us."

"But I can't impose."

"I was all alone when I met Matt," Niana said. "He put himself out to welcome the two children and me. Without this help, I don't know how I'd have coped, so let's say I'm repaying his kindness a little."

The two women's eyes linked and they smiled.

"Thank you," Emine whispered. "Both of you."

*

A scream through the night air woke Matt up. His first reaction was to reach across the bed to comfort Niana but she stirred and didn't appear to be having a nightmare. A second scream followed by sobbing filled the air from the guest bedroom across the hall.

"What is it, Matt?" Niana's voice sounded in the darkness.

"Emine, I'd say. It may be one of the children but I doubt it." He placed an arm around her warm body. "Listen."

Soft sobbing could be heard for a moment before silence replaced the sound.

"Okay," Niana whispered. "I'll go and see. Won't be a moment."

She clicked on the bedside light, slipped out of bed and across to the guest room where a line of light shone under the closed door.

"Emine, can I come in?"

[97]

"Yes," came the muffled reply and Niana entered to find her visitor sitting up in bed with red eyes and a dazed look on her face. The baby was asleep in the cot Matt had brought from the shop the evening before. Emine gave a slight smile. "I'm sorry. I woke you up, didn't I?"

"That doesn't matter," Niana replied. "Did you have a nightmare?"

"More than that," Emine said, her eyes wide. "I remember what happened yesterday."

"I see," Niana said and sat on the edge of the bed. It was one of those typically hot, humid Auckland nights, but the perspiration that soaked the woman's body and saturated the borrowed pyjamas was caused by more than just the weather. "Something frightened you, didn't it, Emine?"

"Yes," the older woman whispered. "Have you heard of Major Konstantin Deuratovich and Lieutenant Nikolai Malkov?"

Niana gasped. "One of them. I think Deuratovich was the guy who torched my shop."

"Malkov works for him. He torched our house. He bragged about killing my friends," came the soft reply.

"You were talking to him?"

"Yes," sobbed Emine. "He threatened me in hospital. It all came back in my dream and I woke up remembering everything."

"Would you like to talk about it," Niana asked in a gentle voice as she reached out to squeeze the woman's hand.

Emine nodded. "Except for the dull corridor security lights, the hospital was in darkness "

*

"Make one sound and I'll cut off your air supply," the harsh snarl in Albanian was the first sense to reach Emine's mind.

The second was pain in her throat and a struggle to get air into starved lungs. A hand had her seized by the throat and was squeezing harder. She opened her eyes and stared, terrified, at the man less than a foot away. It was Lieutenant Nikolai Malkov.

"Understand?"

She gave a frantic nod and felt the pressure on her throat relax enough so air once again rushed into her lungs. Pain gripped her body and her vision blurred.

"I wanted you to know what was happening," the man grunted. "You're going to die, woman, and your child, too." A guttural laugh followed. "In some ways it's a pity you weren't at home. I enjoyed the

[98]

screams of your friends' last seconds on this earth."

"Bastard." Emine managed to hiss but the defiant curse turned to a gurgle as the pressure on her throat increased and blotches of black crossed her vision.

"But there's no hurry," the man snarled. "I always enjoyed taking you. You fought me all the way."

The hand on her throat slackened a little but Emine could feel the vile creature leaning on her and the stink of his sweat filled her nostrils.

Shit. This couldn't be happening. This wasn't the internment camp, was it?

She tried to think. Relax. That was it. Pretend to be unconscious.

With a superhuman effort she gave a soft moan and let herself go limp.

"Blast," the man hissed, relaxing both hands.

That was all Emine needed. She kicked Malkov in the groin, grabbed the emergency button beside her pillow and pushed it. A red light pulsed on the control panel above the bed.

"You whore," he murmured as he released her and sprang up.

Emine screamed, a high-pitched hysterical howl that filled the room and adjacent corridor. "I'll be waiting for you," the man threatened. "You can't stay here forever."

The woman screamed again and then a third time, until, finally, the man was gone, out into the corridor and away.

A flustered night nurse arrived five minutes later to find a semi coherent patient sobbing on a blanketless bed. "There are other patients in the ward, Mrs. Feraj," she reprimanded. "Simmer down. You had a nightmare, that's all."

"I was attacked," Emine gasped.

The nurse just frowned. "Come now," she continued in a more reconciliatory tone. "We're secure here; the main entrances and doors are locked at night, the corridors are alarmed and a security patrol is on duty. You're far safer here than in your own home." She frowned as the baby sighed. "You're lucky junior here didn't wake up."

"I'm telling you the truth," Emine sobbed. "I even know who it was."

"Who?" the nurse asked in a softer voice.

"One of the Serb guards who raped us at the internment camp."

"Twenty thousand kilometres from Kosovo?" The nurse sounded cynical. "You've had a terrible nightmare, Emine. Look, I'll get a sedative for you and, if you like, I'll contact security." She smiled and began to remake

[99]

the bed. "As I said, anyone walking through the hospital would have immediately set off an alarm."

"Okay," Emine relented. She was about to ask the nurse to examine her throat but decided it wasn't worth aggravating the situation any further.

However, when she was handed two pills and a tumbler of water, she only pretended to take the drugs.

*

Nurse Anne Raxworthy was a conscientious and dedicated person but was five hours into a night shift with responsibility for over thirty patients, including two that needed fifteen-minute checks. Gone were the days when two nurses and an aide shared the small hours. Instead, she was by herself with a series of electronic monitors and an emergency number to call if things went wrong.

She tucked her distressed patient in and, as if she regretted her earlier abrupt manner, spoke in a soft voice. "I'll leave your light on, go and call security, and be back. Okay?"

The Kosovar woman nodded. "Thank you," she whispered and rolled over to her side. Her throat still felt like fire and she was sure there were new bruises on her body.

"Peter," Anne said over her radio once she was outside Emine's room. "I'd like you to check out my ward and see if there are any intruders around."

"Sure thing, Anne," the security guard replied. He muttered and gave a brief snort.

"Trouble?"

"Aye, there it is," he said. "The monitors on your block were offline for a moment."

"What do you mean by offline?"

"Static rather than a picture. It happens occasionally but they're all online now. You've got a vase of flowers on a table next to you haven't you?"

Anne glanced around and saw the vase in question then glanced up at the sensor hanging from the ceiling with a green light glowing. She smiled at the device. "And the other views?" she asked.

"Only that old guy waddling off to the restroom again," Peter answered. "If he goes once, he goes a dozen times. I'll do a search on the outside monitors if you like."

"No, it'll be okay." Anne smiled. "I'm sure my patient was

[100]

fantasizing. She's recovering from a traumatic experience and this happens at times. Thanks. See you later."

Anne pressed the disconnect button, waved at the security camera, and walked the few meters back to Emine's room to her patient who had dropped off to sleep. She glanced at the watch that hung from her uniform. Damn, old Mrs. Willox needed to be checked. The nurse gave the sleeping toddler next to Emine a quick grin and headed for room twenty-seven.

*

Morning was a busy time in the hospital with patients being readied for the day, breakfasts provided, patients bathed, prepared for surgery and so forth. Nobody noticed when Emine walked out of the bathroom with her toddler and herself dressed in street clothes. She gathered up a small bag that had been given to her by a volunteer organization, lifted Agron into her backpack and simply walked out.

At the entrance she slipped around the building with senses on high alert in case Deuratovich was waiting. The hospital was built on the crest of a hill with suburbs radiating out so it wasn't difficult to find a side road on which to travel.

Twenty minutes later Emine was in the familiar downtown area, and realized she hadn't planned beyond this point. She wondered what she should do. After all, her home was gone as were the only friends she had in the world. Sure, there were some acquaintances she knew in the city, but she hadn't really mixed a lot. She'd been content over the last few months to be the housekeeper and look after the home and her baby while Ida and Ditra worked, and Rokmane went to school.

The memory of the three brought the tragedy back with a jolt. She wanted to inspect their burned out home and visit her friends' graves but was too frightened. She knew there was always the chance that Deuratovich was watching either of the places. She was as a loss as to what to do.

*

"The rest is confused," Emine continued in her own language. She smiled at Niana sitting beside her on the bed. "I guess shock set in and I had had no medication. I remember studying the card Frances Hoskin gave me and it gave me hope. I withdrew money from my account." She smiled. "You know, the New Zealand government gives us the rights of local citizens and I receive what they call a domestic purposes benefit."

[101]

"We're very lucky," Niana agreed, also speaking in Albanian. "We're treated as equal citizens in every way. I even got preferential treatment for a business loan."

"Yes, we're very fortunate," Emine replied before continuing with her story. "I remember purchasing the airline ticket and being terrified I'd be seen by Malkov."

"Why didn't you report the attack?" Niana asked.

"I was afraid I'd be taken back to the hospital and police, even here, still scare me."

"I know," Niana said with empathy in her voice. "I feel the same at times too, but why did you have that relapse in the bus terminal?"

"It's all confused but I remember my heart pounding and running into the ladies' room." Emine frowned and wiped her hand over her face for a moment. "That's it," she said. "I had just bought my bus ticket and decided Agron needed changing then something frightened me but I can't remember what it was."

"Something to do with that Serb guy who attacked you, perhaps?"

Emine stared at her companion and froze. "That's it," she whispered. "I thought I saw him leering at me through the bus terminal crowd. That's when I ran into the restroom. It seemed to be one place he wouldn't dare follow."

"And was it him?"

Emine shrugged. "I don't know, but if I saw him when I came out with that old lady, surely I would remember."

"So you could have been wrong?"

"I guess. I feel like an old drunk recovering after a night on the town. There still seems to be gaps in what I remember." Tears brimmed in the woman's eyes. "At first I thought you were Ida. She was the dynamic one in our house who made the decisions. Ditra was the stabilizing influence that stopped Ida from rushing into things. Rokmane was a wonderful kid ... Oh God," she sobbed and broke into shuddering tears. "They've gone, Niana, killed by that bastard who blew up our home."

"But you found your children, Emine, and us. You aren't alone. I went through terrible times too. I had the chance of coming to New Zealand, met Matt and," she gave a laugh, "here I am."

"Now I've arrived to ruin things for you," Emine whispered. Her eyes became downcast.

"I don't think so," Niana replied. She placed an arm around her guest's shoulders. "What say we go downstairs and have a cup of coffee? I'm wide awake now." She chuckled. "Would you like to bet Matt's already

[102]

down there preparing a midnight snack for us?"

"I'd like that," Emine said with a grateful smile. "Give me a minute to freshen up and slip something on."

The landing lights were on and, as predicted, downstairs the percolator was bubbling away.

"It was too hot to sleep, anyway," Matt said as his partner slipped into the kitchen, flung her arms around his neck, and kissed him with her usual enthusiasm. "And what was that for?"

"Oh, I just felt like having a big hulk to hold," Niana whispered, and kissed him again.

*

CHAPTER THIRTEEN

When the nurse at Taranaki Base Hospital talked to the security guard outside Emine's room that evening, she wouldn't have been so confident had she realized a shadowy figure watched every movement she made. Lieutenant Nikolai Malkov considered attacking her and going back to eliminate the Kosovar woman. In his warped mind, Emine Feraj was a political enemy who deserved to die.

If he had to kill the nurse before he returned to assassinate Feraj, so be it. One more murder on his bloodied hands didn't really matter. The radio in her hand, though, made him hesitate. He knew the instrument contained an emergency button that, if pushed, couldn't be turned off. The security patrols were more efficient than he anticipated and his attempts to neutralize the monitors were only partly successful. It appeared from the nurse's conversation they were back online already.

"Damn," he said in his own language. He had no doubt that if this nurse raised the alarm the hospital would be sealed and elevators disabled before he could move off the third floor. Malkov shrugged and decided to wait until Feraj was in a less secure area before assassinating her.

"Tomorrow, bitch," he whispered.

He slipped out of the storage room and headed down the three flights of an emergency stairwell to a darkened back lawn. Once outside, he slipped across the grass to some nearby bushes, circled back to the parking lot, climbed into his waiting vehicle and drove away.

*

He'd gone less than a kilometre when he felt cold metal pressed against the soft underside of his chin.

"You will drive down towards the waterfront, Serb," a soft female voice whispered in his ear." The language was Albanian but he understood. "Don't take one finger off the steering wheel or turn your head. One incorrect move and I'll forget I'm a lady."

Lieutenant Nikolai Malkov froze and glanced in the rear view mirror but it had been tilted away.

"Drive slowly and turn onto Devon Street West," the woman hissed. Other instructions were given and soon the car crossed a railway line

[104]

into a darkened area beside a small beach. A hundred meters across black water, the floodlit wharf shone like a beacon to conveniently destroy the driver's night vision.

"Pull onto the grass under the trees," the woman instructed. "Switch off the car lights and engine but keep your hands on the wheel."

The Serb smiled to himself. He was certain he heard a quiver in the voice. So the slut was nervous. As he killed the lights, he suddenly accelerated, swung towards the darkness of the trees and used the steering wheel to propel himself straight up. In the same instant his left arm flung back. It was a violent well-planned move and would have succeeded if there was a slightest hesitation by the woman.

"Oh, I expected better from the Serb security police," she said as she squeezed the trigger.

The discharge was a mere pop as a bullet went through the man's neck and exploded in his brain. He was dead before his bloodied head hit the steering wheel.

*

The car wobbled along the grass but the woman slung the lolling head aside, gripped the wheel and reached forward to turn off the key. Apart from scratching against the low branches of the trees the vehicle came to a controlled stop.

"You won't even have the comfort of visiting The Hague," the woman whispered as she manoeuvred the heavy corpse across the car. She started the motor and drove out of the city to a mountain road where she parked beside a small stream.

"You didn't deserve such a painless death," she hissed and climbed out.

She ripped a long piece of material from a seat cover and, using a nearby twig, pushed it down into the petrol tank. It came up smelling of the fuel and felt damp in the faint light. The woman grimaced and repeated the process until the material was soaked at both ends. This was left dangling from the tank, a match lit and the rag burst into flame.

The woman dived for cover but the car ignited sooner than expected and she was hurled forward down a bank that saved her from being incinerated in the resulting explosion. A gigantic boom split the air and orange flames turned the predawn light into day.

The woman slipped across to a walking track that circled across Egmont National Park. An hour later she walked out another entrance to a

[105]

different road. It was still early morning and the area deserted. With luck, she could be out of the district by noon.

*

"Don't tell me nothing is wrong because I know there is," Niana said in a quiet voice. "Talk to me, Matt?"

Her companion glanced up from the garage bench where the wooden sections of a cuckoo clock were spread out. "Is it that obvious?" he asked.

"Yes." Niana pulled up a wooden stool and reached across to squeeze his tanned arm. "Is it something I've done?"

It was January, the height of the southern hemisphere's summer. New Zealand's silly season had begun, the time when factories and many small service shops closed and the country went on holiday. In line with this custom *Sandwiches and Cuckoo Clocks* was shut until the last week in January when the factories around opened, furniture would begin to sell again and workers wanted food.

Matt turned from Niana's gaze and continued to sand down a little wooden leaf. "Kent cut this out," he said.

"Matt, don't change the topic." She pouted and took her hand away.

"I call it a silent cling," the man whispered. "Everyone is wrapped up in their own thoughts and saying nothing." He coughed. "I know I'm as bad as the rest of you."

"Go on," Niana said.

"Well, Halia is clinging to his mother. Adona, in contrast, is clinging to you almost as if she is afraid you will give her away. You are clinging to Emine's baby and she is clinging to us all. But nobody is saying anything about how they feel or what they want to do. I feel redundant, at times." He grimaced. "That's the truth, Niana."

"Oh sweetheart, don't you realize that you're the person holding us all together?" Niana said earnestly. "You're the silent hulk of a man who has opened his heart and home to this flood of refugees. You're right about Agron. The truth is, he's almost the same age as my baby would have been." She blinked and wiped an eye with a finger.

"And the kids?"

"Halia is torn between us, Matt. He remembers his mother's love back home but has grown to love us, too. Us, Matt. Not just me. Adona hardly remembers her mother, has noticed Halia's attraction to this stranger

[106]

and has turned to us for her security. In her own little way, she told me that last night. We were alone and she bubbled out she never wanted to leave us." Niana reached across and kissed Matt on the cheek. "I love you Matt. More than you could possibly imagine."

"And you still want me?"

"Of course I do," Niana whispered.

"Prove it," Matt's voice was so quiet, the words were hardly heard above background noises.

"Oh Matt, not now. Wait until tonight."

Matt turned, fixed his eyes directly into those of his partner and grabbed both her hands. "I don't mean that," he said. "I want you permanently. I want you to be my wife and have our own family." He grimaced. "Damn, that came out all wrong. I still want Adona and Halia. Don't get me wrong."

"But how," came Niana's hushed reply.

Matt reached into a small under-bench drawer, pulled out a long envelope and handed it to Niana.

She frowned and extracted a formal looking sheet. "From your lawyer," she muttered. "What is this about?"

"My divorce decree," Matt replied. "I am a single man again."

"And you never told me," Niana snapped. "Why not, Matt?"

"I thought it would complicate things."

"So when do you want to do it?"

"Do what?"

"Get married, you silly man."

"You will?"

"Of course..." The rest of her sentence was blocked as Matt swept his arms around her and deposited a kiss firmly on the responding lips.

"Next week?" he added after they surfaced.

Niana wriggled away, stood, grinned and held out her hand. "Agreed, kind sir," she said, giggling. "I heard that on one of those period romances on television. You're committed now, my lad."

"Good. Now, I think we need to get everyone together and have a discussion on what everyone wants. This clinging and doing nothing has to stop."

"Yes dear. You know, Kent clings to you, too."

Matt grinned and nodded. "All these people," he said. "At least I don't get lonely, now. Wait a moment." He walked out and returned a moment later. "I've had this a couple of weeks," he muttered, handing Niana a small cloth-covered box.

[107]

Inside was an engagement ring made up with a cluster of three small but perfect diamonds.

"Oh my God!" she gasped.

"It should fit," the suddenly shy man replied. "If you don't like the design it can be exchanged."

"Like it?" Niana gasped again. "Oh Matt. It's magnificent." She flung her arms around his neck and buried her head in his shoulder while tears poured down her cheeks.

"Why the tears?"

"Memories, my love," Niana whispered. With infinite care she reached across with her right hand and removed the single band wedding ring from her third finger. Blinking back tears she swapped the rings, placing her wedding ring in the red velvet holder and holding the new engagement ring between her fingers.

"Would you mind if I kept Zymer's ring?" she asked.

"No, Niana. Of course not," Matt whispered.

"He was my old life," Niana explained. "You're my new one." She tilted the new ring so the diamonds twinkled in the light and turned back to Matt. "Put in on for me, my darling."

*

"Mummy!" Adona cried out in a loud, gleeful voice less than an hour later. They were lying on the back patio under the shade of a massive yellow sun umbrella. "You've got a new ring."

"Yes," Niana said. "Daddy and I are going to get married. Aren't you happy?"

Adona stared first at the ring and then up to her foster mother. Her small chin quivered and her eyes became troubled. "No," she replied in a determined voice.

"But why, sweetheart? It won't make any difference. None at all. We'll both keep on loving you."

"But Mamma will take me away with her and I'll never see you again," Adona sobbed. Since their mother's arrival, the children called Emine Mamma while retaining Mummy for Niana. It just happened and nothing had really been discussed.

"And you wouldn't like that?"

"No. You're my mummy. Can I stay with you and Daddy even after you get married and have a baby?"

"Forever if you want to, sweetheart." Niana lifted Adona up onto her knees. "We aren't going to have a baby."

"Does Mamma have to go away? She told me she was going away soon as you wouldn't be able to look after her any more."

"Oh Adona, she can stay as long as she wants. We love having her here but she might decide to leave. That's up to her. If she does decide to go and you'd rather stay with us, you can. Okay?"

The little girl nodded. "Then it's okay to marry Daddy," she proclaimed. "Will you wear a pretty dress?"

"Oh yes," Niana laughed. "And so will you, sweetheart. A brand new one in any colour you like."

"A long blue one that touches the ground?"

"Sure."

"I'd love that," Adona said with a big smile.

*

Just inside, a few meters away, Emine stepped back from the curtains. She had hesitated a few moments before when she'd heard her daughter call out. Her eavesdropping had been unintentional but every word had been heard. Deep in thought, she retreated, unseen by the pair on the patio, and walked to the kitchen.

*

"Niana," Emine said late that evening. They were in the kitchen, the children were asleep and Matt was watching television in the front room. "Can I have a word with you?"

"Sure."

"I don't think I ever thanked you for rescuing and looking after the children," the older woman began. "They've grown into fine youngsters who love you and Matt."

"They love you, too, Emine," Niana replied with caution in her voice.

"Halia maybe, but Adona regards me with suspicion."

"No--"

"I overheard your conversation today. She adores you, Niana, and I don't want to disrupt her young life again."

"Meaning?"

"You told me you had identification papers for the children made up with your surname. There is no way to prove their real identity. I want to

[109]

leave it that way..." Emine stopped and glanced, white faced, at her companion. "They're such lovely children and you have provided everything for them, things I can never give them." She stopped again, flushed and turned away so her face was hidden. "Thank you," she whispered with a sob and dashed from the room.

"Wait Emine," Niana called and ran after her.

She reached Emine on the patio and grabbed her arm. The other woman turned, eyes wet with tears. "I'm sorry, Niana. I guess I'm not as rational as I thought I'd be. I was going to thank you for taking me in, tell you to keep the children and that I had decided to return to New Plymouth with Agron."

"Sit down," Niana said in a soft voice as she guided her friend to a patio chair. "You said you overheard my conversation with Adona this afternoon?"

Emine sat down and rested her elbows on the adjacent table. "I don't understand why you want me around," she sobbed. " I'm just a nuisance. You're about to be married to a fine man, and the children love you both. Nobody needs me."

"And who is there in New Plymouth?"

"Neighbours. Some friends. There's an Albanian Society I go to on occasions."

"How do you think Halia would feel if you left him? Adona too. You're their mother, Emine. Nobody can replace that. Sure Adona clings to me but she spends hours playing with Agron. Who does she rush up to after school to tell about her day? You are back in their lives, now. If you left, they'd be heartbroken."

"But I can't just stay here living off Matt and you."

"Ask him," Niana said and she walked over to the sliding doors. "Matt," she called. "Could you come here, please?"

Matt appeared with a bemused look, noticed the slumped woman and caught his fiancé's eyes. "Can I help?" he asked in a compassionate voice.

"Ask him, Emine," Niana said.

"Oh Matt." The sobbing woman glanced up. "I've outstayed my welcome, haven't I?"

"Emine's thinking of returning to New Plymouth and leaving Adona and Halia with us."

"Why?" Matt asked with an incredulous expression. "After all your effort to find the children, do you really think we'd let you leave again?" He shrugged. "Of course, if you want your privacy..." His eyes caught Emine's.

"But you're getting married."

"So?"

"Thank you, Matt," Emine replied, bursting into shuddering tears again. "My God. I'm a nut case, aren't I?"

Matt coughed a laugh and glanced back at Niana. "Emine, you can stay with us as long as you want," he said. "Nobody wants you to leave. Understand?" He walked across and placed an arm around her shoulders, gave her a brief hug and left the patio.

"Us Kosovars have to stick together," Niana added in a hushed voice. "What say we go and have a strong cup of coffee?"

Emine nodded through her tears and smiled. "I'd like that," she whispered and followed her friend inside.

*

CHAPTER FOURTEEN

Major Trent Gillies read a computer readout report and glanced up at his subordinate sitting opposite him in the high rise, inner city office building.

"So there was a connection between the three events, Captain Swenson?" he asked. "What else have you brought to light?"

Though in the military, both men were dressed in civilian suits and could have been two of thousands of civil servants or businessmen who walked the streets of Wellington, New Zealand's capital city, every day.

Both men were members of New Zealand's Army Force Intelligence Group Four, seconded to the Security Intelligence Service and answerable directly to the Prime Minister's Office. Their job, as Geoff Swenson had once told a colleague, was to do the SIS surveillance work within the country and throughout the world where New Zealand's interests were at stake. They often worked directly with allied security services in North America and Europe.

The captain nodded and began his report. "We believe the reason for the time gap between the fires of Niana Balsa's apartment and the one in New Plymouth is that the Serb operatives moved to Australia," he began. "We have reports of malicious fires in Sydney and Melbourne that fit in with our inquiries. "

"So it appears your devious subterfuge was Lieutenant Nikolai Malkov's undoing, Geoff," Trent Gillies said. "He let his guard down and our obliging Kosovar friend killed him."

"It appears so, sir." The captain rubbed his chin. "We were keeping an eye on the Serb when he arrived in New Plymouth and it was sheer bad luck that we failed to intercept him before he started that fire."

"Bad luck that killed two innocent people," Gillies interjected,

"Our sergeant on the scene decided to follow Emine Feraj that morning in case she needed protection. As it turned out, he made the wrong choice and the Serb blew up the house."

"It happens." The major shrugged. "Our resources are stretched thin at the best of times."

"Anyhow when we rescued our young friend it was not difficult to create a fictitious third body for the media to report on. It appears it worked and our enemy was fooled, too."

"Yes but she was one little viper, wasn't she? Sneaked away from under your noses and returned to the hospital where she waited in Nikolai Malkov's car and killed the bastard."

"That's correct, major," Geoff Swenson replied. He gave a tight smile. "She did an excellent job, too. The bastard was shot through the throat at close range before the car was set on fire."

"And you picked her up, I believe?"

"Yes. We scared the hell out of her at what we'd do if she opened her mouth and took her down south where she should be safe. At the moment, the local police theory is that the burned-out vehicle was caused by either an accidental explosion or a suicide, so we're staying quiet on the matter. Emine Feraj left the hospital, headed for Auckland and met up with Niana Bolsa."

"We'll leave that part of it to the police, then," Major Trent Gillies said, nodding at the document in his hand. "Unfortunately, this Lieutenant Nikolai Malkov wasn't working alone. As far as we know, other operatives from his notorious Section Eight are in the country. I want them traced and arrested, Captain. Emine Feraj and Niana Bolsa are still in danger, not to mention other Kosovar women in our country who were interned in those Serb camps. This vendetta appears to be more than just random revenge against Kosovar women, I'm afraid." He pushed a report stamped *Top Secret* across his desk.

Geoff Swenson grimaced as he read the three pages of the computer notes. "I suspected as much," he replied. "So what now, sir. "

"Set a trap to flush the bastards out before anyone else is killed," Trent said. "I want a plan to be implemented, pronto. Time is not on our side, Captain."

"I'll get onto it, sir," Swenson replied and, deep in thought, handed the notes back.

*

Vacation time meant different things to the people associated with *Sandwiches and Cuckoo Clocks*. The children were excited with an endless summer of swimming and fun while Matt took a chance to catch up on work that had been pushed aside with shop customers occupying his time. Six cuckoo clocks, constructed from new and authentic down to the mechanism Matt had managed to import from Singapore were ready for the Japanese firm and three more were waiting to be assembled for local orders.

[113]

As well, another dozen old cuckoo clocks had arrived ready to be restored when time allowed.

"So have you thought of my suggestion?" he said to Kent when they finished packing the new clocks up ready for dispatch.

Kent glanced up and grimaced. "You mean accepting a full time job here and being sponsored by this firm into that arts course at the local college?"

"That's the one." Matt smiled at the boy.

"Dad won't agree. He reckons I need to return to school," the teenager lamented. "It's a waste of bloody time. I'm no academic and will never pass my exams. You have to pass in four subjects. I could manage two at the most."

"Well, think about my offer," Matt said. "I'll need someone fulltime next month but your present job will still be here if you do return to school."

"Thanks, Matt." Kent completed nailing the wooden crate lid on in silence. "I hope they appreciate the hours of work gone into these clocks," he finally muttered in a manner that showed he wanted to change the subject.

Matt studied his young employee and shrugged. The boy had come out of himself since his arrival and had a real talent for carving wooden figures for the clocks. The crouching deer used on all Macolansa Cuckoo Clocks were the lad's own design. However, little more had been found out about Kent's home life. He arrived at the workshop, spent hours on the machines, carving or doing other chores, talked to the children and, in the evening, climbed on his old bicycle and rode away, a lonely figure, unusual for somebody his age.

*

Michael Quinn cast a cold eye over his son. "You're wasting your time down at that used furniture store, time better spent in raising your grades. Next term, you can leave that part time job and concentrate on your studies. It's your last chance to salvage something from your time at school."

"I'm not going back, Dad," Kent replied.

Michael Quinn's face contorted into anger. "Oh, yes you are, Kent. Get those ridiculous ideas of going to that art school out of your mind. You need a business degree to get on in this world today, none of this namby-pamby stuff."

"I am not!" Kent screamed.

The elder Quinn gave his son a none too soft push on the shoulder. "Don't you raise your voice to me," he growled. "And furthermore, you can stay away from that guy at the furniture shop, too. He's put these stupid ideas in your head. Oh, I've heard all about him shacked up with that foreign woman half his age."

"You don't know them, Dad," Kent's voice became hushed. "Matt and Niana are really genuine people. At least they care."

"What do you mean by that?"

"You're no better than Mum," Kent blurted out. "In fact, it was you who drove her out. I can hardly blame her and, as for shacking up, how many women have you slept with since Mum left, Dad? That secretary of yours would be in her twenties, wouldn't she?"

"What are you insinuating?"

"Oh come off it, Dad. Everyone knows of your nocturnal visits to the Blue Ocean Motel with her."

"Why you little…" Quinn's double chin jutted out and angry eyes stared from behind square shaped glasses. He gave his son another violent shove on the shoulder.

Kent's mind went back to the beatings he received as a youngster, the ones that only ceased when he became large enough to receive them without bursting into tears. Without that reaction, Michael Quinn lost some of his authoritarian dominance over his son. Now the man in his mid forties was half a head shorter than Kent, but carried almost twice his weight.

"I wouldn't advise you to get rough with me, Dad," Kent said through clenched teeth.

"Why you ungrateful little bugger," Michael Quinn spat and, using all the force he could muster, slapped Kent across the face.

The teenager reeled back, stared at his father, but didn't slink away this time. The years of violent punishments rushed to his mind, the years of never being good enough for his cold parent, the constant innuendoes and criticisms. He staggered to his feet, wiped blood away from a cut lip and snapped.

For the first time in his eighteen years of life he struck back. With thrashing clenched fists he pounded the unsuspecting older man. For several moments he screamed and pounded, ignored the retaliatory efforts from his father and concluded with an upward punch on the man's jaw that sent blood and a broken tooth splattering.

Michael Quinn collapsed, groaning to the floor and attempted to kick his son away. Kent, heaving and with his own blood running down

[115]

under the chin, stood back with clenched fists and watched the moaning man. This person who had ruled with an iron fist from before he was Halia's age had met his comeuppance.

"Get out." Quinn grunted, his words slurred by his bloodied mouth. "Come back again and I'll--"

"You'll what, Dad?" Kent said, panting. "You can do nothing. You drove Mum out with your violence and unfaithfulness. You're nothing but a pathetic old man, a failure. Your days of threatening people are over."

Quinn grabbed a nearby table, staggered to his knees and attempted to pull himself to his feet. He failed and sank, coughing and spluttering back to the floor while Kent continued to watch with his bruised fists still clenched.

"Get..." Michael Quinn managed to hiss.

"Oh, I am, old man," Kent's voice was now quiet but determined. "And you can rot in hell as far as I am concerned. "

He turned, grabbed his jersey from the couch and left the room.

*

It was seven thirty but already the summer sun was casting its heat across the city when Niana arrived at the restaurant. Though it was closed, like Matt she used her extra time to catch up with chores put off during the normal working day. Today she was going to remove all the curtains and take them home to wash and change some of the furniture around. Matt was home doing some maintenance work on Stubby while Emine had taken the children down to a local bay for a swim before the summer crowds rolled in later in the morning.

She had just parked the car and walked to the back door when a cough made her jump in fright. Anxious thoughts evaporated when she swung around and saw Kent sitting on a bench under the veranda. She relaxed but her emotions turned to concern when she saw his bruised face and cut lip.

"Kent," she said. "What's wrong? You look terrible." She stepped forward. "Your face. Were you mugged?"

"Well, sort of," Kent replied. "I had a difference of opinion with my old man and he kicked me out."

"Oh Kent," Niana said as she unlocked the door. "Come on in and I'll clean you up. What happened?"

Kent wiped a hand over his bloodied nose and shrugged. "I hit back," he whispered. "For the first time in my life, I hit back."

[116]

Suddenly tears filled his eyes and he walked away. Niana caught up to him at the corner of the building and placed an arm around his shoulders. When he turned she reached up and hugged him close.

"Come inside," she whispered as the boy shuddered back tears. "Tell me everything."

*

"He used to thrash me with his belt when I was at primary school," Kent continued his story as he sipped the mug of coffee Niana had given to him." I was terrified of him."

"But your mother?"

"Oh, in hindsight, she tried to help but at the time it seemed as if she only cared for Jenny and Craig, my little sister and brother. She was also beat up by my father. That's why she left."

"So why didn't you go too?" Niana asked.

"She wasn't my real mother." Kent sighed. "Dad was married twice. My real mother took off when I was younger than Adona. I can hardly remember her."

"I see," Niana said. "If it's any help, I believe you did the right thing. You can stay with us and we'll sort things out. Have you any clothes?"

"A backpack full," Kent stood back and wiped his eyes. "I couldn't carry any more on my bike."

"Matt will get your other gear." Niana broke into a grin. "I doubt if your father will intimidate him."

"My father's just a fat slob. I realize that, now." He smiled. "Thanks Niana. You, Matt and the kids are my only friends, you know."

"And friends stick together, Kent. Remember that."

Kent nodded, squeezed Niana's hand and gazed into her eyes. "Thank you," he repeated in a whisper. "Until I came here, I felt so utterly alone. Now you're like my family. Does that sound silly?"

"No." Niana smiled. "I was once all alone, too. I know the feeling. Look, go though to the flat and have a hot shower. Afterwards, I'll have some breakfast for you and you can help me move my tables around."

She watched as the youth left the kitchen and her own thoughts reflected back. It didn't take a war to ruin some people's lives. Here was a young man of extraordinary talent who had suffered for years in one of the most free and stable countries in the world. It made her wonder about human behaviour and feel relieved she'd met Matt.

[117]

The only problem that arose from Kent's move was when the old truck rolled into the Quinn household to pick up some of Kent's personal furniture. Michael Quinn made a half hearted protest but backed down from any real objections when Matt stated quite firmly that, since Kent had turned eighteen a month before, the young man was within his rights to live wherever he liked. He was also within his rights to remove his personal property.

After a week at Matt's place, Kent moved into the empty apartment behind the shop. He assured Niana he would be quite happy by himself, though, in the new term, he might share with another student.

"Okay," she told Kent, "Remember though, you're welcome to come and board with us or even stay a weekend if you get lonely."

"I just might do that," Kent replied, "But, really, I'm okay. Dad was never any company, anyway and I've cooked for myself ever since Mum left."

"And my original proposal?" Matt pushed.

"Yes," Kent answered with a wide grin. "I've already applied for the course and found that my senior year qualifications, especially my art grade, will get me in. A student loan should pay for my fees."

"Great." Matt said. "So I won't need to advertise for an assistant, after all?"

"Not, as long as you don't mind me having time off during the week to attend lectures."

"Part of the deal, Kent."

"And a few baby sitting duties as well," Niana added.

"Your two but not Emine's baby," Kent said with a laugh. "Babies scare me."

Adona's wish came true when she wore a long blue frock, an exact copy of the bride's, for the wedding while Halia looked just as smart in a black suit. The children stood beside their mother and gazed around at the guests who crowded the *Sandwiches and Cuckoo Clocks* workshop where Matt and Niana's marriage ceremony was taking place.

"So by the power vested in me, I now pronounce you man and wife," Cameron Jenkinson the elderly Justice Of The Peace, and an old family friend of Matt's, concluded. He grinned. "You may kiss your bride,

[118]

Matt."

The groom flushed as his wife gazed at him, flung her arms around his neck and gave him a long kiss while the audience hooted and clapped.

"That's the girl, Niana," Ted Wilson, Matt's used furniture friend, yelled out. "Show 'em who's the boss from the very start."

Emine cuddled Agron and grinned at the uncouth New Zealander who looked as if he'd just ambled in from the pub. She reached down and put an arm around her older children as they gazed up at her.

"Mummy and Daddy look almost as beautiful as you two," she commented.

"Men don't look beautiful, Mamma," Adona said, laughing.

"What's the word in English for good looking men then?"

"Handsome." Halia smiled. "Girls are beautiful, boys are handsome."

"So your little sister is beautiful is she?"

"Yeah, she's okay, I guess," Halia said. "Mummy's beautiful, though." He fixed his eyes on his birth mother. "You are too, Mamma," he added in a hushed voice. "I like your new dress."

Emine smiled. Halia had never said anything like that before. "Oh Halia," she whispered. "Thank you, and I think you are a real little man, today. We're all so proud of you both."

The time since she had agreed to stay with her friends had flown. After a big discussion explaining what a honeymoon was, the children agreed to stay home with their mother while their foster parents went away for ten days. After all, they were at home in familiar surroundings. Roseanne from the shop offered to help if she was needed and Kent also promised to call in to visit.

Emine was surprised how Niana and Matt's friends had welcomed her into their circle as if she'd known them for years. At home, there was always a wide circle of family and neighbours around but newcomers in their village were often treated with suspicion. She sighed and wondered if she'd ever see it again. It had, like hundreds of other villages, been destroyed by the Serbs in those dark days in April 1999, perhaps never to be rebuilt.

"Mamma," Halia tugged on her sleeve and jolted her thoughts back to the present. "Mummy and Daddy are going through to the restaurant. Can we go, too?"

"Yes, dear," Emine replied. "We sit at the bride's table right up the front. Remember your table manners, won't you?"

"Yes Mamma," Halia said. "Adona is the only one who slops things."

[119]

"I do not," Adona protested. "At least I don't talk while I'm eating."

"Come on, children, don't argue. It's Mummy and Daddy's day to be proud of you both, isn't it?"

"Oh they are," Adona chirped up and ran ahead to tuck her arm into Niana's.

*

CHAPTER FIFTEEN

In a peninsula separating Tasman and Golden Bays on the northern tip of the South Island, New Zealand, the Abel Tasman National Park offered everything for tourists from sheltered beaches to tall peaks covered in native forests and intercepted by mountain streams. The two honeymooners were into their second day of a sea kayaking expedition. It was an hour after dawn and already the sun was baking the ocean. They paddled northwards out of Torrent Bay where they had spent the previous night. Ahead lay two days of exploring the coastline. That was their plan but with nothing booked until the third night, the time was really their own.

Niana stopped paddling from the front space of the *Southern Sunshine,* a double kayak, and glanced over her shoulder to where Matt was still propelling the craft forward.

"Hold it, big boy," she called out. "My arms are aching already and the blisters on them from yesterday don't help."

Matt grinned and rested his paddle across in front of him." It's going to be a hot day," he said. "I just thought that if we could get up the coast we'd be in front of the crowd. Why don't you relax while I keep paddling?"

"No," his wife grunted. "If you can paddle, so can I."

She leaned forward and dug the paddle into the water. The craft skimmed forward with shuddering bumps while ripples of white wake fanned away from them. The pace, though, couldn't be maintained and after ten minutes both paddlers stopped beyond a headland and gazed ashore. It was low tide and golden sand stretched along beneath a wooden walkway, built to provide access along the shore. Behind, steep hills of native forest rose hundreds of meters into the air.

"We're about half way to that next big headland," Niana said, panting. "We've done well."

"So let's go ashore and have a bite to eat."

"Food." Niana laughed. "All we need is a drink of water, not that potent stuff we drank last night."

"Yeah, you did get giggly didn't you?" Matt chuckled.

"Me?" Niana replied innocently.

Moments later they were ashore at an idyllic spot where the lovers had the area to themselves. Twenty minutes later, after smearing sun block over each other they slipped into their life jackets and Niana scrambled aboard the kayak. Matt was about to push her out and climb in himself when a faint call echoed along the shore.

They both looked along the beach to where a running figure was approaching. A hand waved in an almost frantic manner.

"Someone wants us," Matt said. He stood up in the knee-deep water and held the kayak steady with his hands.

Niana frowned and squinted into the bright light.

Words came through the air, unfamiliar to Matt but they made his wife gasp in alarm.

*

"Albanian," Niana explained as she scrambled out of the kayak and watched the approaching person. "She called out, 'Wait, oh please wait.'"

"You know, I'm sure I noticed a girl running along the walkway when we came in earlier," Matt replied. "Perhaps she's been trying to catch our attention for quite a while."

"Could be."

The figure grew larger and they could now make out a teenage girl. Long hair flew out behind her as she pounded the pathway in a steady stride. Now that it was obvious the pair were waiting, she seemed to be concentrating on running.

Minutes later a perspiring, panting stranger stopped in front of them and bent over gasping for breath.

"Niana Bolsa?" she said, panting after she had recovered. Her brown eyes looked troubled.

"I was," Niana said. "It's Coleman now."

The girl's eyes darted back and forth between the pair. "You're both in danger," she gasped. "You need to get away from the beach. Two Serb assassins are coming."

"How can that be?"

The girl looked desperate. "Please. I'll explain later," she said in accented English. "Do you think I'd run all this way just for a big joke? My name is Meldena Adzovic. I knew Adona and Halia's mother, Emine Feraj back home. Please," she pleaded. "If you get in that kayak and paddle away they will kill you both without mercy. They're from Section Eight." A tremor went through her body as she turned to Matt. "You must understand that these men are totally ruthless. I've been following them. They arrived at the lodge late last night after you'd gone to bed. I was terrified they'd attack

[122]

you before morning but I guess there were too many tourists around. I spent the night on the veranda outside your room but fell asleep. By the time I awoke you were already in your kayak. I've been trying to keep up all morning." She wiped her brow. "If you hadn't decided to stop here I'd never have caught you."

Matt nodded and jerked up. "Listen," he said.

A faint howl of a high revving outboard motor came from beyond the headland. Niana grabbed Matt's sleeve and stared into his eyes. "I believe her," she whispered.

"All right," he replied and flicked his eyes up to where a dark silhouette of a motorboat appeared out of the glare of the morning sun. He dragged the kayak up the beach and pulled three packs from it. He held the smaller backpack out for Niana to slip onto her back and smiled when their new companion offered to wear one.

Niana led the way up where the path turned inland across the back of a second headland. Just before they left the beach, she turned to see the boat slow and circle towards the shore. Their kayak must have been seen.

"Hurry." she gasped. A shudder ran up her back as she reached out for Matt's hand for she had no doubt, whatsoever, that Meldena's story was true.

*

After the trio moved inland through the trees for a few moments, Matt stopped and listened. Everything was quiet with even the lapping sound of surf on the beach cut off.

"We're playing it blind," he said. "You two stay here. I'm going back to see what's happened."

"No," Niana said. "We stick together. I'm coming too."

Matt was about to argue but saw her passionate gaze and shrugged. "And you, Meldena?" he asked.

The teenager frowned. "This track probably cuts back to the beach in a couple of hundred meters. I'll scout ahead and meet you back here."

"Okay," Matt replied and headed back.

They arrived at the edge of the trees and slid forward beneath ferns to a spot where they could view the beach unseen.

"Oh no," Niana whispered.

Two men were deep in conversation at the back of the motorboat idling by the beach. The putting motor drowned out voices but it was obvious some sort of argument was underway. When one pointed to the kayak and waved his hand in anger, the second guy shrugged and slid into the knee-deep water. He waded ashore and went to examine the kayak.

"We left the storage compartment cover off," she whispered. "They'll see we've taken our gear."

A shout from the Serb on the beach reached their ears. He waved and the boat started to move out around the headland.

"Let's get back," hissed Matt. "They're going to try to trap us between them."

He was right. When Meldena met them, her expression was grim. "The boat landed on the beach ahead and one guy is heading this way," she revealed. "We have five minutes at the most before he gets here."

Niana looked pale but said nothing.

"Left or right?" Matt asked, nodding at the thick undergrowth on each side. "We have to leave the track and do it now."

"Inland," Niana replied. "We'll be trapped on the point."

*

The undergrowth was thick and steep with long black vines dangling between boughs of larger trees and the smaller ferns beneath. But these vines were secure and used for leverage as Niana pulled her way up the slope to a small space behind the trunk of a large tree.

After a brief wait to catch her breath, she continued upwards. The foliage caught their backpack and loose debris from Meldena's sneakers fell on her. After several moments the undergrowth cleared a little and she found they'd arrived in a spiky grass covered cutting between steep banks.

"This was probably a slip," Matt explained.

A shout from below and the rumble of angry voices made the three glance back but nothing could be seen. Their pursuers must have met.

"They know we aren't on the track," Meldena gasped.

"Keep going," Matt whispered.

Now that they were out of the dense undergrowth, the climb up the slope was easier. For several moments they continued until finally they reached a rocky outcrop. The three squeezed together, sat down and took a moment to regain their breath. They'd been climbing constantly for twenty minutes and were all flushed and tired. Perspiration dripped from their faces, and their limbs were scratched and covered in grime.

"I doubt if we're being followed," Matt said, puffing. "We would hear them coming."

Niana stretched her weary legs over the edge of the rock and leaned

[124]

back against Matt. The climb had sapped her energy and dozens of sand flies attracted to her sweaty body didn't help. She swiped insects away from her eyes and gave her husband a smile.

"What now, dear?" she asked.

"Keep going up," he advised." Take it slowly."

"Right," Niana agreed, while Meldena just nodded.

The climb progressed at a steady rate and another five minutes passed.

Without warning a rifle report made them jump in fright. Matt swore, Niana gasped in alarm, and Meldena turned a sickly white.

A second shot echoed up the hillside, followed by two more in rapid succession. There was whine and a ping as one bullet ricocheted off a nearby branch.

"Come on down. We have you covered," a voice shouted from the hidden track below.

"Bastard," the girl hissed.

"Keep calm," Matt whispered. "They don't know where we are."

He was correct for the next two shots and the shouts were further along the track.

"I'll check and see where we are," Niana pulled a map from her pocket. "According to this, a track follows the ridge along the top of the hill. She tipped the paper to gather more light and squinted at the tiny writing. *"Original track. Not recommended."*

"Well, at least it's a track," Meldena commented.

"The road into Totaranui is two or three valleys further back," Niana continued. "The map's not very detailed but I'd say the way would be steep and covered in dense bush."

"Okay let's get up to the ridge," Matt added. "If those men decide to follow us, we could still be in trouble." He glanced at the pair. "Have you rested enough?"

"Sure," Niana replied, but indicated to Matt that their companion looked exhausted.

Meldena sat breathing heavily but smiled and pulled herself up when she noticed the Colemans looking at her. "No Serb is going to better me," she grunted. "Never again."

The journey up the cutting was exhausting. Niana said nothing but was worried that they would be exposed if the enemy reached the bottom of the cutting.

"I know," Matt said, as if he'd read her thoughts. "I feel the same. We'll be at the top soon."

[125]

"Poor Meldena looks exhausted," Niana heaved. The climb was affecting her, too with each breath harder to suck into heaving lungs. "I'm no mountaineer, either," she admitted and grinned when Matt placed his hands on her rump and gave her a heave upwards.

"You're doing well," he encouraged.

Five minutes later they scrambled over a ledge and back beneath the trees. Below, the deep blue bay stretched away with several kayaks and one motorboat in sight. Their own craft was out of sight but portions of the walkway could be seen far below.

"We've come a long way," Meldena panted.

"And there is a sort of track," Niana added. "The creeper has encroached from the sides but you can see bare earth."

*

They followed the undulating track north along a narrow ridge with views in all directions. To their right, the Tasman Bay glittered turquoise while the opposite valley was covered in dense native forest. The ridge widened and finally curved into a hillside that blocked the view of the ocean. They entered the bush, cooler temperatures and dull light. The foliage closed in with ferns and creepers almost obliterating the track.

Ten minutes later a mud stained Meldena, who had slipped to the rear, glanced at the other two. Her hazel eyes were wide in anticipation and lips pouted in a determined way. "Someone's following us," she whispered. "I heard branches being pushed aside."

They listened. Cicadas could be heard with their constant clattering, an occasional bird chirped and even their heavy breathing added to the hushed sounds. But there was also another noise. Behind, faintly at first but increasing in volume, a swishing sound of branches being thrust aside reached their ears. A faint cough confirmed that Meldena was correct. Someone was coming.

"Let's go," Matt hissed. "I'll keep at the back."

For twenty minutes they surged forward with no concerns about minor scratches or insects flying in their faces. The situation was becoming desperate.

They continued around a tight corner and stopped. Their hill stopped at a massive canyon that cut across at right angles. Opposite was another cliff backed by dense native forest that towered up a high peak. Far below and out of sight under a canopy of trees and ferns the gurgle of a stream tumbling over rocks was heard.

The trampers' attention though was focused straight ahead at an ancient swing bridge that spanned the chasm. Two steel cables anchored in the foliage behind them, reached up above tall poles at the edge of the vertical drop. From there, the cables dipped down across the gap before curving up to two poles poking out of the undergrowth on the opposite bank.

Suspended below, like an elongated wire basket, was a swing bridge. Meter wide planks formed the decking that curved down to a lowest point in the middle of the canyon before it rose again. The only handholds were a couple of arm-height wires. However, the structure hadn't been maintained for years. The planks looked rotten and slippery with several missing. The wire appeared firm but was coated in rust and a dull grey moss. An ancient sign nailed across the entrance read, *Condemned* in faded paint.

Meldena stared at the bridge and gasped. "We can't cross that."

"But we have nowhere else to go," Niana said. She glanced at Matt and attempted to sound confident. "That bridge has been here for years. It's not about to fall down now. I'll go first."

Matt frowned but nodded. "Meldena, you follow Niana while I watch the track behind us and warn you if anyone comes."

"Right," the teenager replied in a determined voice.

*

Perspiration made Niana's hands sticky as she gripped the two guide wires and stepped forward onto the bridge. As soon as she was beyond the shelter of the trees a wind buffeted her. Her arms shot outwards and caused the bridge to shudder.

"Pull your arms in," Matt called in a hushed voice. "That will steady the planking."

Niana stared straight ahead and followed the instructions. She knew she shouldn't, but felt a strange urge to glance down. For one brief second her eyes dropped.

Through gaps between the planks, the stream was hidden beneath the undergrowth. Huge ferns and trees growing out of both banks reached up but their tops were still many meters below. Niana swallowed back bile and stopped. The murmur of the stream bubbling through rocks below and the buzz of insects helped to calm her nerves.

She glanced back up and focused on the opposite bank. Her feet carefully found the planks before she risked moving the weight of her body forward. In this deliberate fashion she advanced to the middle dip and

[127]

ascended the other side. Once her forward foot found no plank. In panic, she glanced down, noticed a board missing and forced herself forward to the next one.

Finally, she reached the end of the bridge and stepped onto the security of a little muddy path surrounded by tall grass and ferns. She turned and waved at Meldena who was waiting to begin.

The girl nodded and stepped out. She gripped the two wires, moved slowly down to the lowest part, skilfully crossed the missing planks and walked more confidently up to the opposite bank. Once there, she grabbed Niana's extended hand and almost ran forward the last couple of meters.

"That was scary," she gasped.

Back on the other side, Matt had already started to cross. Niana grinned as he gave a nervous wave when he reached the halfway point.

"Oh, my God," Meldena exclaimed. "Look."

Niana saw a stranger burst out of the bush opposite. The man stopped at the bridge and raised the rifle he was carrying.

"Matt!" Niana screamed, "Someone's arrived. Move it."

Matt turned, sized up the situation and made a dash forward. In his haste he actually made a rhythm that steadied the decking. The seconds it took to reach the end seemed an eternity. Matt had just reached solid ground when a shot rang out.

This was followed by another report, so loud Niana's ears buzzed, a flash of orange flame dazzled the periphery of her vision and cordite choked her nose. A gun had fired from right beside her. She snapped her head around and saw Meldena with a small handgun in her hands. A whisk of smoke curled up from the barrel.

"Bastard," the teenager sobbed. The girl's face was taut with a quivering chin and tear filled eyes stared across the bridge. Her hands, though, were steady.

With infinite precision her firing finger squeezed the trigger and a second explosion sounded through the air.

The man on the bridge screamed, turned and ran the few meters back to the far bank with his body arched over and one hand holding the other.

Whether Meldena would have fired a third time was never discovered for Matt reached across, seized the girl's wrists in an iron grip and forced them down. At the same time, his other hand took the weapon from her hand.

"No," he whispered in a compassionate voice. "He's not worth it."

The girl glanced up, ashen faced, burst into quivering tears,

[128]

wrenched herself away from Matt and attempted to run up the track.

Niana leapt up, grabbed and spun her around into her arms. A trembling body clung onto her and the girl's tears streamed onto Niana's clothes.

"You don't understand," she sobbed. "These aren't men. They're animals who would kill us with as much pity as if they were swatting flies. They killed my family. My father and two brothers were taken from our village and shot in cold blood." Her speech became almost incoherent as sobbing replaced speech.

"I do understand," Niana said as she clutched the sobbing teenager to her torso. "I was shot by the Serbs and my unborn baby killed. But we're not in Kosovo now, Meldena. As Matt said, those criminals aren't worth it. We will get out of here and report them to the police."

"The police? They do nothing," Meldena spat. She squeezed Niana's arms and allowed herself to be guided along the track until the canyon and bank disappeared behind them.

"Well you achieved something," Matt added in a soft voice. "I'm sure you winged that guy. I doubt if they'll risk crossing the bridge for a while." He glanced up at Niana. "Can you keep on eye on her, I want to slip back to see what is happening?"

"Stay in the trees," Niana warned. "They have a rifle."

Matt grunted and slipped away while Niana sat Meldena on a small grass bank.

"That was a marvellous two shots you got away," she whispered. "Where did you learn to handle the gun?"

"Papa taught me," Meldena sniffed. "He knew the troubles at home would get worse but we left it too late." She glanced up. "Oh Niana, when I found out about you and discovered they were tracking you down, I had to help."

"And you did. If you hadn't reached us we could have been floating, head down, in the harbour by now." Niana's voice shook.

Their conversation was interrupted when Matt returned. "One guy was certainly hit," he reported. "At least two men are across the canyon but are staying back from the bridge."

"So what do we do?" Niana asked.

"Move on," Matt advised. He glanced at the small handgun still in his hand. "This will be of little value against a rifle if we get in line of sight. There are only two bullets left in the magazine."

"That's all I have," Meldena whispered. "It was in the car they had."

Niana glanced at Matt. She had no idea what the girl meant.

[129]

CHAPTER SIXTEEN

If it wasn't for their situation, the tramp through the valley surrounded by dense native bush would have been enjoyable. The hot summer sun beat down, but trees shaded the trio and kept the temperature at a bearable level. Niana studied her map and worked out that they would circle back to the coastal track within half an hour.

"We should be safe there," she commented. "At this time of day there should be trampers everywhere."

"We haven't got half an hour," Meldena added. "Someone is keeping pace behind us."

"So you heard," Matt whispered. "Every time we stop, so do they. I think they have respect for your gun and are biding their time."

"But why?" Niana asked.

"Who knows?" Matt shrugged.

However, the reason for their pursuers hesitance soon became apparent. They came to a bend in the track and found themselves at the edge of the trees on a hill facing the bay. Far below, ant like trampers could be seen walking along the shoreline. The hillside between them and the shore was scrubland, secondary growth that had grown over what was once a farm. Any attempt to go down the hill would leave them exposed to anyone standing in their present position.

"If we go through down there they'll be able to shoot at will," Meldena gasped.

"So what do we do?" Niana said.

Matt gazed around. "Play chess," he muttered. "The edge of the bush goes down on our right and the scrub narrows. That would be the logical way to go." He grimaced and nodded the other direction. "So we follow the line uphill. Take a look."

Niana followed his gaze and saw the slope in that direction levelled off at a ridge that curled around the scrub. After an initial climb to this ridge, the way looked relatively flat.

"We should be able to circle back the way we came," Matt said. "If I was chasing someone, I'd assume they'd head downhill to the track, wouldn't you?"

"Which is the very reason they'll guess we will go the other way,"

Meldena argued.

"We have a third choice," Niana added quietly. "Slip back in the undergrowth and let them go by. As long as we are careful not to flatten any vegetation we'll be as safe as anywhere."

Matt nodded and held a finger up to his lips. The two women watched as he swished through the grass on the downhill side. He returned and examined his efforts. It wouldn't fool an expert but would have to do.

"All right," Matt whispered. "Let's hide."

*

It was hands and knees stuff with backpacks carried in their arms, but within a few minutes, the trio were sheltered in a grotto of soft leaves surrounded by ferns, scrub and vines. Two enormous tree trunks provided further shelter and, by lying down and parting the foliage, they could see a sliver of the area just left.

The wait was short. The sound of footsteps and smell of cigarettes reached them before two men dressed in shorts and bush jackets strolled into the clearing. One carried a rifle. Neither showed any sign of an injury so could not have been the guy Meldena hit on the bridge. They stopped and muttered to each other in a foreign language Matt couldn't understand.

But Niana could. She squeezed Matt's hand and listened.

"Well, where are they?" the taller of the two growled.

"You'd hardly expect them to go straight down the hill through that stuff, would you, Otakar?"

His companion shrugged. "That damn girl. If it wasn't for her, Dmitri..." his voice trailed off as he walked out of Niana's line of vision. The cigarette smoke clung to the air and footfalls could be heard pounding around before the voices became clear again.

"Stupid fools." Dmitri's voice, hoarse and loud and still in Serbian vibrated through the foliage. "They tried to make us think they went downhill."

"So they went up," Otakar replied.

"Or are waiting to ambush us. That girl is dead accurate with that gun. Another couple of centimetres and she'd have shot Sergi in the back of the neck just like Lieutenant Nikolai Malkov back in New Plymouth."

"So you reckon she's the one that killed him?"

"Of course. The little bitch has been on to us for months. I reckon she's had help though, military police probably. It's too much of a coincidence. We only found out about this Bolsa bitch coming here a week

[131]

ago and she was here waiting to warn her."

Niana frowned and stared sideways. She noticed Meldena looked as blank as Matt. Many Kosovars didn't speak Serbian so perhaps the girl didn't understand the conversation.

"And the man?" Otakar asked, still in his native language.

"Just a local guy that fell for Bolsa's charms. He's probably as dumb as an ox. I'd say she's the one that wears the pants."

Niana glowered and bit back a snort of denial.

"Anyhow let's head uphill to that ledge. I bet you a week's salary they'll be up there. For God sake keep under cover." Dmitri coughed and once again the voices and footsteps faded.

"So what did they say?" Matt whispered.

"Not a lot," his wife replied casually. "Your trail didn't fool them and they're heading uphill " She grinned at Meldena. "I think they're worried you'll take another shot at them."

"And I would, too, if Matt didn't take my gun," came the hushed reply.

Niana frowned and, like the Serbs, wondered about their companion. It was strange that she just happened to be here to warn them. "Where now?" she said aloud.

"Back the way we came," Matt suggested.

"Right," she replied, glanced at Meldena who nodded, and crawled out through the undergrowth.

*

The apartment was everything Kent hoped for, and more. Though smaller than the original living quarters behind the old shop, it was more contemporary and faced the morning sun. Better still, a door opened out into a small corridor that led onto the shop staff room while the main entrance opened to a veranda and private enclosure separated from the parking lot by a head-high wooden fence.

Though a part of the whole building, it was private and away from the noise of the road at the front. Contrary to Niana's fear, Kent wasn't lonely but enjoyed managing for himself. Without his father's authoritarian presence he spent more time with his friends but found, as usual, he was on the periphery of the groups. While accepted, nobody really cared whether he was with them or not and the girls ignored him. It had always been that way but now Kent realized what they were like and appreciated Matt, Niana, Emine and the children as genuine friends. Even though Matt and Niana had only been away a few days, he missed their companionship and support.

He grinned as he wiped the breakfast dishes and turned to the frame of a cuckoo clock spread out across the kitchen table. The mechanism that sprung the cuckoo out of the Lilliputian doors was crooked and needed adjustment. With his tongue out the corner of his mouth in deep concentration he leaned over the table and levered the spring across to a new clip.

"That should do it," he muttered to himself, poking the wooden bird in and clicking the doors shut. He swung the clock hands around to the hour and smiled as the cuckoo sprang out. Now he had to get the sound synchronized.

He was about to turn the clock over when the telephone rang. A high pitched anxious voice sounded in his ear. "Kent, is that you?"

The youth frowned. "Yes," he replied.

"It's Halia. Mamma's sick. We need help," came the sobbing reply. In the background a baby was bawling.

"What is it Halia? Is Mamma sick to her stomach?"

"No, she just sits on the sofa and gazes into the air. When we talk to her she says silly things and she won't look after Agron. We tried but it is too hard. Will you come and help us? Please." The last word sounded desperate.

Kent swallowed. It sounded bad but what could he do? The kids were obviously desperate so he needed to go and see what had happened.

"Look, give Agron a bottle of warm milk or his veggies. I'll come over in Matt's truck. See you in about twenty minutes. Okay?"

"Yes," Halia sounded relieved.

"That's a boy. Mamma probably forgot to take her medicine or something. You were right to ring me. That's what friends are for, isn't it?"

"That's what Adona said."

"Good. I'll see you soon. Bye."

The teenager hung up and grabbed the truck keys. Matt had given him permission to use the vehicle in an emergency. If anything could be classified an emergency, this was.

*

Adona and Halia rushed out to meet Kent when he drove Stubby into the drive. Both looked anxious but pleased to see him. Adona had the toddler on her hip and, while the little fellow seemed cheerful enough, his tuft of hair was uncombed and breakfast remains covered his face. He'd

[133]

been changed into a clean shirt, but an attempt to pin a diaper on had been less successful as it dangled around his ankles.

Inside, the kitchen was not too untidy but breakfast dishes were piled on the sink, a saucepan of burned vegetables sat on the stove and baby clothes were strewn in a corner.

"Where's Mamma?" Kent asked as he glanced around the room.

"In the other room," Halia replied.

He led Kent through to the sitting room. Emine was sitting in an armchair dressed in a nightgown with her eyes strangely vacant and staring at the wall.

"Emine," Kent whispered and walked over to the woman. "It's Kent. I've come to see how you are."

Emine's gaze switched and, for a second, focused on his. "Hello Kent," she replied. "I'm fine, thank you."

Kent swallowed and squeezed her hand. "The children are worried about you, Emine," he said.

"The children?" She looked up again. "You mean the baby?" Suddenly her voice rose in volume. "My baby," she cried. "Where's my baby?"

"Agron is fine," the youth said. He frowned and was at a loss as to what to do. "Halia and Adona fed and dressed him. It's you we're worried about."

"I'm fine, thank you," the woman repeated, and then she stared back at the wall. "Will Ida and Rokmane be home soon?"

"Who are they?" Kent turned to the children.

"Mummy said they used to look after Mamma," Halia replied. "That was when they were in New Plymouth."

"Okay," Kent replied, remembering that Niana had mentioned the tragedy in New Plymouth. So Emine had forgotten her friends were dead. It sounded as if her mind had gone.

"Can Leanne help?" Adona asked.

"Leanne, who's she?"

"The nurse who visits us. Her name is at the front of the telephone book. She told Mummy to ring her any time Mamma got sick."

"Right," the teenager sighed in relief, pleased there was something he could do. "I'll phone her."

*

In the fifty minutes it took public health nurse Leanne O'Brien to

[134]

arrive, Emine didn't move from the armchair. Any questions Kent asked were either ignored or answered in a vague manner, but as far as he could gather, she thought she was back in New Plymouth with the three other women and Agron was a baby, not a chubby toddler. She only mentioned Halia and Adona in the past tense and didn't realize the children staring at her were her own.

Leanne, a woman built like a tank but with a bright personality, examined and talked to her patient for several moments, asked the children where their mother's medicine was, checked the packages of prescriptions and turned to Kent.

"It's as I thought," she confessed. "Emine has stopped taking her medication. Together with being left in charge of the family by herself, she's had a relapse." She sighed. "This can happen. The patient appears and feels normal and thinks the medication isn't needed any longer."

"But nothing went wrong," Kent protested. "The kids are all fine."

"I know," Leanne replied." When someone has been through trauma, sometimes it's some innocent unrelated incident that causes the brain to switch in this defence mechanism."

"So what now?" Kent asked.

"We'll need to hospitalize her, give her booster doses of medication and hope she comes around. Usually, patients return to normal and remain so if they continue their medication."

"But how does it help?"

Leanne grimaced. "Part of her condition is caused by a chemical imbalance. It's complicated but basically, if her body senses that she's in danger, it produces vast quantities of adrenalin and deprives her of other chemicals used to maintain her health. This puts her in a trance like state as her body attempts to recover from this latest anxiety. The medication provides vital chemicals and is also a mild tranquilizer."

"Sort of withdrawal symptoms like a druggie has?" Kent asked.

"Similar, in a way," the nurse replied.

"Will Mamma be herself again?" Adona cut in. Her eyes were wide and mature beyond her years.

"Yes," Nurse O'Brien replied. "Mummy and Daddy will be back in a few days and, in the meantime," she glanced up a the tall scraggy teenager, "if it's not too much to ask..."

Kent didn't hesitate. "Don't worry, I'll look after them," he whispered.

"Good," Leanne said. "If you stay with Emine a few moments, I'll get Agron changed and arrange for an ambulance to come." She turned to the children. "And who did the marvellous job of dressing Agron?" She smiled.

"We both did," Adona replied. "It was hard, though. He kicks and screams all the time."

"Yeah," Halia added. "That's why we called Kent."

"Everyone will be proud of you both," Leanne added. "Now don't worry. Mamma will be fine soon."

*

Like all return journeys, it didn't seem long before the trio were back searching through the foliage at the swing-bridge that glistened in the late morning sun. On their side of the gorge the hill just stopped at a vertical cliff that disappeared through treetops, thirty or more meters below. The scene was a vision of tranquillity with only distant bird cries and the constant chirp of cicadas complementing the faint gurgle of water in the hidden stream below.

"Looks okay," Meldena muttered.

Matt rubbed his cheek. "Could be," he said as he shaded his eyes with his hand and studied the opposite bank. "But I don't like it. Once on the bridge, we're completely exposed."

"Well, we can't go back," Niana said in a tired voice that was little above a whisper. "If we're going to cross we should do it now. The longer we wait, the bigger the chance those Serbs will circle back and trap us here."

"You're right," Matt said. "I'll go first this time. When I check the other side, I'll wave an all clear and you both come together. Once on the bridge, don't stop. Just walk firmly ahead. Okay?"

Niana frowned but nodded. "We'll keep out of sight here and watch the path. Be careful, sweetheart." She reached across and kissed Matt lightly on the lips.

He squeezed her arm, tapped Meldena on the shoulder and pressed the handgun into her hand. "Careful, it's all ready to fire. I hope you don't need it," he grunted and slipped out into the sunshine.

*

Matt was half way across the swing bridge when a shot rang out.
He froze.
His heart pumped adrenalin through his body. He looked up to see a man on the opposite bank with a smoking rifle aimed straight at him. At

[136]

this very second, the gunman was steadying the weapon to fire again.

Now another sense entered his cat-like mind.

A sound.

A voice. Niana's voice!

"Lie down!" she screamed. "Matt, get down."

So he did. Almost in defiance to his body's thoughts of self-preservation, he made his left hand let the guide-wire go and reach down to seize the edge of a plank. His front foot moved back and he flung himself down.

The rifle fired.

Matt's other arm was jolted back as if hit by an express train and almost wrenched from its socket. For a microsecond his body toppled, the bridge swayed and the trees became a blur. Excruciating pain shot through the arm and finally the report of gunfire reached his ears.

He was now horizontal on the bridge. Blood poured everywhere and his arm hung limp like disembowelled flesh that didn't belong to him. Only with superhuman effort, he concentrated on his other hand and gripped the support wire to save himself from being pitched sideways to a certain death in the depths below. The low groan he heard was from his own lips.

A third shot echoed across the canyon.

*

"Lie down!" Niana screamed a second time just before the second shot flashed and, microseconds later, the report sounded.

"Oh my God." Meldena gasped when the pair saw Matt stagger and crash to the decking. He tipped sideways when the guide-wire moved out. For a second, his body was at a forty-five degree angle and above nothing but the chasm below.

Niana screamed in absolute terror and, without any thought of her own safety broke cover and ran towards the bridge. She stopped at the bridge when a hand grabbed her from behind. It was Meldena

"Wait," the teenager gasped. "Matt's still there."

Niana stopped and watched, shaking, as her husband managed to steady himself. He was on his knees and the wire moved back. But something else was wrong, too.

"Shit," she gasped and her body froze. After the second report, she studied the gunman and the rifle he was holding. It was one of those older rifles that had to have the bolt manually shifted to bring another shell into the firing chamber. The man had just expelled the empty cartridge and was moving the mechanism ready to fire a third time.

Meldena held the handgun but it was facing nowhere in particular.

"Give it to me," Niana hissed and reached forward.

The girl's fingers released the small weapon into her companion's hand.

Niana's nervousness was gone and had been replaced by a cold fury. Her face turned gray but her mind was crisp as ice. No bloody Serb was going to kill her husband.

With infinite slowness she raised the pistol with both hands as steady as a statue, shut one eye, lined the vile creature in the minute sights and squeezed the trigger.

*

A scream followed the report.

Blinking back tears of pain, Matt found he was facing the bank and could clearly see his assassin, so close there was no way the man could miss. The man's sadistic grin could be clearly seen and the weapon was raised for the coup de grace.

The report that reached Matt's ears, though, sounded different, the pitch was higher. He cringed but nothing happened. No bullet hit.

He opened his eyes and saw the dark green blur of trees below. Dizziness and clouds of purple crossed his vision as he fought to remain conscious as he again collapsed onto the decking. Something caught his eye. His mind focused and eyes lifted so he could see the opposite bank.

The rifleman had gone.

*

If the first shot winged the man, the second killed him.

Niana would have continued to fire but on the third squeeze, the firing pin only clicked. The weapon was out of ammunition. She realized this, tossed the gun into the canyon and shock set in.

Meldena recovered first, and tucked an arm around her shaking companion. "That's even better shooting than mine," she croaked.

"Yes," Niana whispered. "It's one skill I never thought I'd need to use again."

She gazed across at the carnage on the bridge with haunted eyes. The rifleman lay crumpled against the far bank and only Matt's hairy legs and tramping boots were visible in the middle of the swing-bridge. One arm dangled down into the void.

"Come on," Meldena spoke in a soft voice. "We need to get to Matt."

"Yes," Niana responded and, without hesitation, walked out onto the bridge with eyes riveted on her husband. "Oh my God," she gasped when she reached Matt. His right side was covered in blood that flowed out across a plank and dripped into the abyss below.

But he was conscious. "I'm okay, sweetheart," he said. "The bastard hit my arm. That's all." Using his good hand to grip a wire, he staggered to his knees and turned to smile at Niana.

"Let me help." Niana bent forward, placed an arm under her husband's good shoulder but staggered when the bridge swayed. Another hand, though, had her gripped from behind and she realized Meldena was clinging to her waist with one hand and the swaying wire with the other. Without her assistance they would have both slipped.

As it was, the bridge still shuddered, the planks buckled and the guide-wires parted. Niana held her husband with one hand and pulled the guide wire in with the other. The bridge steadied and Matt managed to stagger up into a standing position.

*

While Niana concentrated on finding Matt a place to sit, Meldena walked across to the slumped body and pulled it over by the collar. Vacant eyes would stare no more.

"He's the one I winged this morning," she reported in a monotone. "They must have left him here to guard the bridge in case we circled back."

"Is he dead?" Niana asked with as little emotion as her young compatriot.

"Very," Meldena said. "Now what?"

"Leave him," Matt said in a quiet voice. "The police can sort it out."

"But we shot him," Meldena interrupted. "We need to hide the body. Toss him over the edge."

"No," Matt said, looking at Niana who nodded in support. "It was self defence. If we hadn't fired, I'd be dead and probably you two as well. If we remove the body it could be construed as an admission of guilt."

"I guess," Meldena whispered. "I'm not used to police forces that are honest. Back home..." She shrugged, turned to a white faced Niana and

[139]

sighed, "... You know."

"Yes, I know but we aren't in Kosovo anymore."

"If you can call being hit by a bullet lucky, you were, sweetheart," Niana whispered a moment later after she'd moved her husband's arm slightly to examine it. "It appears the bullet went clean through the fleshy part of your arm just below the shoulder."

"I was holding the wire," Matt said. "If I hadn't sat down at that moment." His eyes caught hers. "I heard your shout," he whispered. "It happened so quickly. I was watching the other bank but didn't see the man until after the first shot was fired."

Niana opened Matt's backpack and brought out a small first aid container, and dabbed the wound with disinfectant. Matt gritted his teeth in pain but merely smiled when she hesitated and glanced into his eyes.

"Keep going," he whispered. "It has to be done."

She nodded, found a bandage in the kit and wound it around the whole shoulder. Blood seeped through but soon stopped expanding. Niana finished bandaging Matt's wound and handed him a tumbler of orange juice, fizzling with two aspirins.

"We have to go," Meldena interrupted. "The enemy has arrived."

Two men appeared out of the trees across the canyon, stopped, saw them and dived back out of sight.

"Stalemate," Niana grunted. "They think we have a gun."

"We have," the teenager replied. "This guy's rifle."

"No more shooting," Matt ordered.

"Just one," Niana replied. She reached over, grabbed the rifle, waited until she saw some branches shift on the opposite bank and fired.

Once again the loud discharge rattled through the canyon, foliage opposite vibrated and a red shirt could be briefly seen as one Serb made a hasty retreat

"That'll give them something to think about," she retorted. She withdrew the magazine and heaved the rifle away. "Let's go before those guys pluck up enough courage to cross the bridge."

*

CHAPTER SEVENTEEN

"Well, it proves my theory," Dmitri grunted after the bullet whined through the branches above them. "Somebody over there is deadly with a rifle."

"Yeah," muttered Otakar as he squinted across the canyon. There was no movement beyond the swing-bridge. "It looks as if Baristra's had it. The stupid bugger should have known better than to remain in the open. "

"So we need to follow them. Sitting here like cowards won't solve anything."

Otakar stubbed a cigarette on an adjacent rock. "Okay, you run across. I bet the bitch will have you in her sights before you're half way."

"We'll wait ten minutes and if there's no sign of anybody, we move."

The other man nodded grimly and lay studying the far bank. There was no movement, not even a flash of the sun reflecting off metal.

After ten minutes Dmitri grunted. "It's time. You go and I'll cover you."

"Okay," came the nervous reply. "I'll bloody run. Keep your eyes peeled and aim at the flash if the bitch fires."

The Serb swallowed, loaded his rifle and gave a slight nod. Otakar stood and charged at the bridge. He was three quarters of the way across before anything out of the ordinary happened. He slipped and crashed to the deck with a mighty thud but no shots came. All remained silent.

He staggered to his feet with nothing more than his pride hurt and walked the rest of the distance to where his slain compatriot lay by the bank. He grunted and gave the corpse a slight kick.

"Bitch," he hissed.

Though it appeared the Kosovar bitches had gone, he was too much of a professional to take any more reckless chances. He waved across at his partner and a moment later was joined by Dmitri. They examined the body, muttered and, with no further remorse, hid it beneath some foliage.

"Now let's get them," Dmitri said. "Baristra winged one of them in the middle of the bridge. There's blood everywhere. They'll be making slow progress."

His companion nodded and the pair set off at a fast pace to follow their targets. Otakar and Dmitri were killers, every bit as ruthless as their commander Konstantin Deuratovich and their immediate superior officer, Lieutenant Nikolai Malkov. His death would be revenged.

*

Niana, Meldena and an exhausted Matt arrived back at the shore by the kayak and motorboat. During their absence the tide had come in and was now half way out again so there was wet sand to make their journey easier.

"Don't count on it being any help to us," Matt muttered when Meldena ran over to the Serb's boat with an expectant expression.

He was right. Not only was there no key but also the whole outboard motor was tilted up and locked with a steel clamp.

"Trusting sods," Niana said.

"If we incapacitate their boat you can use the kayak," Meldena suggested.

"What do we do?" Niana asked

"Remove the rotor," Matt said.

He explained what it was and before long Niana had removed the vital parts while Meldena searched the cabin and reappeared a moment later. "I thought there might be a radio or mobile phone aboard but there isn't."

"You did well but we'd better get going." Matt heaved and attempted to hide the pain he was feeling.

"No," Niana replied with a stubborn frown. "You're all in. We'll use the kayak."

"But it'll be too slow." he protested. "We'll continue walking."

"No," his wife answered. "Climb aboard and we'll put it along the beach,"

"I guess," Matt replied.

After Niana and Meldena refloated the kayak and loaded their gear aboard, Matt wedged himself into the front section and smiled at the pair. "Okay, ladies, away we go."

They set off towards the lodge. It was blistering hot but the ocean surf helped to cool them as they waded knee deep in the water with Meldena pulling the mooring rope and Niana pushing from the rear.

Matt grabbed a paddle and attempted to help by using his good arm but realized he was more of a hindrance than help so stopped and watched the two soaking wet women guide him along. His shoulder ached but didn't appear to be bleeding so he relaxed and spent time gazing back behind

[142]

them. Once again, they were terribly exposed though he doubted if their pursuers would try anything on this main track. With a little luck, trampers would appear soon.

However, during the next quarter hour nobody, friend or foe, appeared. Of more concern was the beach itself. They had reached the end of the sand and progress was blocked by a hilly headland with the water lapping right up to a cliff that dropped down from dense foliage. The walking track took a sharp turn inland and disappeared beneath high trees.

"Now what?" Meldena puffed.

"We walk," Matt said but Niana shook her head and turned to the teenager.

"Look, can you run ahead and get help, Meldena? There must be somebody around tramping or paddling kayaks. I'll paddle the canoe out around the headland and head back towards Awaroa."

"It's a long way," the girl protested. "Can you manage?"

"I can try. Also, we'll be safer from the Serbs if they appear."

"I hate to admit it, but Niana's idea sounds the best available," Matt added. "If we don't see you at the beach around the point, meet us back at the lodge." He gave a slight shrug. "Unless you have other things to do."

Meldena sucked on her bottom lip and stared, deep in thought, at Matt. "No," she replied. "I'll get help. Keep an eye on the shoreline and don't come too close in. Those guys could take a shot at you. See you at the lodge, if not before."

She helped Niana in the rear section of the Kayak, checked that the clamp on the middle luggage compartment was shut and pushed the two Colemans out into the bay until the water was up to her waist.

"Bye. See you later."

Niana waved and concentrated on moving away from the shore. A small breeze had sprung up so the glass like surface of the morning was replaced by choppy waves that appeared to be bigger beyond the sheltered headland.

"You're going well, sweetheart," Matt encouraged as she obtained a momentum and propelled the craft out parallel to the cliff.

"The tide's helping us," she said, panting, red faced and with her wet clothes clinging to her skin. "I can feel a distinct rip carrying us offshore.

"Then just relax and let the water do its job," Matt advised." He glanced back and swore. "On second thoughts, paddle like hell."

"Why?" Niana called back.

"Our friends are on the beach."

[143]

Niana pushed the paddle into the water, pulled back, switched across to the other side and repeated the process. The kayak bumped on the chop but with every paddle, they moved further from the beach and were soon directly across from the point of the headland.

She edged away from the pounding shoreline surf and cursed as a side rip buffeted the kayak and sent water spraying over them.

Matt turned and glanced around. They were about a hundred meters offshore and the waves here were more rolling than choppy. Back on the beach the two figures had climbed out of the motorboat and were now jogging along the beach.

"It's them all right. They've found their boat won't go," he muttered. "I think we should stay out here rather than bothering to meet Meldena at the next beach.

"But she's all alone," Niana said, panting

"She'll be okay. That young lady could run the whole distance back without getting a sweat up, I reckon. She's a survivor." He shrugged. "I wonder if we'll ever see her again."

"We will, sweetheart," Niana replied. "I'm sure of that."

The two men on the beach had already reached the end of the bay and were just standing at the water's edge staring in their direction.

"We're sitting ducks if they fire at us," Matt muttered, and once again he attempted, unsuccessfully, to use his own paddle.

Niana nodded and concentrated on paddling. "One, two, three," she counted every time her paddle hit water. Her arms soon ached from the effort and she had to stop. But it was for only five seconds before she grimaced and did another burst. After the fifth bout of counting to twenty, her arms ached right through to her shoulders and a row of red blisters began to form across her hands. Stomach muscles cramped and she stopped and bent forward gasping for breath.

"I've got a stitch," she cried and held her stomach, perspiration poured from her bright red face and wet hair plastered down each side of her head. "Oh hell," she gasped as a second spasm of pain shot through her.

"Relax, sweetheart," Matt comforted. "We're well away from shore and almost out of sight. Let the water carry us now."

"I have to," Niana said. "My arms are like jelly." "How are you, sweetheart?"

"There's not much feeling," Matt admitted, wiping his brow. "The bleeding has stopped, I'd say." His face was also red but without the perspiration he looked almost civilized compared with his exhausted wife.

Now that it was obvious they were out of range from the Serb's weapons, Niana set her mind to the next task in hand. With a prominent peak as a reference point, she started paddling, slower now but with steady strokes that she could maintain without reaching an exhausted state.

Matt continued to talk, pointing out odd items around and maintaining their morale while Niana stayed silent and concentrated on paddling. Thirty minutes slipped by before Matt called a halt.

"Stop," he said in a quiet voice. "We're getting nowhere."

"What do you mean?" Niana panted. She pulled the paddle from the water and rested it across her knees.

"See that headland?" Matt replied.

"Yes, that must be Awaroa Head," Niana replied.

"It isn't, sweetheart," Matt continued. "It's where we came out."

"But I've been paddling almost an hour."

"And getting nowhere. The outgoing tide or perhaps a rip is carrying us north. All you managed to do is keep us more or less in the same place."

"Shit." Niana swore in her own language that often rose to the surface in an emergency.

"What?" Matt queried.

"I said shit, S-H-I-T. I'm bloody exhausted, burned to a crisp, feel like hell and my throat's on fire."

"But I still love you." Matt turned and smiled at his wife.

"Oh Matt," Niana's eyes were wide. "I'm sorry. It's all going wrong."

"Not really. We escaped from those louts and I'm sure our new friend will get help."

"Okay, but what do we do?"

"Go with the flow," Matt advised. "Rest up and let the kayak carry us along the coast for a while then paddle across the rip towards shore." He grinned. "That's what we intended to do originally, anyway. We have food, water and our tent. Even if we have to stay overnight we'll be okay."

"But your arm?"

"I don't think it will get worse," Matt said. "Anyhow, it's Hobson's Choice isn't it?"

Niana's English was excellent but at times she couldn't comprehend what Matt meant. This was one such occasion.

"It's just an old English saying," Matt explained. "Hobson was a British admiral, I think, who was fighting the French or Spanish a couple of hundred years ago and his fleet was trapped. His only choice was to fight his way out. The saying means that, because of the circumstances, you have no

[145]

choice."

"I see," the woman nodded. "And did it work for him?"

"Who."

"This English admiral."

"I think so but can't really remember."

"Okay, Hobson's Choice," Niana replied. She reached down between her knees to a small pack and brought out a tube of sun block and bottle of water. "It's a bit late for the sun block," she muttered as she smothered her face, arms and legs with yellow paste and handed it forward to Matt.

*

The sun was high in the cloudless sky, the day too hot and the reflection off the waves so intense it became almost painful to look at. Niana sucked on a piece of candy and took stock of the situation. She could feel that her eyebrows, lips, ears and the back of her neck were scorched. Matt, now with his hat on, didn't look quite as bad but she was concerned about his wound. The bandage was soaked and must be giving him hell.

"Sweetheart," she said. "I'm so sorry."

"Me too. I'd rather be under those cool trees on shore, next to a bubbling brook making mad passionate love to you."

Niana laughed. "In about a week," she replied. "It'll take that long for my aches and sunburn to go away."

"Aw hell," Matt said, trying to look upset.

The light-hearted banter made them both feel better as the kayak carried them northwards along the shore. The headland retreated into the distance and they were now drifting by unfamiliar scenery.

"Head in, Niana," Matt advised a few moments later. "We should make progress by going across the current and we're well north of any Serb gunmen."

Once again the paddling started with Niana determined to make progress while Matt broke into an old romantic ballad from a movie they'd seen a few weeks earlier. Niana joined in and the paddling became automatic with tired limbs forgotten. Once again, spray shot over them and the hills gradually became closer.

Progress was being made.

Niana's watch said three twenty when she finally paddled into a small deserted bay. Golden sand stretched in front of a forested hill. There was no stream but everything else was as they'd hoped with light surf breaking on the sand. She slipped overboard and pushed the sturdy craft the rest of the way until it crunched on the shore.

Matt grimaced as he stepped into knee-deep water and helped as well as he could while Niana dragged the kayak up the beach. When she stood and stretched her aching back, a massive arm tucked around her sunburned shoulders and Matt gave her a passionate kiss. They stung from the pressure but she responded before standing back and looking into his eyes with intense concern.

"Come on, get in the shade and I'll examine your wound, you naughty man," she said.

*

The isolated bay was idyllic except for one thing, sand flies. Seemingly, millions of them descended on the pair as Niana unwound the wet, blood coagulated bandages from her husband's wound. He grimaced as she pulled away the last bit and blood began to flow.

"It looks clean," she murmured as she dabbed the wound with ointment and used the last clean bandage to wrap it again.

"Thanks, sweetheart," Matt said. "That feels better."

They lubricated their parched throats from the plastic bottle, ate an apple and took a brief stroll along the beach. But it was scorching out in the sun so they retreated into the shade of overhanging trees and the sand flies.

"This is stupid," Niana said after a few minutes and walked across to the kayak's storage compartment. In ten minutes she had the bright orange tent assembled in a shady spot. "See," she grinned as she unzipped the front to show a second flap of mosquito netting. "Go inside, hubby."

Matt grinned and slid into the small space just large enough for two. Niana arrived with a can of insect spray, squirted the interior liberally and crawled in beside her husband.

"So we wait," she sighed.

Time passed and Matt fell asleep. Niana crawled out of the tent, started a small bottled gas burner and began cooking a can of stew. The smell of onions and meat was quite appealing.

"I thought you might be hungry," she said when she noticed that Matt had awoken. "How are you feeling?"

"Stiff and sore but, thanks to you, I've no insect bites." He stood up and glanced out at the empty ocean. "Have you considered that Meldena may have just gotten on with her life and never told anyone of our plight?" he said.

"She wouldn't do that," Niana replied. "My worry is that the Serbs caught her."

"But you don't really know her. She came out of nowhere, spun us a story that we only have her word for. She may have even been in with the Serbs."

"She's an Albanian Kosovar so you needn't worry about that."

"So you trust Meldena, then?"

"I do."

"Funny," Matt whispered. "I do, too. It's just getting so late, I hope she's okay."

"We're in a pretty isolated bay and in the wrong direction from where we said we were heading. There's not even a track here. Someone might have been looking for us for hours."

"I hope they find us soon," Matt whispered." I reckon if nobody comes in the next hour we'll be here for the night. Now, how about that lovely stew I smell?"

"Coming up, sweetheart. I have hot coffee, too."

Matt reached across to kiss his wife. "Thanks," he said in a serious voice. "For everything."

*

Fifteen minutes later, a large blue helicopter with *Rescue* painted in white letters across the fuselage thundered up the coast line from the south, hovered above the two waving castaways for a moment and landed on the sand.

"We've been looking for you guys," a loud speaker blared out as the rotors wound down and two crouched medics came running towards them.

It was early evening when they landed at the public hospital in Nelson. This small city was the largest centre in the area and, though a hundred and twenty tortuous kilometres from Abel Tasman National Park, in a direct line across Tasman Bay it was barely a third the distance.

*

The surgeon came out of the operating room and walked up to Niana. "Your husband is fine with what is basically a flesh wound," he said. "The projectile went in his upper arm below the armpit. No bones or major blood vessels were hit. We've cleaned and stitched the wounds" He grimaced. "You don't look too well yourself, Mrs. Coleman."

[148]

"A little too much sun, doctor," Niana replied. "Really, I'm okay"

"You are not," the man insisted. "Second degree burns and dehydration, I'd say." He pulled a pager from his pocket and pressed a button. An officious looking nurse appeared within seconds.

"Yes, Doctor Simonsen."

"Mr. and Mrs. Coleman are both to be admitted for the night. I want a double room please."

"But what ward, doctor? Male or female."

"A private room, Head Nurse Thompson. They're honeymooners." The surgeon glowered. "See to it, now."

"Yes doctor," the nurse responded, flashed a smile at the pair and disappeared.

"There's one other thing, I'm afraid," Simonsen continued in a neutral tone after the woman had gone. "All gunshot wounds have to be reported to the police." He glanced over at a pale Matt. "They will be sending an officer in to interview you both in the morning. Meanwhile, Mrs. Coleman," he added. "We'll get one of our doctors to attend to your sunburn."

After Niana was examined, given two injections and had her severe sunburn treated, she was wheeled along to a bright room where Matt was sitting up in bed with his arm heavily bandaged.

"Hi," he said. "You look beautiful again."

Niana smiled. "Whatever they did sure works. I feel fine."

"Probably got us both pumped full of morphine. You'll feel like hell again in the morning."

"Thanks," she sighed and lay back on the soft pillow. "We won't forget our honeymoon in a hurry, will we?"

"No." Matt replied. "We certainly won't."

*

Niana realized someone was beside her bed when she woke up from a dreamless, drug induced sleep. She opened her eyes to see Matt in the glare of a bed lamp grinning at someone behind her. She turned and broke into a smile.

"How did you get here?" she asked.

Standing beside the bed holding a bunch of flowers, stood a smirking Meldena.

"Drove," the girl chuckled and produced a familiar key ring from her pocket. "Your Honda is in the parking lot. I thought you might need it."

[149]

"But how?" Niana gasped. They'd left her car at the Awaroa Lodge and had intended to pick it up after the kayak trip.

"I sort of borrowed your keys," the girl said. "Picked your pocket, actually."

"What?" Niana didn't know whether to be angry or relieved.

"One resourceful lady, I'd say." Matt chuckled. "Now, would you have given her the keys if she'd asked, sweetheart?"

"I might have."

"I used your credit card to pay your bill for the lodge and kayak rental," Meldena continued and handed a Visa card over to Niana. "They said they'd send a crew out to collect the kayak from that bay where you two lovebirds sneaked off to."

"We didn't sneak off," Niana retorted. "And my credit card. You've got a nerve, girl."

"Well, I've no money of my own. You don't need to go all the way back, now."

Niana stared at the teenager and suddenly burst out laughing. "And the twenty dollars in my pocket?"

"It's still there. What do you think I am, a thief or something?" Meldena said.

"So what happened to you after we left," Matt asked.

Meldena shrugged. "Not a lot. About twenty minutes after I left you, I ran into a group of trampers. One of them had a mobile phone and called the police. Most of the time was spent searching for you."

"And the Serbs?" Niana asked.

"I don't think anybody knows where they went. At least I wasn't told. The cops questioned me for an hour but I never told them about that guy you plugged." She sighed. "They knew about him, of course but never mentioned it, so I didn't either."

"How do you know," Matt asked.

"Body language," Meldena said. "Bloody amateurs after those NATO cops I talked to in Albania."

"So what now?" Matt asked.

Meldena turned serious. "Can I come home with you," she whispered. "You said..."

"Yes, of course," Niana said. "Tonight, I think Matt means."

"Oh that. I'll sleep in the Honda in the parking lot." The girl laughed. "Don't worry. The whole area is floodlit."

CHAPTER EIGHTEEN

Captain Geoff Swenson cursed the insects as he strutted back from the middle of the swing-bridge. The first strip of sunlight poked over the eastern hill and already the temperatures were too high for the business suit he was wearing.

"There've been two shootings here, sergeant," he muttered to the police officer who accompanied him. "In the middle of the bridge and on this side." He grunted and walked to where the body had been discovered. "This guy underestimated his adversaries."

"So what's your scenario?" Sergeant Chris Proser asked. He was the typical policeman, heavily built and clean-shaven with a naturally dour expression.

"One of our friends got winged while crossing and a return shot killed the Serb from the far bank."

"Why Serb? It could be anyone."

"Oh, it was them, all right," Swenson said. "We've been on their trail for weeks and used Niana Bolsa's honeymoon to flush them out." He sighed. "If only Meldena Adzovic had waited for us instead of rushing off to warn her."

Proser shrugged and turned to the constable waiting patiently in the background. "We need forensic experts in here. Call base, please."

"No," Swenson interrupted. "A crew to remove the body will do." He fixed the police constable with a dark stare. "This was a tramper, illegally hunting in the national park who tripped and shot himself while crossing the swing-bridge. Get it?"

Constable Patty Kubavat pouted but her sergeant gave a minute nod.

"Yes sir," she whispered. She spoke on her police radio, listened and glanced up at Proser. "Matt Coleman was the one shot, sir," she reported.

"Any sign of the men?" Geoff Swenson asked, silently cursing the delay. It had taken all the daylight hours of the previous evening to find this unmarked track and by then it was considered too late to proceed until first light.

"No reported sightings."

"Damn. They could be anywhere. That girl should have waited like we ordered."

The police sergeant broke into a craggy smile. "She's a teenager, Captain Swensennot one of your highly trained personnel," he replied. "Anyway, the Colemans could have all been dead if she'd waited for us to arrive yesterday morning."

"I guess," Geoff said with a shrug. "I must admit we didn't expect the suspects to be on to them so quickly. The girl used her initiative by phoning ahead and finding where Niana Coleman was staying, then hitchhiking in."

"Sergeant," Patty Kubavat interrupted. "You're wanted on the radio."

The sergeant nodded and listened to the incoming call. He muttered a few comments and frowned. "Your idea of covering up the facts hasn't worked too well, captain. If I'd been left on my own, I would have had those Colemans in custody on suspicion of murder by now. At least they'd be safe at the police station."

"What do you mean?" Geoff Swenson retorted.

"The Nelson police questioned the pair and they were let go. Matt Coleman's injuries weren't too bad and he was released from hospital."

"And where are they?"

"The only info we have, is that Adzovic drove their car back to Nelson and they all headed east out of town, probably back to Picton."

"The ferry terminal. Shit, that's a two-hour drive. They could be intercepted anywhere on that windy road over the ranges." He took out his own phone, snapped instructions into it and glanced up. "I assume you have the car's description and plate number."

"Yes sir, and more news. Their booking is for ten tonight."

"All right. We'll try to intercept them and I'll get some staff on the boat." Swenson grimaced. "We've botched this up like a couple of cadets, sergeant."

Chris Proser glanced at Patty behind the other man's back and raised an eyebrow.

*

Twilight turned to darkness as the Honda continued its journey on a quiet State Highway 6. Niana navigated a tight corner and braked. In front, pulled off to the side of the road, was a late-model white vehicle reflected in the dull light. Closer though, was a woman standing on the road waving

[152]

them down frantically.

"A breakdown," Niana muttered. She switched her turn signal on and slowed to a crawl. By now they were alongside the car and Meldena stared at the car less than three meters away.

"Don't stop, Niana!" she screamed. "It's a trap. Keep going."

Niana heard the desperate tone and immediately responded. She accelerated, tires spun, the car wobbled, gripped the seal and sped forward.

"What is it?" Matt asked.

"Serbs," Meldena hissed.

They came to a corner and the stationary car disappeared from view. Niana realized she was travelling too fast and slowed. She frowned into the mirror at Meldena. "How do you know?" she asked. "It looked perfectly ordinary to me."

"It was all wrong."

"How?"

"Two things. There were two men sitting in the car. We were so close I could see the outline of their faces. Now, why would two men sit in a broken down car while a young woman waves someone down?"

"A good point," Matt admitted. "And your second one?"

"The vehicle had its lights turned off. If it was a genuine breakdown they'd have them on." She bit on her lip. "You think I'm being paranoid, don't you?"

"No," Niana said. "I think you have fantastic reactions. You were asleep a moment ago."

"There are lights coming up fast behind us," Matt interrupted

Lights were blaring down on them, full beam and dazzling. It was a hair-raising twenty minutes. Niana, though, was an expert driver and held their distance in front of the chasing car while Meldena kept her eyes peeled out the rear window and gave a continuous report on the distance to the lights.

At times the glare disappeared behind a corner only to reappear seconds later. No opposing traffic came along the lonely road so Niana risked cutting corners to gain that little extra distance. The other car wasn't gaining, but neither was it dropping back.

"Bastards," Niana hissed as she braked and swung around yet another corner.

She watched the other car's headlights reflect off the trees on the far side of the bend, but this time they didn't sweep back around to dazzle into her eyes again. For the first time, it remained dark.

"They've gone," Meldena shouted from the rear.

The pursuing car swayed and a loud bang jolted the passenger's ears.

Dmitri cursed. Something was wrong. The whole car screeched sideways out of control and veered across the road in a scream of tires. It swung back and came to a crunching halt on the opposing grass verge.

"What the hell's wrong?" Otakar snapped while the third passenger, the young woman who'd tried to wave the Colemans down, ran a hand over a bruised head that had just rebounded off the roof.

"A back tire's blown." Dmitri swore and banged the steering wheel in frustration.

But the three Serbs were due for another shock. The vehicle's doors were flung open and two heavily armed solders dressed in full camouflage gear covered them with automatic rifles.

"All hands in sight and then don't move," a voice commanded.

Otakar reached down but stopped when he saw the rifle barrel move up and point directly at him.

"Don't," a granite-like voice sounded.

Within moments the three found themselves being frisked. The girl stared with hatred but said nothing when a soldier slammed her against the side of the car. A handgun was pulled from her shorts and a revolver extracted from Otakar's belt.

"There's an automatic pistol in the car sarge," a voice came through the darkness followed by a whistle of surprise. "A hand grenade, too."

Sergeant Bill Rangi grunted. "All right," he said. "Get them to the chopper. "

The three were grabbed by steel-like hands, propelled up a slope and through a clump of trees to a clearing where the silhouette of a military helicopter sat in a small dip. No lights shone but three air force personnel could be seen, all grim and on full alert.

After the three were forced aboard and handcuffed to a bulkhead bar, Bill Rangi walked across to where another soldier appeared from the trees. "Great shooting, corporal," he complimented.

"No problem, Sarge," the man replied as he took a steel cased instrument off his helmet. "These infrared glasses make it as clear as day. I got the bugger's back tire."

"So the captain was right," Rangi added in a philosophical tone. He turned to the pilot leaning out the helicopter's open window. "I reckon these are the villain, sir," he reported. "Beats me how they got all this hardware in the country."

"Desperate men, sergeant," the pilot replied. "Embittered to the end. They'll never change."

"Woman, too, sir," the sergeant replied. "That girl with them eats nails for breakfast, I reckon."

*

"So it could have been some hooligan just wanting a race," Matt said as the trio pulled into the small town of Picton and headed to where the inter island ferry waited beside a floodlit wharf. The rail and car ferry carried passengers and freight through the Queen Charlotte Sound and across Cook Strait to Wellington.

"It wasn't just hooligans," his wife replied. "We're just lucky something happened to them."

"I agree with Niana," Meldena added. "We're damn lucky."

Matt nodded. "Okay," he relented. "We'll report the incident to someone tomorrow. Let's get the car aboard." He glanced at his watch. "A quarter to ten. Just in time."

After leaving the vehicle deck, the three walked through a crowded lounge just as the ferry pulled out. It was a three and a quarter hour journey on a hot calm summer's night. Matt gazed at Niana and that warm honeymoon feeling returned.

"Come on," she said. "Let's go up on the top deck and watch the harbour lights."

The trio made their way through crowds of holidaymakers to a top deck, just as the ferry moved into the sound. Quay lights reflected in the still water and layers of house and streetlights sparkled from the hill Picton was built upon. Overhead, a million stars glittered in the sky and warm salt laden air buffeted the passengers.

"Oh Matt." Niana sighed as she stared at the white wake radiating behind the ferry. "It's beautiful. "

For a moment, the troubles of the previous two days were forgotten. Even Meldena relaxed and watched the harbour lights disappear behind a dark hillside. "I've never been on a boat before," she said with a sigh." It's like a picture postcard."

Without thinking, she tucked an arm around Matt's waist and smiled when he looked down at her. "Do you mind?"

"No," he laughed. "Two beautiful women on my arms must make

[155]

me the envy of every male aboard."

"Just this time," Niana responded with a grin, "but don't make a habit of it."

"No ma'am," the smiling Meldena replied in an exaggerated tone, still clutching Matt's waist.

*

"Meldena is sound asleep. I'm just going to freshen up so see you in a few minutes," Niana whispered as she reached across to Matt, kissed him lightly on the cheek and squeezed his hand. "Keep my deck chair for me."

Matt grinned, gave her a playful slap on the posterior and leaned back to admire the view. The ferry was out of the sheltered sounds now and began to roll a little in the exposed Cook Strait. The South Island disappeared in darkness, white wake reflected the faint light from a crescent moon and, off to the left, flashing pilot lights showed where a freighter headed away to a distant land.

Niana walked past teenagers still drinking, yelling or playing loud music and down two flights of stairs to a quiet passageway where the women's restrooms were situated.

Inside, every cubicle had the little ivory sign turned to *Vacant* and the row of handbasins was empty. She ran warm water into a handbasin and glanced at her reflection in the mirror. Tired eyes looked back at her.

"God, I look a mess," she muttered and took a small make-up kit from the bag strapped around her waist. She reached for a hairbrush when a faint squeak interrupted the solitude.

The door to one of the stall doors opened and a man burst out.

A man in the ladies room? Something was wrong! Before Niana could react, two powerful hands grabbed her; one around the throat while the other pinned back an arm. She was literally spun around and a rough face rubbed her chin.

"One sound and I break your neck," whispered a harsh voice.

The petrified woman tried to move but the hand on her throat squeezed harder. At the same time she was frogmarched into a small cubicle used to change babies and the door kicked shut. She could smell the stinking breath of stale smoke and realized the situation was desperate. Another wriggle and the clutch on her throat grew tighter.

"No screams and I'll release the pressure," the man growled.

Niana's vision filled with purple spots and her lungs felt as if they'd burst but she managed to nod. Very slowly the pressure was released so she could breathe. She found herself swung around.

The man leering at her was like so many she had seen in the journey out of Kosovo. He was a Serb militia policeman. Everything told her so, from the shaven head and two day's growth of stubble to the cold impassive eyes. A long stiletto knife appeared in one hand.

"I'm afraid your tender life is about to end Mrs. Niana Coleman." He turned his nose up in distaste and smirked. "Your new English name will not help you."

Niana's face drained white, bile blocked her throat and her body began to tremble violently. Eyes bulged and thoughts screamed through her mind. It was a nightmare. It couldn't be true. But it was.

The man pulled her in towards him in a massive bear hug. Niana kicked out and spat at him, the only defence she had available.

"Spirited little bit," he said as he wiped the spittle off his face.

Terror gripped her but nothing could be done. The nightmare was back. Visions of the Serb guardhouse blotted her vision and the violation of her body that followed. She thought of the baby but opposing thoughts told her there was none. Not now. Not here on the inter-island ferry.

The man ogled her and his hand come off her throat as he reached to fondle her breasts.

Niana screamed.

"You bitch," the man snarled. He slapped her across the face and grabbed her in another strangle hold with her chin bent back so she could only see the ceiling. Niana could only manage a gurgle. It was Kosovo again.

The edge of the counter cut into her and she waited for the rifle butt to slam into the small of her back if she didn't co-operate. In her groggy mind she once again attempted to return her mind to the present. There was no rifle butt. She was on the ferry. Surely someone would have heard her scream and come to the rescue.

The hand on her throat gripped tighter and Niana moaned as consciousness faded away and her body slumped.

"That's more like it," the man said, chuckling.

A faint movement of cooler air as the door behind opened just a fraction went unnoticed.

There was a faint pop and Niana felt the man go limp. His eyes changed to utter surprise and glassed over. There was a hole through his skull and blood spurting out. She just stared with her mouth opened in a silent scream of frozen terror.

A man dressed in a formal business suit stood in the opened door holding a revolver; one with a huge cylinder screwed in the front of it. Niana

[157]

realized this was a silencer.

"You're safe now, Niana," the man spoke with a kind voice. "The bastard is dead."

Niana found her voice. She screamed hysterically again and again before bending over and bursting into tears of distress and humiliation.

Another man dressed in a white coat appeared and wrapped a large towel around her shuddering shoulders. Before Niana could react again, the door was shoved back, the man brushed aside, and Matt appeared. Her distraught husband took one glance at the gruesome corpse lying on the floor and swept her into his arms.

"Niana! Niana!" he cried and smothered her in kisses. "I heard your screams."

She held onto the man she loved and sobbed uncontrollably while the strangers stepped outside to wait. For almost five minutes Niana continued to cry until finally her sobs slowed and her body stopped shaking. All the time Matt just held on, kissing her face and neck as he stroked her hair and talked quietly.

"It's all okay, my darling. It's all right. I'm here now," he whispered and tried to stop his own tears from coming. "I decided to come down and meet you when I heard your screams."

Finally Niana regained control of her emotions and kissed Matt. "He came from nowhere," she wept. "It was just like at the internment camp. I wanted to freshen up and put on my lipstick because I know you like the colour."

"Oh Niana," he said. "You're not hurt. That's all that matters."

He turned and suddenly realized the men were still there. "Thank you," he said. "From the bottom of my heart. Thank you."

"I was almost too late," the man in the suit, replied as he offered his hand to Matt. "Trent's the name."

"Police?" Matt asked as he stared at the corpse slumped in the corner.

"No," came the slow reply. "New Zealand Army. Actually, I'm Major Trent Gillies from Intelligence Group Four, seconded to the security intelligence service, here to flush out this terrorist and to protect your wife and young friend." He grinned. "I almost failed my assignment. "

"Meldena," Niana spluttered in alarm. "She's still on the top deck."

"And safe. Two police officers were watching you all from the moment you boarded." Trent Gillies gave the corpse a kick. "We got him in the end. The name is Konstantin Deuratovich. Have you heard of him?"

"Yes," Niana retorted. Now that the terror was over, her emotion turned to anger. "He was responsible for killing my friend's companions and, I believe, the one who burned our shop down."

Trent grunted. "We've been trying to find him for months now but thought he'd escaped out of the country. I confess we used you to flush him out."

"So Meldena has been working for you?" whispered Niana.

Before Gillies could reply, there was a cough and the second man appeared. "There's a crowd outside, Sir."

Trent stared at him. "Well, don't just stand there. Get rid of them."

*

CHAPTER NINETEEN

Though still distressed, Niana held her chin high as she and Matt followed a constable into a day cabin and sat in a comfortable armchair. The constable excused herself and, for the first time, the pair were by themselves.

"Well, we never got bored, sweetheart." She sighed and managed a faint smile. "You being shot, me attacked and two corpses lying around."

Matt nodded with his own face creased in worry lines. "It's not bloody fair," he whispered and crouched down to take his wife's trembling hands. "Nobody deserves this."

"No," Niana replied, and suddenly found herself in tears again, long anguished sobs that shook her whole body.

Matt grabbed her in his arms and just held her until the sobs stopped and she buried her head in his chest. "Let it all out," he whispered and then kissed her forehead. "Just let it all go, my dear."

And she did, all the strain of the previous day rose inside and poured out, memories of her past, thoughts of the fire, her stillborn child, the terror and deprivation. Everything was washed away in tears that rolled down her cheeks and dropped onto a torn blouse. When they finally subsided, she blew her nose and turned cold lips up to be kissed.

"Your arm, sweetheart. I'm hurting it."

"No," Matt said. "It's fine and we're going home."

"Yes, we're going home."

They stood and walked over to the two small rectangular windows that faced the darkened ocean. In the far distance a light blinked. "The North Island," Matt whispered. "My home of thirty years."

"And ours for the next thirty," Niana added. "Oh Matt, I thought he'd rape and kill me. It was worse than in Kosovo, because I've been so happy here with you."

"But he didn't, sweetheart. You're safe and sound now. God, Niana, if Gillies hadn't killed him, I would have."

A cough interrupted their thoughts and the constable poked her head in. "Would you like a visitor?" she asked.

A worried Meldena brushed by and stared at Niana. "Are you okay, Niana? They told me what happened."

[160]

"The bastard was shot," Niana replied. "It's getting to be a habit."

"Konstantin Deuratovich," Meldena whispered. "He was the one we were trying to find, the leader of the gang that killed my friends, Ida, Ditra and Emine."

"Emine?" Matt interrupted. "Not Emine Feraj?"

The teenager stopped and stared at Matt. "Yes," she whispered. "Ida and Ditra died in the fire and Emine was killed in the hospital afterwards. I don't know what happened to her little boy."

"Agron is home with Emine but she never mentioned your name," Niana said with a strange expression on her face,

"What?" the teenager yelled. "You mean..."

"She's alive and well. At this moment she's looking after Halia and Adona, her two elder children. I brought them out of Kosovo with me."

Tears arrived again but this time it was the teenager who broke down. "The bastards never told me," she sobbed.

"But who are you?" Matt pushed.

"Meldena Adzovic is an assumed name, my mother's maiden name, to tell the truth. My real name is Rokmane Mucoli. They should have told me Emine was still alive. All those weeks of mourning, hell bent on revenge." Her tone was bitter.

"So you took your mother's name and then what?"

"I spent some time in Christchurch with a family. They were very nice but didn't really understand." She shrugged. "We had an argument and I walked out. I was offered a chance to keep an eye on you two." She stopped and walked across to stare out the cabin window to where a silhouette of a headland could be seen as an inky hill in front of the stars. "I don't think the buggers told me the full story about you either, just that you, Niana, are a Kosovar like myself who was being chased by this notorious Section Eight."

"It was true, but we didn't realize this Deuratovich was tracking us," Niana whispered.

"So it's all over except for one thing," Meldena, or Rokmane as the Coleman's now had to get used to calling her, said with a sigh.

"What's that?" Niana asked.

Rokmane stared out at the ocean and broke into a smile. "Emine and Agron are alive. They were all I had left."

"So you now have someone to look forward to seeing at our place, don't you?"

The teenager swung around and linked eyes with Niana. She didn't notice the crumpled blouse, dishevelled hair and tear-stained cheeks, but

[161]

saw the intense eyes of a friend. She stepped over and took her hands. "I will," she said in Albanian. "I thought I was completely alone in this world but fine ... Oh hell," she sobbed. "You know what I mean."

"Yes," Niana spoke back in her native language.

"Our house will be full," Matt said.

Rokmane's lip dropped until she saw the twinkle in his eyes and realized he was teasing. " I won't be a burden."

"So you'd better settle down more than you did with the Burkharts," a male voice sounded.

Rokmane spun around to see Trent standing in the cabin. She sucked on her lip again and frowned at him. "It wasn't all my fault."

"The Burkharts were the family Rokmane stayed with in Christchurch," Trent explained. "They had a slight disagreement just before Christmas."

"I told them I didn't recognize Christmas and they went bonkers. I said they were as narrow minded as the Serbs and--"

"Okay," Trent laughed. "I admit they were a bit churchy but you were no angel, young lady."

"I suppose." The girl pouted and turned to Matt. "Can I call Emine, please?"

"Tomorrow," Matt promised. "We thought we'd forego travelling home by car and take an early flight to Auckland. You can see her by noon tomorrow."

"Great." Rokmane broke into a smile. "Look, I'll go and get our gear. It's still on the top deck. See yah."

She disappeared out the door.

Trent turned to the pair. "She was a handful down south," he admitted. "We were worried she'd go completely off the rails after she walked out of the Burkharts. She needs security and good, old fashioned love."

"We all do," Niana replied softly.

"Well, yes," the secret service agent coughed and placed a satchel on a small side bench. "But there are more serious concerns."

Niana glanced at Matt.

"These... err... accidents," the man continued. "To put it frankly, if the police had their way, our young friend would be up on a murder charge. Forensic experts can prove Lieutenant Nikolai Malkov was shot in the throat before his car was incinerated in New Plymouth and there are these latest two shootings, not to mention Matt's gunshot wound."

"You said--" Matt began but stopped when Trent held up his hand

[162]

and extracted two sheets of paper from his satchel.

"Could you sign these, please," he said, handing them each a copy.

"What are they?" Niana frowned.

"The Secrecy Act. By signing these, you both agree to keep secret everything that happened over the last forty-eight hours and also everything else you know about the arson in New Plymouth and of your shop in Auckland. In return, the police will drop all investigations into the incidents."

"Otherwise?" Matt responded, his voice hard.

Major Trent Gillies turned professional. "Both your wife and new friend will be arrested on suspicion of murdering Serb immigrants." He turned to face a flushed Niana. "Your shot across the swing-bridge with that handgun was dead accurate, wasn't it?"

"I had to."

"I know that," the major reassured in a softer tone. "But imagine what the public would think?"

"Does this cover Meldena, too?" Matt asked.

"She's a minor and can't sign a legal document but, yes, if you read the fine print, the wording means you sign on her behalf." He shrugged. "We had a long talk and she won't say a word. I can promise you that."

Matt still appeared doubtful. "And what happens the next time?"

"God willing, there won't be one," Trent said. "This Deuratovich and his so called Section Eight are all dead or in custody. The three who attempted to stop you on the road from Nelson will be deported. They deserve to be thrown in jail but we don't want the publicity. Mind you, when they arrive at their destination, they'll be arrested for crimes against humanity, taken to The Hague and tried."

"Slimy business." Matt glowered. "Doesn't anyone have morals anymore?"

The army officer caught Matt's gaze. "Probably not," he replied.

"Then we'll sign," Niana responded. She grabbed the ballpoint pen Trent held out and placed her signature on the paper.

Matt gave a brief chuckle and also signed. "And I didn't even read the fine print," he said.

*

The final fifteen minutes of the ferry's journey into Port Nicholson with twinkling lights from houses, highways and high rise buildings made Niana relax. The trio moved back to the top deck leaned on the railing and watched the throbbing city draw closer.

Rokmane glanced at Niana and smiled. "Where now?" she asked as they walked down to the Honda and waited while the ferry backed in, gangplanks lowered and vehicles began to drive off.

"We're a day early so can't get the honeymoon suite in the Pan Pacific Hotel," Matt replied. "Instead, I managed to get a room at a motel on the way out to the airport. Sorry, that's all I could order from the ferry."

"And I'll pay my share," Rokmane said, taking out her purse. "Trent paid me for my services so I've got money, now." She grinned. "All cash, too."

The motel was easy to find and the proprietress completely unfazed by their late arrival or unkempt appearance. She chattered away, led them to a small unit and apologized for not having a larger one available.

"I'll make us some coffee." Niana yawned and Matt tucked an arm around her.

"No, I'll make a drink. You go and have a nice hot shower." He glanced at the teenager. "You too, Mel ... I'm sorry, Rokmane. You look all in."

"Me?" the girl chided. "I'm the only one here in one piece."

*

An hour later, Rokmane lay covered in perspiration and exhausted but sleep would not come. The rumbling snores of one of her companions filled the air. "I hear you're still awake, Niana," she whispered. "How are you?"

"I can't sleep," Niana replied. "Every time I drop off, horrible dreams jerk me awake. Hell, it's so hot, too. They need air conditioning."

"I can't sleep either," Rokmane said. "I keep thinking about everything."

"What say we slip through to the kitchen and I'll put the kettle on," Niana suggested. "There are some muffins I bought on the sink."

"Okay," Rokmane replied, and she almost bounced out of bed. A few moments later the pair sat on stools beside a small table sipping coffee.

The teenager grinned at her companion. "How's Matt?" she asked.

"It took a while but he's asleep now." Niana chucked. "Snores like a bull, doesn't he? I still love him, though."

"You're so lucky."

"I think so but tell me about yourself. I'm curious."

The two were silent for a moment before Rokmane whispered.

"What do you want to know, Niana?"

"I guess the bit about how you knew Emine."

"We were all such great friends," Rokmane began. "We shared a tent in the refugee camp together and they helped me to rebuild my life. Ida was…" her voice drifted on with an account that, in many ways, reflected Niana's own experiences. "… In New Plymouth, we had everything, until that bastard blew our house up." The youngster sniffed back tears and sipped her coffee.

"Stop if it is too hard to discuss. I understand," her companion cut in.

"No, I'd like to talk about it. It's all bottled up inside me. Everyone since then has tried to be kind but they didn't really understand. You're different. You've been through it all." The tears began. "It was such a beautiful morning " Rokmane began her story.

*

It was quiet when Rokmane awoke in their New Plymouth home and realized Emine had left to go for an early morning walk.

"Damn. She could have woken me up," she muttered to herself as she hastily dressed and decided to try to catch up with her friend.

The bedroom reflected the red light from the eastern sky and felt so comfortable the teenager relished the atmosphere and didn't turn a light on. Outside, the ocean could be heard lapping on the rock wall beyond the adjacent parking lot, a sign that it was high tide, and the usual harbour navigation light blinked at the head of the breakwater a couple of kilometres along the shoreline. It was going to be another hot day.

Like Emine a few moments earlier, Rokmane paused when she was outside to take in the view but, unlike her friend, she noticed something different. Instead of the salty sea spray wafting by her nose there was a distinct smell of high-octane aviation fuel. It brought immediate memories of the crowded airport in Albania before they flew out to Italy.

She hesitated and sniffed the air. Strange, the local airport was up the coast a dozen kilometres and even the main highway was one hill inland. This smell had never been around before. She shrugged. Perhaps the breeze was bringing it in from the wharf where tankers loaded fuel from a local gas to gasoline extraction plant.

With this reasoning in her mind she set off towards the small pedestrian bridge where she knew Emine and Agron had gone.

Her walk, though, went no further.

[165]

A hiss hit her ears and, as she turned, this changed to an almighty crack that made her leap in fright.

"No!" she screamed.

The world in front blew apart in a tower of orange explosive. Hot superheated air hit the side of her face and, in the same second, she was hurled sideways into a grass bank like a paper puppet.

Her senses tried to cope but couldn't. She could feel the heat, burning and terrible but the noise was worse. The screaming roar of flames followed by putrid black smoke seized her, and sent her coughing and spluttering along the path; eyes smarted and oxygen ripped away. She couldn't breath. Her throat was like fire but her friends were in the building. She had to help. The girl staggered around to find the light so bright she had to shut her eyes.

"No!" she shrieked again in shock and stepped towards the house.

Towering flames, three times higher than the building itself filled the air. Millions of hot sparks floated by, followed by a series of earth shattering cracks as roofing iron exploded and rocketed into the air.

Rokmane sheltered her face and attempted to move closer but it was too hot. Nothing could survive the carnage. With tears that evaporated almost as quickly as they formed so her eyes felt tinder dry, she swung back and searched frantically for help.

The hand that grabbed her was calloused and rough. She screamed again, that high-pitched shriek of sheer terror.

"Shut up, Slut." The voice pierced her mind with self-preservation now her only thoughts. She screeched again ...and again.

From the corner of her eye she noticed something coming and instantly pulled back. For a second she could see wild eyes fixed on her, a face, lips and even smell stale cigarette smoke then the metal object connected with the side of her head.

The excruciating pain!

The feeling was only momentary though as blessed unconsciousness arrived.

*

Rokmane awoke to find herself choking. She couldn't breathe... or move. Her arms ached and her legs felt numb. Vomit filled her throat and she was dizzy. What was wrong?

She shook her head and it cleared slightly. Her tongue seemed to fill her whole mouth and her teeth ached. Another sputtering cough made

[166]

saliva slither down her throat to cause an automatic swallow that helped to awaken her.

An evil smelling rag bound her mouth, her hands were aching because they were behind her back and held securely by ropes, so tight she had burns from them. She was lying sideways on a cold metal floor that was shaking. That was why she felt so ill.

She was in the back of a vehicle but it was pitch black. The air stank of rubber, sweat and fumes.

She kicked out and realized her legs were also tied together and her torso was twisted in a claustrophobic space. Shit, the vehicle swayed and her head banged against steel.

Panic.

An attempted scream sent her into a choking fit.

Air. She had no air.

Bang! The noise sent her in quivers of terror until she realized it was the sound her sneakers made when she had kicked against the metal side of her prison.

There was another violent lurch to the left and a shaft of light, filled with specks of dust cut across the space. This small beam of light helped her to focus her attention and she begin to think rational thoughts again.

Her racing pulse slowed and she managed to breathe through her nose. Stuffy air that stunk like a crowded room raced into her screaming lungs but it was air.

Rokmane began to fathom what was happening. She appeared to be in a metal space of a moving vehicle. When she moved, her head banged metal above her and she could hardly move from a foetal position. No wonder every bone in her body ached.

She was in the trunk of a car. A small rubber mat dug into her posterior and she could feel something harder beneath, a tool-kit maybe.

Once more she was tossed sideways as the vehicle swerved and a shattering blow hit her head and the shaft of dusty light disappeared. She struggled to breathe but choked and again the world went black.

Her next sense was that of being lifted. Sunlight shone in her eyes.

"Just hang on, Miss," a compassion-filled male voice said. "We'll get you untied."

"Where am I?" the teenager spluttered after realizing the gag around her mouth had gone and she could breathe the air. It was fresh air, too.

She opened her eyes to see blue sky and a face above her. It belonged to another man but this one was clean-shaven, smelt of aftershave

[167]

and the eyes that gazed down at her were soft like a baby's.

"Hi," the man said. "My name is Geoff Swenson. I'm a police officer. We managed to stop the men that kidnapped you."

*

Rokmane smiled at Niana and placed her empty coffee mug on the counter. "I found out later the secret service were following the terrorist but were too late to save our house. They followed the car I'd been slung in and stopped it with those road spike things on one of the back roads. I was taken to a house somewhere in New Plymouth and had the situation explained to me. They said Emine was safe in hospital with Agron but the others dead. After the initial shock, I was interviewed and agreed to help catch those responsible and the media were informed I'd been killed, too. Later I was flown out to Christchurch and given my new identity. I chose my mother's name so I'd remember it easily

That first day, I was told to stay away from Emine or my cover would be blown. I didn't believe them so sneaked out one night," she laughed. "Told the young constable guarding me I needed to go to the restroom and just walked out. At the hospital I walked in a side door and just wandered around until I found the ward Emine was in." She shuddered. "Then it all went wrong."

"How?" Niana asked quietly.

"She began screaming, high pitched hysterical screams like those I heard at home. Then they stopped. There was utter silence. That was when I walked almost slap bang into the Serb who had kidnapped me."

"How did you know him?"

"The eyes. I'll never forget those eyes under the thick eyebrows. He was just sort of waiting there. I panicked, I guess but was certain he must have killed Emine. The rest is blurred. I remember the empty parking lot with one car in it, slipping inside it and--" She stopped and bit on her lip.

"Go on."

"I was sure it was the car I had been tossed into the back of. The smell or shape, I suppose. Anyhow, I found a gun in the glove box and hid in the back. When the bastard returned I killed him," she said in a matter-of-fact tone.

"Oh my God," Niana muttered.

"Yeah...bad as you aren't I?" Rokmane stopped and sipped her coffee. "Major Gillies said if breathed a word to anyone except Matt and you about anything that happened, I'd be arrested and charged for killing the guy in New Plymouth. He'd do it, too, the bastard."

"Probably," Niana replied, catching Matt's eyes. "So we keep quiet, don't we?"

"I have no regrets," the teenager replied bitterly.

"I know but try to put it behind you," Niana said in a soft voice. "If you carry the bitterness inside, you'll only destroy your own life. It is hard. I know it is. Hardly a night goes by when I don't think about what happened but it doesn't eat into me any more." She grimaced. "Until I was attacked tonight," she whispered.

"So we both have to forget," Rokmane answered. She glanced up.

"Yes," her companion answered. She smiled, stood and peered out the kitchenette door. "Matt's still asleep," she whispered. "He can sleep through anything."

*

He stared helplessly across the swing-bridge while his wife screamed for help. But he couldn't get to her. The bridge was wrecked with the steel wires and planks dangling vertically down into the abyss below.

"Help me," she screamed, and he could hear the Serb grunt as the pink pyjamas were ripped from her slender body and the foul beast ogled her heaving breasts.

Matt raised his rifle so it was aimed at the Serb's back as the man lashed at his young wife and fired. But the weapon merely clicked. He was out of ammunition.

"Help me!" Niana screamed as the grinning Serb pushed her back and forced her down out of sight in the foliage. Her screams turned to pitiful sobs while Matt seethed with rage from his side of the gorge.

The Serb turned and grinned across at Matt before dragging the screaming woman across to the edge of the ravine. "See yah, slut." He roared with laugher and tossed her over.

"No!" Matt shrieked with tears streaming from his eyes. "Niana!" The white body just tumbled through the air. Strange, though he was there, too, falling... falling straight down....

Matt jerked up and realized he was lying in bed and Niana was beside him. She had one arm out from the hot sheet. It was early but already the sun bathed the room in warm light.

The nightmare was so realistic that Matt shook in fright. He studied his wife beside him, her breasts enhanced rather than hidden by the shiny, pink shortie pyjamas, and forced his mind back to reality. He wanted to

[169]

hold, love and protect her. However, he hesitated and remembered they weren't alone. Another bob of hair and arm hung out of the next bed. The young stranger that came into their lives was sighing softly in her sleep.

"Bugger," Matt whispered. He bent over, kissed Niana's dry lips and slipped out of bed. God, it was hot and his wounded arm ached like a rotten tooth. He knew it was useless trying to sleep again and was amazed that both his companions managed to do so in the sticky heat and everything they'd been through.

He washed up, gave himself an awkward shave using the wrong hand, and was combing his hair when, the dream flashed back into his mind, so vivid his hands shook. He stared at himself in the mirror and erupted into sudden and unexpected tears that rolled silently down his cheeks.

Nothing like this had happened for years. At boarding school, he remembered being bullied and the only refuge was the restroom where he'd cry in loneliness and frustration before blowing his nose, wiping the eyes and leaving to survive another day. Boys, after all, didn't cry, they played sport and got in fights but they never cried. Only wimps cried.

But Matt was crying now; the shock of the previous day also caught up to him. He had tried to protect Niana but failed. It was sheer luck that the secret service agent had intercepted the assassin. It should have been him who came to her rescue.

"Stupid bugger," he swore at his reflection, wiped the tears away and slipped his clothes on.

Niana and Rokmane were still asleep so Matt let himself outside. The ocean was only across the deserted road and below a stone retainer wall. He walked down a set of steps and ambled, bare feet along the surf line. Ahead, the high-rise buildings of the city centre could be seen while behind the motel, houses towered up the steep hillside.

Matt wandered on and began to feel more at ease with the world. It was so peaceful here in the middle of New Zealand's capital and, at this time of the day, the city was silent and glittering in the morning sun. After mounting more steps he walked back across a grassed area to a park bench. He sat down and was immediately approached by a dozen seagulls looking for a morsel of bread.

"Sorry, birds," Matt said. "Perhaps I'll bring you something after breakfast."

For fifteen minutes he sat and absorbed the view but his mind played through the events of his life since meeting Niana. He was so deep in thought, he never noticed the young woman approach until she was a few meters away, standing on the sand with white surf twisting through her

[170]

ankles. He looked up, saw her wide smile and blushed.

My God, she was beautiful in a simple white cotton top, bare sunburned tummy and brown shorts with a brief view of blue lace beneath.

Without a word he stood, stepped out, almost jumped down the steps and swept her in his arms. His kiss almost smothered her but she responded and sent a quiver of passion through him.

"Whoa, big boy." Niana gasped. "What's all this about?"

"I love you, my darling," Matt said in a serious voice. "I never want you to be hurt again. When I saw you in that restroom "

Niana held onto him and glanced up. Tears were rolling down Matt's face. "Sweetheart, I'm fine," she whispered. "Really I am."

"I left my stiff upper lip at home," Matt responded and kissed her again.

"Silly Man," Niana scolded but she felt proud as they turned and walked, hand in hand, back to the motel.

*

CHAPTER TWENTY

The deal Matt arranged to have the car taken by rail to Auckland wasn't too expensive and he was pleased when the hotel where they'd booked to spend two nights, refunded his deposit after they'd heard of the reason for the cancellation.

"Well with your bandage, Matt, and Niana looking as if she's had a fight with a gorilla and then burned to a crisp, they couldn't not believe your story," Rokmane said when Matt told of the refund.

"And what story did you spin, sweetheart?" Niana asked.

"I said I had a fall while we were tramping and decided to return home early." He grinned. "I was looking forward to that honeymoon suite, though."

"Yes, but we saved a few hundred bucks," Niana laughed.

"About the cost of the air tickets to Auckland," Matt replied as he slid into the passenger seat of the Honda. "Let's drop the car off and head to the airport."

*

Later that morning an Air New Zealand flight landed at Auckland International Airport and three weary travellers moved out of the domestic terminal to find a taxi.

But it was not to be.

"Mummy," screamed a high-pitched voice.

Niana glanced along the walkway to see not only Adona and Halia running towards her, but also Kent who stood back with Agron in his arms.

"We heard you were coming home early," he muttered after all the hugs and kisses were over. "The truck is over in the far corner near the main entrance. It is too big to bring any closer."

"Oh Kent," Niana said. "You shouldn't have." She glanced over and noticed Rokmane standing back looking embarrassed. "Rokmane, come and meet Kent, Matt's right hand man at the factory."

She grinned as the tall scraggly youth and slightly chubby, tanned girl in shorts and tank top, muttered to each other. The girl's eyes, though, were on the toddler.

"Agron." she yelled. "My haven't you grown? Remember me?"

[172]

The little boy grinned, his eyes twinkled in recognition and he held his arms out to her. "Rok Rok," his voice called.

"Of course," Niana exclaimed. "He often says that. We thought he meant up, up but it was your name."

"I used to lift him out of his highchair." Rokmane smiled and turned back to Kent. "I'll take Bubbs, if you like. You're holding him all wrong, anyway."

"Be my guest," Kent replied, laughing. A look of relief flashed across his face as he handed Agron to Rokmane. "He's wet," he cautioned.

But the girl wasn't listening. She cuddled the toddler with tears in the corner of her eyes." Oh, Bubbs," she sniffed. "I thought I'd never see you again."

"Do you know him?" Kent asked with a quizzical expression across his brow.

"Yes," Rokmane answered and kissed the wee boy. "Sure do."

"But where is Emine?" Niana asked in a puzzled voice. "And why have you got Agron?"

"Mamma's in hospital," Halia replied. "Kent's been looking after us all week."

"What?" Niana became serious. "Kent, tell us what happened."

"The doctor called it a relapse," Kent began and explained what had happened. "I tried to contact you. Then late last night, this guy phoned me and said you were flying home. He also hinted there's been some sort of trouble so we decided to meet the incoming flights. You were on the fourth one in from Wellington, this morning."

"And you looked after Bubbs and the children yourself for almost a week?" Niana sounded dumbfounded.

"We helped," Adona cut in.

"Oh sweetheart, I'm sure you did," Niana picked her foster daughter up and placed a kiss on her cheek while, at the same time, Matt tucked an arm around an appreciative Halia.

When they looked in the back roll up door of Stubby, parked just inside the main entrance road, Matt and Niana grinned at each other. The enclosed back of the truck had all the work tools removed and in their place were sleeping bags, a couple of beanbags, bundles of clothes, boxes of food, baby stuff and a small portable gas cooker that Matt recognized came from the shop. Everything was neatly arranged around the walls and quite snug.

"We didn't know when you'd come," Kent explained.

"So how long have you been here?" Niana asked.

"Since yesterday afternoon," Halia continued. "It got a bit scary last

[173]

night when a policeman came to see what we were doing."

"Yeah, it was a security guard, actually," Kent explained. "He said we couldn't stay but when he saw the kids, gave us until noon today to move."

"And we had breakfast at McDonald's," Adona added as she cuddled into Niana's neck. "Kent even got them to warm up Bubb's bottle and open a can of his food."

"Cheeky." Rokmane smiled warmly at Kent.

He caught her eye and flushed. "We didn't want to miss any flights," he muttered.

"And we're proud of you," Niana added.

Kent grinned back at her. "Where did you get the shiner, Niana? Matt rough you up a bit?" He switched his gaze to the man's bound arm. "Looks like you won the fight in the end, though."

"She ran into a door and I tripped on a mat," Matt replied dryly, "We're suing the lodge for negligence."

"Sure," Kent said and glanced at Rokmane again. "There's not much room in the cab."

"Okay," Niana replied. "I'll drive and Matt can come up front with me, if you don't mind all sitting back here."

"It'll be great," Rokmane cut in before anyone else could reply.

She placed Agron on board and started to load her backpack on. Kent raced to help while Niana gave Matt a discreet dig in the ribs.

"Come on, sweetheart," Niana said. "Let's get up the front. Kent and Rokmane can put the rest of the luggage aboard."

Moments later the old truck headed out into the morning motorway traffic and they crawled their way across the city. Matt leaned back and sighed. "Dear old Stubby," he said

"I know what you mean," Niana said as she shifted gears and moved the truck forward a few meters.

"If I'd realized what was going to happen..."

"If we'd gone somewhere else it still would have happened, Matt," Niana reasoned. "Both sides knew we were on our honeymoon and followed us."

"I suppose but what about Emine?"

Niana frowned. "Yes, that's a worry. We shouldn't have left her in charge but she seemed perfect when we left." She turned to her husband. "Kent rose to the occasion, though, didn't he?"

"Yes, but I'm not really surprised. In many ways he's very mature for his years."

[174]

"Like Meldena?" Niana chuckled "Rokmane, I mean."

"They'd be a similar age, you know. I noticed the hormones at work."

Niana laughed and slapped Matt's shoulder. "They're just kids."

*

At the back, Adona and Halia had cuddled in beside Kent on one beanbag while Agron was asleep in Rokmane's arms on the other.

"Are you like Niana and the kids?" Kent asked Rokmane.

"What do you mean?"

"A refugee from Kosovo?"

The girl frowned. "Yeah, I am. I guess my accent gives me away. Does it matter?"

"Not at all," Kent said and squeezed his arms around the two children beside him. "All my friends come from there." He shrugged. "Not counting Matt, of course."

Rokmane smiled across at him. "We can't pick our parents or where we're born on this earth," she said in a quiet voice. "My parents were everything a girl could ask for but they've both gone now." She was silent for a moment before changing the topic. "How's Emine?"

"Not good," Kent admitted, and told her everything that had happened.

"She was like that for months. Then one day she came out of it. Perhaps it'll happen again."

"That's what the doctor said but he also warned me if she didn't show signs of improving soon it could become permanent. God, when the children told me what happened I didn't know what to do."

Rokmane grinned and glanced around. The sun shone in through two skylights and a shaft of bright light flickered around the interior. "You did, okay," she complimented.

*

Rokmane gasped after she'd jumped from the truck and stared, enraptured, at Matt's house. "Is this your place?"

"Matt designed it," Kent said with pride in his voice. "It's really cool inside with four bedrooms, a massive living area, satellite television; just about everything."

"Wow," the girl said. "I love those light collared bricks and

[175]

windows that stick out."

"They're called bay windows."

When they walked inside, the visitor just stood and stared while Niana noticed that the kitchen looked spotless. She walked through to the laundry and it had also been tidied, as had the rest of the house. "Kent," she said, smiling. "You're a wonder. I don't even keep it this tidy."

Kent shrugged but looked pleased.

"Come and see my room, Mummy," Adona said. "I tidied it myself."

"No you didn't," Halia corrected. "I helped you."

"A little," Adona admitted. She took Niana's hand and led her through to where one single bed was made up and the second covered with teddy bears and toys with a wooden tractor and wagon in a prominent place.

"If you don't mind, you can share this room with Adona," Niana told the teenager.

Rokmane just stood, almost mesmerized. "The tractor and wagon," she said. "They're so authentic, just like the ones at home."

"Matt made them for the kids," Niana explained. "Adona had to have one just like Halia's."

"And why not?" Rokmane said. She walked to the bay window and stared out at the parched lawn and small vegetable garden before turning and wrapping her arms around her host. "I'd love to share this room with Adona but are you sure?"

"You are welcome here, Rokmane," Niana said with finality in her voice. "We told you that."

"But I didn't realize you had such a beautiful place."

"What difference does that make?"

Rokmane grinned. "None, I guess. All the rich people I've met were as mean as hell."

"We aren't rich." Niana laughed. "Matt's just worked hard, that's all." She watched the teenager's enthusiasm and felt proud of her home and the wonderful man who was her husband. "Come on," she said. "We'll freshen up, have a bite to eat and then we'll go and find Emine."

*

Emine was sitting in a deck chair on the veranda of the hospital reading an old Albanian language magazine someone had found for her. It was one of those light women's magazines that bored her but she didn't have the heart to tell the lady from the Albanian Society she wasn't interested.

Massive dosages of various drugs left her dozy but her mind was alert and a patchwork of memories of recent events returned. The accompanying stress that played on her mind brought the curtain back. But she was determined to remember everything.

"Hi Emine." Pauline Bromley, the therapist walked across the concrete floor and pulled up a second deck chair. "How are you this morning?"

"I let everyone down," the woman replied without looking at her visitor. "My baby, the other children, everyone."

"What children?" Pauline clicked on a hidden recorder and leaned forward. This was the first time her patient had mentioned anyone except her baby.

"Halia and Adona," Emine answered. "I was looking after them and let them down. Bubbs, too. You said he's fine but when can I see him?"

"Today," the therapist replied. "Now, can you describe Halia and Adona?"

"Sure," Emine responded and gave a very accurate description of the two children.

"And why were you looking after them by yourself?"

Emine frowned and scratched her head. "This isn't New Plymouth is it?"

"No, we're in North Shore City over the harbour bridge from Auckland."

"Of course," Emine answered. "I found them here. Niana Bolsa was looking after them." She frowned and stared out at the lawn. "That's it. Niana and Matt are on their honeymoon and..." She turned and tears sprang into her eyes. "I remember it, Pauline. The fire. I came home to find my friends had been killed. Oh shit." Tears appeared in her eyes.

"Relax," Pauline said in a quiet voice. "Just tell me what you remember."

Emine's account was almost complete. She still had no recollection of how she got from New Plymouth or anything about the bus station but knew of her friends' deaths, being in hospital and walking into the restaurant.

"But I let Niana and Matt down," she repeated. "The one time I could pay them back for their kindness, I had to go and..." She stopped and wiped her brow. "You say Kent is looking after them?"

"Yes, and they all visited you yesterday morning. Can't you remember?"

Emine shook her head. "Sorry." She sighed. "Some things are so clear while other events are a blur like a dream out of focus." Her fearful eyes looked up at the therapist's. " Will I be okay, Pauline? "

"As long as you keep up your medication you should be fine," the other woman replied. "Today's session is a good indication you can lead a normal life. "

The therapist was about to take her leave and visit her next patient when a nurse approached.

"Emine has visitors," the young woman said. "Is it okay if I bring them in?

"Would you like to see your friends?" Pauline turned to Emine.

"Yes, very much," came the soft reply.

*

Emine glanced up and saw a dark haired girl walk through the open doorway carrying Agron. Emine frowned and shook her head. Was she hallucinating again? It couldn't be.

The young woman walked closer. She was smiling and crying at the same time as she hugged the toddler close and searched Emine's face for signs of recognition.

"It can't be," Emine cried. She stood up and stepped forward. "Rokmane!"

"Yes," replied the tearful girl. She stood the little boy on the floor and ran the last few steps into her friend's arms. "I followed you out that morning and... Do you remember me, Emine?"

"Yes, of course," sobbed the older woman. "How can it be? They told me you were dead." Her lips quivered and she couldn't talk as the teenager squeezed her close and kissed her cheek.

"It's a long story," Rokmane began, "But you remember me, Emine--that's all that matters now."

Emine wept and finally looked over her young friend's shoulder to see Niana, Matt and her children standing there... Kent too. Everyone was smiling.

*

"Are you sure you'll be okay?" Niana asked for a second time as she inspected the small house Emine had just moved into. Much of the furniture had come from Matt's store but it was all serviceable and with the

[178]

new curtains the women had just finished making, the house looked very cosy.

"Of course," Emine replied. "I've got Rokmane and we're only a few blocks from your place. I promise, if anything goes even the slightest bit wrong I'll call you."

"Or I will," Rokmane added.

It was March and several weeks after the honeymoon, a busy and crowded time with the Coleman house full and both sections of *Sandwiches and Cuckoo Clocks* having a busy new season. Emine's condition was as normal as she'd ever be but doctors warned Niana, Matt and Rokmane that she would never be completely cured. However, as long as she kept on her preventative medicine and didn't suffer from unexpected stress or responsibilities, she should be able to live a normal life.

The honeymoon experiences brought back many bad nights for Niana with a return of life-like nightmares. Matt was always there, though, when she awoke. She heeded his advice and returned to the doctor who prescribed a mild course of sedatives that were now being slowly phased out.

Kent had begun his arts course but still worked in the factory while Rokmane flatly refused to attend any school or educational institute. Instead, she accepted a part time job working for Niana in the restaurant and spent the rest of her time helping Emine, or with Kent, doing things teenagers enjoyed.

It was Emine who first suggested she rent her own place and Niana's opposition was squashed by Matt who told her the move was necessary for them all. The older children were asked where they wanted to live and, to Niana's relief, they both stated they wanted to stay with Mummy and Daddy. Emine said little but seemed to be also relieved so, with Rokmane and Agron, she was prepared to begin this new phase of her life.

"Our place will certainly be empty," Matt said as he drove home with Niana and the two children.

"No it won't Daddy," Adona's now expected interruption came from the back seat. "There's Halia, me and also Misty the cat."

"Our family." Matt grinned. "More or less how we started."

"Yes," Niana laughed. "Most things have clicked into place."

"Yeah," Matt sighed. "Most things."

Niana frowned but Matt's expression told her no explanation was forthcoming. "Well sweetheart," she said instead. "What say we all go out for a meal tonight, one of those little restaurants that provide for children and isn't too expensive.

[179]

Matt's face lit up. "That sounds great. Now I think I know just the place. You know that little restaurant over in Brown's Bay…"

*

The tall red headed woman Niana almost bumped into at the supermarket somehow didn't look as sophisticated as when they'd last met. Sure, the red hair was immaculate and long fingernails were still there, but the simple overcoat couldn't hide a very pregnant torso.

"Well, Mrs. Niana Coleman," Judith said with a trace of sarcasm in her voice. "How do you like the new name?" She glanced around at the two children and at the toddler sitting in the shopping cart. "My God. Not more children." Her glance moved up to Rokmane who was doing the weekly grocery shopping for Emine while her friend relaxed at home. "Yours too? What a large family."

The teenager stared coldly at the pregnant woman and immediately jumped to Niana's defence. "Who are you to talk about something large?" she retorted.

Judith had the grace to flush. "Okay," she said and turned back to Niana. "I'm Mrs. Doyle, now. How's Matt, anyway?"

"Fine, thank you, Judith," Niana replied.

"And the house?"

Niana froze and remembered a previous comment from the woman about wanting the family home.

"Don't worry." Judith laughed. "I need nothing more from Matt. Graeme, that's my husband, provides me with all I need."

"That's obvious," Rokmane muttered.

Judith ignored the scowling teenager and continued her conversation with Niana. Now that the initial jibes were over she became almost pleasant. "I heard about your wedding and these children's poor mother," she continued. "Tell me, will the children all have Matt's surname?"

"Emine, Rokmane and Agron have their own home, now," Niana replied testily. Her eyes bore into the other woman. "Halia and Adona are still called Bolsa."

"Fair enough," Judith replied. "Not that it affects me now I'm not a Coleman, does it?"

"No," Niana replied. "It doesn't."

"Okay, I was a bit of a bitch," Judith confessed. "Tell Matt, he's welcome to the house and I now consider the divorce settlement was quite

[180]

fair." She shrugged. "He was quite generous, actually."

"He's that sort of man," Niana added in a quiet voice.

Judith's eyes met Niana and she nodded. After a few brief words to Halia and Adona, and a goo at Agron she departed out of their lives.

"Who's the old bag?" Rokmane said.

"Matt's first wife," Niana answered. "We thought she might cause us trouble a while back but nothing came of it."

"Yeah, I'd say he was lucky to get out of her clutches," the girl said, staring down the empty aisle.

"Daddy's got Mummy now," Adona, who'd taken in every word, added.

"Yes," agreed Halia. "We don't need that lady."

Rokmane caught Niana's eyes and smiled before turning to the children. "Come on kids," she said. "Let's find the ice cream counter. I'll treat you both. Nothing too big, mind you."

"Me too, Rok Rok," Agron looked expectantly up with a smiling face.

"If the boss says so," the teenager laughed. Niana nodded and watched as her family disappeared behind the shelves, Rokmane pushing the shopping cart with Bubbs inside while the other two attempted to keep up behind.

Somehow the chance meeting with Judith had been profitable and she couldn't wait to tell Matt about his pregnant ex-wife.

*

Matt's reaction to the news, though, was unexpected. "Damn," he muttered. "Trust her to get pregnant before the ink even dried on our divorce papers. Just to show me up, no doubt."

Niana stared at her husband, realized he wasn't jesting and a pang of jealousy ran through her slender body. "What's wrong Matt?" she asked. "I thought you'd be thrilled to hear Judith isn't going to try to get any more money out of you. Have you still got feelings for her?"

Matt turned. "Oh no, sweetheart. It's you I'm thinking of."

"Me," gasped his wife. "How do I come into the equation?"

"Judith's pregnant," Matt said miserably.

"So."

"It proves what I had suspected all along but was too afraid to admit."

"You're talking in riddles, Matt. I repeat, how does the fact that

[181]

Judith is pregnant affect us?"

"Oh sweetheart," Matt said and pulled Niana down beside him on the living room couch. She almost brushed him aside and stood back up but, once again, noticed his body language and hesitated.

"No secrets," she whispered and huddled in close.

"One of the reasons my first marriage broke up was that Judith wanted a family," he started. "It wasn't the only reason, of course but sort of started the rot in our marriage, I guess."

"Go on."

"We tried to have a child for years and visited specialists." He coughed. "I had tests and the specialist said it was a seventy to thirty chance I was the reason Judith never got pregnant. It seems he was right, doesn't it?"

"Possibly but does it matter?"

"Us. If I couldn't father a child then, it will be the same now, won't it?"

Niana smiled in relief. Her earlier thoughts that there were still feelings between Matt and his ex-wife, dissipated. "Oh Matt," she whispered and reached across to kiss him. "I don't care."

"You don't," Matt replied, still in a sombre voice. "I thought all young brides wanted a family."

"Sweetheart," Niana said, "I've been pregnant and really don't want to start again, anyway. We have our business, the two children and possibly Agron if things go wrong with Emine. Another baby would just be too much trouble, at least at the moment."

"So you don't mind? I was going to tell you ages ago but…"

"Coward," Niana replied and kissed him again.

Matt grinned and returned the kisses. "So Judith can have her infant," he said. "Good luck to her and…"

"Yes."

"I am glad she'll be off our backs over the house. My lawyer said she had no chance but you never know how court cases come out."

"And you're sure you have no feelings for her?"

"Not a one," Matt said, smiling. "They died well before I met you, my love."

*

[182]

CHAPTER TWENTY-ONE

Matt didn't like Prue McKenzie very much, probably because the woman reminded him of Judith. Mind you, she was a very profitable customer who'd spent hundreds of dollars at the factory purchasing antique furniture, none of that new artificial stuff, but genuine oak cabinets and bedroom furniture from a bygone era that Matt had restored to pristine condition. She'd also bought one of the cuckoo clocks after Matt discreetly forgot to tell her it was one of his own designs, only a few weeks old and the minute figures gathered around the chalet door were all designed by Kent.

"It will look simply exquisite in my entranceway," Prue said in her private boarding school accent the day she picked it up.

Today she was examining a china cabinet Matt was in the process of restoring. It was solid oak with lead framed coloured glass doors and came from an estate he'd won a bid for. Much of the property was junk but this cabinet made it well worth the purchase price.

"I want it, Mr. Coleman," she cooed. "When can it be ready?"

Matt eyed the twenty-five hundred dollar price tag and mentally kicked himself for having the price on display. If he'd known she was interested he'd have upped it to three grand and got it. Niana would chastise him for profiteering but it was all supply and demand and if he didn't provide Prue with the goods she wanted, no doubt she'd move on to someone else only too pleased to relieve her of her money.

"It'll take a while, Mrs. McKenzie," he drawled and rubbed his chin. "All the coloured glass will have to come out so the fittings can be sanded down and restained. I have a back order for three cuckoo clocks and hadn't intended to get back to this for a month or so."

Prue glared at him. "Sales talk, Matt," she said. "Look, I'll pay you three thousand if it's ready by August first."

"Thirty-five hundred and it's a deal," Matt replied. Their bartering had become quite a feature of past sales.

The woman glanced in his eyes but Matt never flinched. "Okay," she muttered and pulled a chequebook from her purse. "Half now, as usual."

"I'll write a receipt," Matt smiled. "Come through into the office."

[183]

"And are you going to the charity ball?" Prue asked a few moments later as she sipped a cup of coffee, another protocol Matt pampered her with.

"What charity ball?"

Prue sighed. "The combined service clubs on the North Shore are having their ball next month. This year the funds raised from it will be sent to Kosovo to help buy equipment for a children's hospital in Pristina. Niana would have heard about it."

"She may have but it's never been mentioned.

"I have the tickets," Prue continued and placed a glossy pamphlet on Matt's desk. "Read it and if you're interested, call me. Tell your friend Rokmane, too. We're trying to encourage the younger set to attend, not just us old timers." She laughed at her own joke and poked him in the ribs.

Matt grinned. Prue was forty-five if she was a day but with dyed hair, makeup, long red fingernails and sharp clothes, she tried to maintain a perpetual twenty-eight. It didn't work but Matt certainly wasn't about to point this out.

"It could be something we would enjoy," he replied as he browsed through the pamphlet. "And, as you said it's a good cause."

"Yes," Prue replied. "It's formal and upscale but Niana will love it. Now, if I was her age and had a figure like hers I'd..." her voice rattled on but Matt had stopped listening.

*

"Hello, Niana," said the man who walked up to the counter in the *Sandwiches and Cuckoo Clocks* restaurant the next afternoon.

Niana glanced up from the sandwiches she was spreading margarine on and instantly recognized the visitor. "Major Gillies," she replied in a cautious voice. "What can I do for you?"

"Call me Trent, please." He smiled. "If you can free yourself I'd like to have a short talk with you and Matt."

"Of course. Roseanne, can you take over on the counter, please?"

"Sure, Niana," her ever faithful assistant replied and walked over from where she'd been placing dishes in the dishwasher. "Take your time. The rush isn't due for half an hour and Rokmane will be in by then."

"How is the youngster?" Trent asked. "I've heard nothing so that must be a good sign."

"She's one of the family," Niana replied, still with caution in her voice. "Why do you ask?"

[184]

"Just being polite." Trent didn't say anything further until they met Matt in the staff room and the door was closed. "I promised no civil action against you or Rokmane would be taken and the New Zealand Police have respected that request."

"So why are you here, Major Gillies?" Matt asked. "You're hardly likely to be up here in Auckland just to drop in on a social visit."

"True," the man replied. "I assure you it's nothing sinister. We could have written you a letter but they can be so formal,"

"So." Niana leaned forward in her seat, noticed the man's body language and relaxed a little. "I'm sorry Trent, I'm being unsociable. Can I offer you a cup of coffee?"

"From your coffee bar? I'd be delighted and one of those delicious blackcurrant muffins I saw on display too, if that's possible."

Niana grinned. "Sure," she said and slipped out.

When she'd gone Trent turned to Matt. "I have news about your wife's family, Matt but it only confirms their deaths. Will she take it okay?"

"I think so," Matt said. "I'm sure she would appreciate any information you have. After all this time, I doubt if she'd expect any positive news."

"Right," the major replied and took a document from the briefcase he carried under his arm. "As you know," he started after Niana returned with three mugs of coffee and a plate of muffins to hand around, "police from around the world seconded to the United Nations have been investigating crimes by Serb police, special forces and army from April through to June 1999 when the Serbs withdrew from the province. Have you heard of the village of Besden, Niana?"

In spite of herself, Niana paled. "Yes, it's the village where my grandparents lived and my mother grew up. The last I heard from her and Poppa was when we considered evacuating Pristina. They both returned to Besden but I stayed in Pristina with my first husband." Her hands shook as she stirred her coffee. "I was in the last stages of my pregnancy," she whispered.

"I know," Trent said. "It is one of the many villages where atrocities are being investigated. On Tuesday the eleventh of May 1999, a Serb unit called Section Eight surrounded Besden and every villager who hadn't managed to escape to the mountains was herded into the local school and systematically shot."

"My family?" Niana's voice choked with emotion.

"They were among the victims later exhumed from a mass grave behind the village. Dental records and other forensic identification

[185]

procedures confirmed the bodies of your mother, father, grandmother and other family members."

Niana's chin shook. "Grandpapa?" she asked.

"Your grandfather feigned death and escaped the massacre. Later, he returned to take a video of the scene. It appears the Serbs discovered this had happened and attacked their mountain camp and he was captured then."

"Go on," Niana said with her eyes glued on the major.

"We believe Konstantin Deuratovich was determined to have the video cassette destroyed. He thought it had been given to you. He wanted to kill you so you couldn't be a witness against him if he was arrested."

"I'd left Kosovo by then and never knew about any video," Niana replied in a hushed voice. "Grandpapa would never implicate me or try to put me in danger, I know that much."

"We don't believe he did," Trent answered. "It's possible, though, he made up a plausible story that the video was out of the country to protect the remaining villagers further up the mountain at that time. They had the video and turned it over to KFOR troops when they returned home after the war.

We pieced together information and are almost certain he never divulged your name to the Serbs. Deuratovich, however, had access to an extensive spy network and, we believe, came to his own conclusion it was you who had the cassette. He knew your age and the fact you'd come to New Zealand but not your name so he arrived here looking for a Kosovar woman in her twenties. Less than a thousand of your people emigrated to New Zealand so it wasn't a very difficult job to trace where you all went."

"So they attacked Emine's home in New Plymouth on the off chance the video would be destroyed?"

"It appears so. Open revenge against Albanian Kosovars who, in his eyes, now controlled his country was also a factor. He was a killing machine responsible for hundreds of deaths. A dozen or so more meant little to him if, in the long run, he could save his own hide."

"Poor Grandpapa," Niana said. "Do you know what happened to him?"

"I'm sorry Niana," The major's voice was sympathetic. "They killed him. Villagers found his body after the war and all your family were buried together. Your late husband's grave has never been found, I'm afraid."

"Thank you," Niana replied and placed her coffee mug on the table. Her eyes were dry but haunted.

"What happened to the three who tried to stop our car near

Nelson?" Matt asked.

"They and two others from the same unit were arrested, deported to Kosovo and released," the major shrugged.

"What?" Niana snapped. Her face turned to a scowl.

"Yeah," the major continued in a slow voice. "Apparently some unknown person followed them from Pristina airport and intercepted their car. They were all found shot on the side of the highway." Gillies sipped his coffee. "Each one had a bullet wound in the back of the head."

"Now, that was a coincidence, wasn't it?" Niana's sarcasm was not hidden.

"Yes, very," the major said. " Most of the revenge shootings have been stopped by the British who control that sector of Kosovo but a few still slip through. It's still a volatile country."

"Makes me appreciate being here, Major Gillies," Niana replied. She reached out and squeezed Matt's hand.

"So the whole case is closed," Trent concluded. "Your friends and family have nothing to fear from local authorities or any terrorists."

He stood, shook hands with the pair, remarked on the delicious muffins and departed. Niana gazed at the empty door for a full moment before she turned and looked into Matt's eyes.

"You would have liked Grandpapa and my parents," she whispered.

"I'm sure I would have," Matt replied and wrapped his arms around his wife.

It was only then that she began to cry.

*

The Grand Charity Ball was a night to remember. Hundreds of guests jostled each other on the dance floor of the Memorial Stadium while the thirty-six-piece orchestra played an old fashioned waltz. Near the centre, a graceful woman in a long dark blue frock of sleek satin material cuddled in close to the tall slightly overweight man dressed in a tuxedo and black bow tie.

"Where did you learn to dance so beautifully, sweetheart," Niana sighed as her partner guided her around the dance floor.

"My ex," Matt said. "It was something necessary in the social circle Judith aspired to. She never had your grace though. And you?"

Niana's eyes clouded for a moment. "We had a high school graduation ball and Papa insisted on paying for professional tutoring. I went to classes for several weeks and attended the function with a nervous young

[187]

guy who tripped over me all night and ruined the evening." She smiled up at her husband. "I remember I walked in the door at home afterwards and burst into tears when Papa asked me how it went."

Their conversation was interrupted when the music stopped and dancers moved off to the tables spaced around the massive stadium. Matt had just held out a chair for his wife when a panting Rokmane rushed in with Kent almost dragged behind her.

"Hi guys," she puffed, and then ungracefully plunked herself down in the third chair. Like Niana, she had a long sleek gown but hers was a charcoal colour that exposed her shoulders. She also wore long white gloves and looked twenty or older. Kent stood beside her looking sophisticated in his own tuxedo and grinned at his friends.

"God it gets hot out there." Kent ran a finger around the back of his tight collar and smiled at his partner. "Can I get you something to drink, Rokmane?" he asked.

"Yes. Some of that punch please, Kent."

"Sure." Kent pushed his way through to the junior bar, one purposely set up for the younger guests. The massive bowl of punch there was empty, so he shrugged and edged his way to the adjacent table, took two glasses and filled them from the punch bowl there.

"Aye lad," a barman interrupted. "That's pretty potent stuff."

"So?"

"Well, it's your head in the morning," the man shrugged and switched his attention to another customer.

Rokmane liked the taste and after two refills over the next hour was decidedly giggly while Kent had lost his usual shyness and chatted away nonstop to his partner.

"Matt," Niana said in the early hours of the morning. "Those two. What have they been drinking?"

"Hell, I don't know," Matt said. He was feeling quite cheerful himself and kept peering down Niana's cleavage. "Stuff from the junior bar, I think." He pulled her close and slopped a kiss on her cheek.

"Matt," Niana retorted. "Behave yourself."

"Ladies and Gentlemen," came an announcement from the MC. "Take your partner for the penultimate dance."

"Do you mind?" Matt asked and nodded Rokmane's way. His wife shook her head and smiled when he tapped Kent on the shoulder and swept the girl away.

Kent stood looking uncertain until Niana tugged his sleeve. "Come on, Kent," she said. "You can guide an old woman around, can't you?"

"You aren't old. No way near it," the youth responded. "In fact I'd say you're the second most beautiful woman here today."

"Why thank you, Kent," came the surprised reply as they began to dance. "And who's the most beautiful?"

Kent blushed a bright red. "You know," he muttered.

*

Across the floor Rokmane looked into her partner's eyes and turned serious. "Thank you, for all you've done for us all," she whispered. "Taking me in, looking after Emine and the kids. Everything. I know Niana loves you very much but you took all us hanger-ons in without one complaint. I doubt if any of us could have survived without you."

"It works both ways," Matt replied. "Until I met you all I was pretty screwed up."

*

Kent's hand slid around to Rokmane's back and pulled the back zipper down. "If you want me to stop just say so," he said in an unfamiliar calm voice.

It was the early hours of the morning and, on the girl's suggestion, the taxi dropped them off at Kent's apartment behind the shop rather than at Emine's house.

Very tenderly, he pulled her gown down so it slid to her waist. He turned the young woman around, glanced at her smiling face but couldn't resist glancing down. She was wearing a black lace bra, which scarcely covered the cleavage showing through the material.

The young man swallowed, mentally cursed an erection that had been up half the night, grabbed her tightly and kissed the receptive lips. Their tongues touched and the first light kiss became passionate. Slowly his hand found and squeezed her right breast. Rokmane hung on and said nothing. It was as if she needed him as much as he wanted her.

The youth's trembling hands ran along the top of her bra as he gaped at the breasts beneath. His fingers slipped beneath the material while she kissed him without complaint. She yanked away his bow tie and undid his shirt buttons.

"Kent," Rokmane groaned and slung her arms around his neck. Tongues lashed. Her breasts were now pressed against his bare chest.

"Oh, Rokmane," Kent gasped as she cuddled in close and they just

[189]

sort of rolled onto the floor. Clothes disappeared and the frantic teenagers made wild, passionate love in that apartment living room.

"Stop," Rokmane whispered with a grin, as they lay exhausted on the carpet for what seemed like an hour.

"What?" replied Kent.

"Well, you told me to tell you when to stop. I just did."

"Oh my God, Rokmane. I wasn't going to..." he apologized.

"Why not?" Rokmane whispered.

Kent kissed her firmly on the lips and stared into her eyes. This was more than an erotic one-night stand. Feelings that he never knew he was capable of were flowing through his body.

"Rokmane," he whispered and kissed her again.

"My God," she said loudly. "Did I do that?"

Kent wondered what she was talking about until he realized his neck smarted. Blood was oozing from a love bite.

"Oh you poor dear," laughed Rokmane. "Just call me a vampire."

She stood up slipped her gown on and disappeared into the corridor, only to return a moment later with a first aid box in her hand. "I knew there'd be one in the shop," she said.

"Kent," Rokmane sighed as he tucked an arm around her. "You're a real man."

Kent laughed. "Come on. I'll take you home."

"In your state?" the girl replied. "No way."

Kent frowned. "A taxi?"

"Oh Kent, you can be gullible at times. You have a bed here haven't you?"

"Just just mine," he stuttered.

"Good," Rokmane laughed, "that's all we need. Loan me some of your pyjamas and you can take me home in the morning."

*

Across the city, a bedroom stood vacant with clothes, sheets and blankets strewn all over the floor but screams were coming from the bathroom.

"Get out, Matt!" Niana shouted as the grinning man pulled back the sliding front of the shower and slipped in under the warm water to embrace the sensuous body he'd only made love to moments earlier.

"Matt!" she shrieked as hands pushed her gently back against the steaming tiles. "There's no room."

[190]

But there was.

"I love you, Matt," Niana whispered a few moments later. She reached around and handed Matt a towel. "I hope Kent enjoyed himself as much as you obviously did."

"What do you mean?" Matt grunted.

"I doubt if Rokmane would let him slip away from her tonight without doing what we just did."

"But they're just kids. I bet Rokmane's at home and Kent is sound asleep in his apartment."

"How much?" Niana smirked.

"Fifty bucks they did nothing more than a simple kiss goodnight."

"You're on."

Niana slipped her nightgown on and headed out to the bedside telephone. She picked it up, clicked the speaker and memory buttons. It rang for a count of eight before a husky voice answered.

"Hello," Kent's hesitant voice filled the room.

"Hi Kent, Niana here. I know Rokmane's with you. Can I speak to her, please?"

The room went silent, Niana grinned at Matt and waited. They could hear some scuffling noises and a girl's voice. "Hi Niana. What do you want?"

"I hope you took precautions," Niana said in as formal a voice as she could muster.

"Oh shit," the girl retorted. "How did you guess?"

"Well, did you?"

"None of your bloody business," the retort came and the line went dead.

Niana turned to Matt. "You owe me fifty bucks, sweetheart."

"Oh hell," Matt replied when the telephone rang in his ear. "Hello," he said.

Rokmane's voice filled the room again. "I know you're listening, Niana," she said. "Sorry I hung up on you. I love you both. See you in the morning."

"Bye, both of you," Niana replied.

"Bye Niana," came Kent's embarrassed voice and the phone was hung up.

"Oh hell," Matt repeated. "When I was his age I wouldn't have gotten up enough nerve to kiss a girl goodnight let alone..."

"It's a new millennium, sweetheart." Niana chuckled.

"I know but ..."

[191]

"Oh Matt," Niana laughed and grabbed his hand, "Come on, I'll remake the bed and we can get some sleep. I have a strange feeling our heads will be complaining in the morning."

*

Four very subdued people met late the next morning at Emine's place where the children had spent the night. Emine glowered at Rokmane who appeared from Stubby dressed in one of Kent's shorts and shirt. The youth couldn't look anybody in the eye and Niana had to poke Matt to stop him from grinning.

"I'm going to take a shower," Rokmane announced and slipped away before anyone could say a word.

"Why didn't Rokmane come home?" Emine stated with an annoyed expression across her brow. "And why the two vehicles? "

"It was so late we didn't want to disturb you," Matt lied. "We all stayed at our place and, as for the truck, Kent and I are going to pick up some furniture later."

"Oh," Emine's voice relaxed. "I was worried. You should have called."

"Sorry Emine," Kent replied and flashed an appreciative glance at his employer. "We arrived home late and sort of slept in."

"Lazy," laughed Adona. She gripped Kent's hand. "We've been up for hours. Agron's been miserable but another tooth has come in."

Her excited voice rattled on while Halia slipped his own hand in Niana's and grinned up at her. "Did you like the ball, Mummy?" he asked.

"I did, sweetheart," his foster mother squeezed his hand. "We all had lots of fun."

She caught Kent's eyes and the teenager's face burned.

*

A month slipped by. Matt drove the old yellow truck in beside the house, gathered up a box of items he'd brought home aand walked into the kitchen.

Niana stood there with a strange expression on her face. "Hi, Matt" she whispered and reached up to kiss his cold lips.

Matt frowned. Niana had left work midway through the afternoon but hadn't told him the reason why.

"What's wrong?" he asked.

[192]

"Is it so obvious?" she replied.

"It is," he said. He stroked her hair as she snuggled into him, kissed her lightly and held her back with both hands so he could look into her eyes. "Well?"

"We have a pregnancy in the family," Niana whispered.

Matt's heart lurched. "Not Rokmane?" he muttered.

"It's me Matt." Niana couldn't stop the smile. "Isn't it wonderful, sweetheart? I visited the doctor and my suspicions were confirmed. That's why I've been so grouchy lately. Everything is fine and I was told there was no reason I can't have a perfectly normal pregnancy."

"Really? Oh, Niana!" Matt grabbed his wife in a passionate embrace. She turned her face up and their lips met.

"Mummy," screamed Adona from the kitchen door.

"Leave them," her older brother said from behind. "They're just smooching again."

"Yeah," the little girl retorted. "But why does Mummy always cry when she's smooching?"

Halia shrugged. "They're adults," he said. "You know adults do strange things."

They turned and, as usual, the boy's hand slipped into his sister's as they walked into the living room to watch television.

The End

www.ingramcontent.com/pod-product-compliance
Lightning Source LLC
Chambersburg PA
CBHW071235130626
46556CB00003B/1019